"There's something going on here that doesn't have anything to do with the job."

He was right—this wasn't about the job. It was about what had started in the tower and was moving out of her control with frightening speed. "Perhaps you just have an overactive imagination," Sloane said, fighting to keep her voice even.

"I don't know. Let's test it. Empirical method." Nick leaned in, sliding his fingers along her cheek. "Experiment and observe."

"You're out of your mind, Trask."

"Nick," he corrected softly, so close she could feel his mouth form the word.

"What?"

"Call me Nick." Then his lips brushed hers.

Dear Reader,

Well, we're getting into the holiday season full tilt, and what better way to begin the celebrations than with some heartwarming reading? Let's get started with Gina Wilkins's *The Borrowed Ring,* next up in her FAMILY FOUND series. A woman trying to track down her family's most mysterious and intriguing foster son finds him and a whole lot more—such as a job posing as his wife! *A Montana Homecoming,* by popular author Allison Leigh, brings home a woman who's spent her life running from her own secrets. But they're about to be revealed, courtesy of her childhood crush, now the local sheriff.

This month, our class reunion series, MOST LIKELY TO…, brings us Jen Safrey's *Secrets of a Good Girl,* in which we learn that the girl most likely to…*do everything* disappeared right after college. Perhaps her secret crush, a former professor, can have some luck tracking her down overseas? We're delighted to have bestselling Blaze author Kristin Hardy visit Special Edition in the first of her HOLIDAY HEARTS books. *Where There's Smoke* introduces us to the first of the devastating Trask brothers. The featured brother this month is a handsome firefighter in Boston. And speaking of delighted—we are absolutely thrilled to welcome RITA® Award nominee and Red Dress Ink and Intimate Moments star Karen Templeton to Special Edition. Although this is her first Special Edition contribution, it feels as if she's coming home. Especially with *Marriage, Interrupted,* in which a pregnant widow meets up once again with the man who got away—her first husband—at her second husband's funeral. We know you're going to enjoy this amazing story as much as we did. And we are so happy to welcome brand-new Golden Heart winner Gail Barrett to Special Edition. *Where He Belongs,* the story of the bad boy who's come back to town to the girl he's never been able to forget, is Gail's first published book.

So enjoy—and remember, next month we continue our celebration….

Gail Chasan
Senior Editor

Please address questions and book requests to:
Silhouette Reader Service
U.S.: 3010 Walden Ave., P.O. Box 1325, Buffalo, NY 14269
Canadian: P.O. Box 609, Fort Erie, Ont. L2A 5X3

KRISTIN HARDY

WHERE THERE'S SMOKE

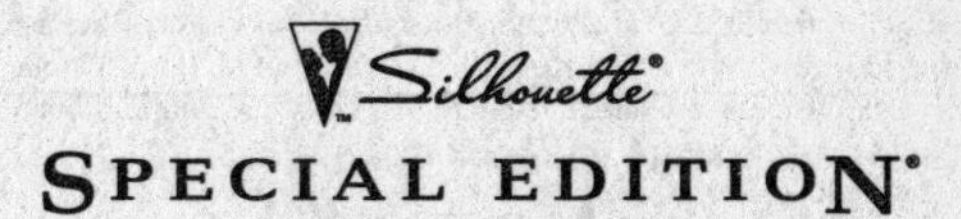

Published by Silhouette Books
America's Publisher of Contemporary Romance

For their invaluable assistance in my research, thanks to Scott Salman of the Boston Fire Department, Joel Schwartz of the Dorchester Bay Economic Development Corp. and most of all, Stephen Hardy of the Merrimack Romantic Development Corp.

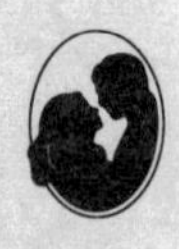

SILHOUETTE BOOKS

ISBN 0-373-24720-6

WHERE THERE'S SMOKE

This edition published by arrangement with Harlequin Books S.A.

Visit Silhouette Books at www.eHarlequin.com

Printed in U.S.A.

Books by Kristin Hardy

Silhouette Special Edition

Where There's Smoke #1720

Harlequin Blaze

**My Sexiest Mistake* #44
**Scoring* #78
**As Bad as Can Be* #86
**Slippery When Wet* #94
†*Turn Me On* #148
†*Cutting Loose* #156
†*Nothing but the Best* #164
§*Certified Male* #187
§*U.S. Male* #199

*Under the Covers
†Sex & the Supper Club
§Sealed with a Kiss

KRISTIN HARDY

has always wanted to write, starting her first novel while still in grade school. Although she became a laser engineer by training, she never gave up her dream of being an author. In 2002, her first completed manuscript, *My Sexiest Mistake,* debuted in Harlequin's Blaze line; it was subsequently made into a movie by the Oxygen network. The author of nine books to date, Kristin lives in New Hampshire with her husband and collaborator.

Dear Reader,

The publication of *Where There's Smoke* is a dream come true for me. About twenty years ago (when I was two, of course) I picked up a Silhouette Special Edition novel at the store and I got the bug to write a romance. Fast forward through several false starts and *long* hiatuses from writing. Even though I never finished a book, I always knew that one day I'd make my living as a romance novelist. Then in September 2001, I finally typed "The End" on a story and sold it to Harlequin's newly launched Blaze line.

My heart has always been with Special Edition, though. When Gail Chasan bought the HOLIDAY HEARTS trilogy I couldn't have been more thrilled. I have so many stories to tell, so I hope that this is a journey we can go on together as I continue to write for both lines.

I'd love to hear what you think of my first effort, so please drop me a line at kristin@kristinhardy.com. Stop by my Web site at www.kristinhardy.com for contests, details on upcoming books, recipes and more.

Happy holidays.

Kristin Hardy

Chapter One

It was beyond him how so much paperwork could stack up in such a short time. Nick Trask stared balefully at the forms piled up on his desk and sighed. He'd joined the fire department to battle fires, not to generate his own personal fire hazard.

When people asked him why he loved firefighting, he usually shrugged and said it was rewarding. It was true, that much of it, but there was more he didn't say. He didn't tell them of the fierce pleasure of firefighting, the euphoria of saving a life or the way the adrenaline blasted through him as he risked everything against the ravening beast of the flames.

Those were the moments that made it all worthwhile. Those were the times that made up for days like this one, he thought, raking an impatient hand through his cropped hair. It had been crazy from the get-go. They'd hardly had time to go over the morning announcements at the start of shift when the bells had sounded for a house fire in a triple-decker just blocks away. Climbing to the roof to ventilate the blaze, hands full with a chainsaw, Bruce Jackson had found out the twenty-foot ladder had a bad rung. The hard way. All things considered, it was a lucky thing he'd only fallen eight feet—if you could call a broken collarbone lucky.

And the day had just gone downhill from there.

Accident reports, damaged property reports, defective equipment reports…Nick was tempted to put a lump of coal underneath them and see if he could make a diamond. It wouldn't have been so bad if it hadn't been for the rescue call, the inspections and the car fire. Not to mention the medical aid calls. Three of them. Even after spending every moment in between calls filling out forms and cursing the department for not having it all online, he was only a little over half done, and everything had to be shipshape by the time they made the shift change.

Nick shook his head and glanced at the books he'd optimistically spread out, hoping to study for the promotional exam. His chances of getting any time to look at them this shift were about as good as his chances of winning Powerball.

"Yo, cap, give me a hand for a minute?" The question was shouted up from the garage area below, rising above the sounds of rock music on the radio. If he craned his neck, Nick could see out the open door of his office and through the stair railing to the long, gleaming red shapes of the fire engine and ladder truck, massive yet oddly sleek under the fluorescent lights of the cavernous garage. Something of the boy in him smiled then, something of the man felt a swelling pride, underlain by a breath of challenge, a taste of danger.

Firefighting was his life. It touched the essence of him in a way nothing else ever had.

Feet thumped up the stairs. "El capitan?" A burly, middle-aged firefighter with a blunt-featured face leaned into the office. From behind him came the sound of U2 singing about a beautiful day.

Nick put down his pen. "Still stuck on these reports, O'Hanlan, sorry."

"Remember the other day when you were asking me why I didn't want to take the exam to move up? 'Nuff said. You officer types, you gotta love paperwork. Me, I'm an action guy."

A corner of Nick's mouth quirked as he looked at O'Hanlan's florid face. "An action guy, huh?"

"Every minute of every day."

"No wonder your wife looks scared. Look, I've got to keep working on this pile if I'm going to get through it by shift change, so if someone else can help you, go for it."

"No problem. I understand. Some people are born bureaucrats. But if your hand starts getting tired and you want to be reminded what the apparatus looks like…"

Nick stopped and considered, tapping forms-in-triplicate with his pen and eyeing the door where O'Hanlan beckoned.

"Were you ever in sales, O'Hanlan?"

"Just pointing out your options." He tipped his head in the direction of the apparatus floor, wagging his eyebrows.

It *was* Nick's duty as captain to take care of any problems, and God knew he could use a break from the endless writing. Nick grinned and tossed down his pen. "All right, you got me."

"Cap." Todd Beaulieu, compact and dark-haired, met them on the stairs, a slip of paper in his hand. "I just found this note by the phone. Looks like you got a call sometime yesterday."

"Yesterday?"

"I guess the other shift forgot to tell you." Beaulieu squinted at the paper. "Jeez, O'Hanlan, this writing looks as bad as yours."

"Hey, I've won awards for my handwriting, I'll have you know," O'Hanlan protested.

"Probably for cryptography," Beaulieu shot back.

Nick reached out for the message. "Eq tes tom?" he asked squinting at the scribbles. "Anybody want to guess?"

O'Hanlan considered. "Abusing a cat?"

"Leave your personal life out of this," Beaulieu told him.

Nick struggled for a moment to make sense of the hasty scrawl. "Looks like someone's doing something tomorrow. Which means today. I guess we'll find out eventually." He shrugged and turned to the stairs. "What did you break this time, O'Hanlan?"

Down on the garage floor, Nick and O'Hanlan threaded their way around the pumper to the ladder truck. The music on the radio segued into a no-nonsense woman's voice reading the morning news.

"In Dorchester, Councilman Donald Ayre, running for re-election next month, spoke again about his new safety plan for Boston firefighters."

"We can't have fire safety in Boston until our firefighters are safe," Ayre said self-importantly. "That's my mission, and that's why I'm looking for reelection."

O'Hanlan rolled his eyes at the sound bite. "Looks like old Hot Ayre is at it again," he said, climbing on top of the ladder truck. "Funny, the last time he got yapping about firefighters it was an election year, too."

"And the time before that, I think," Nick said, following him. "'Course, he doesn't talk about how he pushed for department budget cuts once the voting was over, does he?"

"He's probably shy about his accomplishments," O'Hanlan guessed. "Besides, if the equipment was good enough for our great-grandfathers, it's good enough for us, right?"

"Sure. Just ask Jackson." Nick's lip curled. "Twenty bucks says that inside of two weeks we've got our illustrious councilman in a photo op with some high-tech gizmo the department will buy one of for tests and never use."

"C'mon, how's he supposed to enjoy the budget cuts unless he cleans out the miscellaneous fund, too? Cut him some slack."

"I'd like to cut him something." Nick shook his head in disgust. "If we don't give them something to yap about on the campaign trail, we don't exist for those guys."

"Cushy life, though. Think about it: nice, soft chair in the City Council meetings, free parking anywhere in town. Free lunches, too." O'Hanlan's eyes brightened. "Maybe I should go into politics."

Nick looked him up and down. "I'm not sure you could handle any more lunches, O'Hanlan."

"That?" O'Hanlan slapped his comfortable belly. "That's muscle, sonny boy, and don't you forget it."

"I'll work on it. So what's the problem that you had to drag me all the way down here for, anyway?"

O'Hanlan bent down to the giant aerial ladder that lay folded up in sections on top of the truck. "The ladder felt sticky at that last fire. She didn't open up like she should have. I took a look and this bolt right here is loose and partly sheared." He pulled at the ladder and the bolt rattled in its hole. "I think it'll be okay if we just switch it, but with these mitts of mine I can't get at it."

Nick glanced at it briefly, then at his watch. "Why don't I write it up for repair?"

"Because"—O'Hanlan made a futile attempt to reach the back of the bolt—"you write it up, the motor squad'll take a month to get to it and a month to fix it. Or we'll get stuck working with one of those Civil War relics they keep around."

"I'd think an action guy would want the challenge."

"I have to save my valuable strength for firefighting, not for pushing the truck to the scene." O'Hanlan's voice was aggrieved. "Here I'm trying to save you some writing and you're not even appreciating it, ya bureaucrat."

"That's the trouble with you, O'Hanlan, always thinking of others first." Nick squatted down to get a better view. "Give me a wrench."

Sloane Hillyard strode down the sidewalk toward Firehouse 67, narrowing her eyes against the glare of the October sun, wishing she'd remembered her sunglasses. A group of teenaged boys hanging out on the corner turned to watch her pass.

"Yo, baby, what you in such a hurry for?" the boldest of them called. "Y'oughta stop and be more sociable." He trailed after her a few steps, while his buddies nudged one another and laughed. "C'mon, baby, stop. I'll show you God."

Sloane ignored him and kept going. An angry tangle of graffiti covered the walls of the building she passed. Here where the southern Boston neighborhoods of North Dorchester and Roxbury came together, even the sidewalk looked hard used. Sloane genuinely didn't notice. She wasn't concerned with young boys or with her surroundings. She was only concerned with the men in the firehouse ahead.

Her stomach tightened.

When she stepped through the doorway, she would start the final phase of five years of intense—some might say obsessive—effort. Five years to design equipment that would help ensure no firefighter, anywhere, would be lost in a blaze. Five years to help ensure that no more men would be devoured by the gaping maw of the flames.

The main doors of the station were open as she walked up.

She slowed as she reached the dark crack in the concrete that marked the threshold. It had been a long time since she'd set foot in a firehouse. She'd thought she was ready for it.

She'd been wrong.

Just do it, she told herself grimly, fighting to ignore the quick twist of anxiety. She was so close to achieving her goal, so close. This was no time to let the past take over the future.

Taking a deep breath, she crossed the line and passed into the fluorescent cool of the garage. A compact, dark-haired man with a boyish face stacked air canisters against the wall. A young firefighter in a Red Sox cap swept the floor around the trucks. The sweeping came to an abrupt halt as he glanced up, hastily setting the broom aside and wiping off his hands as Sloane approached. "Can I help you?"

The click of her heels rang in the cavernous garage. "Hello." She smiled, wondering if he could have been a day past nineteen. "I'm looking for Nick Trask."

The boy was blushing, trying to act cool. "The captain? I think he's up in his office. I'll go get him."

The dark-haired firefighter turned before they took two steps. "Yo, Red! She looking for Trask?"

Sloane froze, her chest suddenly constricted.

"He's not up in his office. He's with O'Hanlan." The man pointed toward the ladder truck at the far side of the garage. "Over there."

"Thanks, Beaulieu." The boy smiled shyly. "My mistake." He looked at Sloane more closely. "Are you okay?"

Sloane forced herself to breathe. "I'm fine, thanks." She saw it now, bright auburn hair curling around the edges of his ball cap. "I knew someone else called Red once."

"My name's Jim Sorensen," he said ruefully, taking his hat

off and scrubbing it through his wavy brush. "But you know how it goes. They took one look at my hair and that was that."

"I know how it goes," she agreed.

"Okay, I've got hold of the nut if you can get the bolt through," Nick muttered, jaw set in concentration. "Let's give it a push and get the holes lined up." They leaned on the ladder together and the metal creaked as it moved.

"Let me get my hand in there. It's just about…ah!" O'Hanlan cursed to the ceiling as he barked his knuckles on unforgiving metal. "I signed up to be a firefighter, not a damn mechanic."

"You were the one who was dead against calling in the motor squad," Nick reminded him. "Come on, action guy, repeat *power steering* to yourself three times and let's try it again."

"Power steering, power steering, there's no place like home, there's no place like home," O'Hanlan's voice rose an octave. "There's no place—" Abruptly he gave a low whistle. "Well, well, well. Looks like I should have volunteered for clean-up detail."

Without turning, Nick knew it was a woman. Her voice floated over to them, low, slightly rough, a smoky contralto that belonged in the bedroom and made him tighten before he ever looked at her. When he did, the first thing he saw was her hair. She had it pulled back and looped up in a clip, but not bound into submission. It was thick, nearly down to her waist, he'd guess, and flamed a deep, splendid red. The face…the face went with the voice, decidedly, recklessly sensual. Slavic cheekbones, challenging eyes, a mouth that made him wonder how it would feel on his skin. Her narrow, forest-green suit played up the sleek curves of her body enough to make his imagination temporarily run rampant.

There was more, something about the lift to her shoulders, the cool self-assurance in her stance that intrigued and enticed him.

"Look at Red." O'Hanlan chuckled. "He's falling all over himself, poor kid." He turned back around. "Hey, Nick?"

He'd been staring, Nick realized, shaking himself loose. "And you, of course, are a master of self-control." He gave O'Hanlan a derisive look before bending back to the ladder. "C'mon, let's finish this."

"I'm a happily married man," O'Hanlan reminded him, grunting as he leaned on the ladder and threaded the bolt in place. "And Leanne would skin me alive if she caught me looking at another woman." O'Hanlan peeked over his shoulder at the approaching redhead. "Which is why I do it here."

Nick squeezed his hand in between ladder struts to work a nut onto the bolt. "Stick to fighting fires," he advised, manipulating the wrench expertly. "It's safer."

"Hello? Excuse me?" The words echoed up from beside the truck. "I'm looking for Nick Trask."

At close range her voice whispered over his skin and into his bones, mesmerizing, arousing. He leaned across the top of the ladder until their eyes locked. Up close, she was all the glimpse had promised and more. "I'm Nick Trask. Give me a minute, I'll be right with you."

"A minute?" O'Hanlan grinned. "Take over for me here and I'll be down there in thirty seconds."

"Easy, big fella." Nick passed the wrench to O'Hanlan and patted him on the shoulder. "Skinned alive, remember? Save your strength for Leanne."

She'd always been a sucker for men in uniform, Sloane thought, watching the lean, stripped-down lines of his body as he swung down from the ladder truck. That was all it was. Of course, he filled the uniform as though it had been designed for him. Off limits, she reminded herself. She didn't do firefighters. He neared and Sloane's pulse skittered unevenly, then steadied.

"Nick Trask," he said, wiping his hands on a rag.

Dark, Sloane thought, and dangerous. His looks hit her with the slamming impact of a hundred-mile-an-hour collision. Black hair, tanned, almost swarthy skin and eyes darker than jet combined on a face that simultaneously compelled and alarmed. It was a face that was not so much conventionally handsome as it was filled with the essential character of the man.

Her guard was up in a heartbeat.

"Sloane Hillyard, Exler Corporation." She reached out her hand when he drew near. "Councilman Ayre's office asked me to stop by." She wasn't sure what she found more disconcerting, the almost imperceptible chill that swept over his face as she spoke, or the flush of heat that assaulted her at the touch of his hand. Nerves, she told herself. She was just on edge over being in a firehouse again. "Nice to meet you, Captain Trask."

"And you." There was a cursory politeness in his voice but no warmth. This close to him Sloane could see that his eyes weren't black. They were deep gray, the color of darkest smoke, the color of a stormy sky at dusk. "What can I do for you and the councilman?"

Focus, Sloane reminded herself. "I'm here for our meeting."

"Our meeting?"

"I called to confirm yesterday."

"I didn't get any…" He checked himself and pulled a pink slip of paper covered in illegible script from his pocket. "Ah. This must be you. Sorry, but I didn't get this until about five minutes ago and it's been a really hectic day, so if—"

"That's all right," she cut in smoothly. "I'll only need a few minutes of your time. We need to talk about the gear."

"The gear?" He put his hands on his hips and gave a nod. "Ayre doesn't waste time, I'll give him that."

Sloane didn't need to know the reason for the sarcasm to understand that she was at least a partial target. Irritation pricked at her. "We need to talk about scheduling, plan the testing," she continued, not about to be derailed. "Councilman Ayre's office—"

"Yeah, I know, Councilman Ayre's office." Nick cut her off, glancing at the number of men with sudden, pressing business in the immediate vicinity. "Look, let's go to my office and you can tell me what Ayre's up to this time."

He didn't offer it as a choice, but in the clipped tone of command. "Yes sir," Sloane muttered, following him up the stairs. Perhaps the man could put out fires, but graciousness was clearly not his strong suit.

Nor, she thought a moment later, was neatness.

"Right through there. Have a seat."

Sloane stood in the doorway of his tiny office and threw a glance of disbelief at the jumble of paperwork and books everywhere. "Which stack of paper did you have in mind for me to sit on, Captain Trask?" Her tone was deceptively sweet, as was her face. The sarcasm lurked only in her gaze, which warned him not to push too hard, not to presume too much.

Nick shifted a pile of books to the floor. "There." The telephone jangled for attention and he answered it impatiently. "House sixty-seven, Trask. Oh yeah, right. Giancoli says the brakes on the pumper are down." He slid into his chair, instantly absorbed, leaving Sloane standing in the middle of the room.

Setting down her briefcase, she took the opportunity to look around. Photographs covered the walls: smiling firefighters in front of shining engines, men crowded together at the kitchen table, competing in the Firefighters' Olympics. A newspaper clipping showed grim men in helmets and turnouts, lines of exhaustion etched into their soot-streaked faces as they carried stretchers out of a smoke-filled building. Hillview Convalescent Home Burns but the Fire Claims No Victims, the caption read. The men in the picture were from Ladder 67.

Sloane glanced further along and her interest sharpened. Stacked haphazardly atop the filing cabinet were a pair of plaques, the top one an award of valor presented to one Nick Trask for action above and beyond the call of duty. Impressed in spite of herself, Sloane glanced over to where he sat at his desk, absorbed in his call.

She'd been wrong when she'd thought his face held more character than perfection. Clearly, the sharp slashes of his cheekbones, the compelling shape of his mouth translated into above-average looks. It was simply that the force of his personality was so strong that it overwhelmed the handsomeness, carried it past simple good looks to a more dangerous realm, giving him the ability to hypnotize, the power to obsess.

The sudden flicker of warning ran through her to the pit of her stomach. In defense, she moved to stare out the window. Outside, a dog barked and boys shouted as they threw a football in the street. Inside, a subtle tension filled the air.

Nick shifted in his chair impatiently. "Yeah, okay. Let me know when it'll go. Great, talk to you later." He hung up the phone, turning to where Sloane stood. Perhaps it was a trick of the light, but for just an instant her hair blazed the exact color of flame. For just an instant, he watched without speaking. He shook his head and forced his mind to business just as she turned from the window.

"All finished?"

"Yes. Sorry about the wait." Because he was still having a hard time concentrating, Nick plunged in without preamble. "So, Ms. Hillyard, what has the councilman's office promised that we would do for you?"

His tone was more brusque than he'd intended. It made Sloane's mouth tighten and she took her time coming back to her chair. "I believe the councilman's office is taking a sincere interest in your safety, as I think you'll see. Now, I made an appointment through the city weeks ago," she said frostily. "I assumed you'd be ready to discuss this."

Nick silently cursed the man who'd taken the garbled message, then cursed the fact that it had been uncovered so late that he'd had no time to sort it out. And he added Ayre, just on principle. No matter how gorgeous she was, whatever the woman was selling, it was going to take time he didn't have. "Yes, well," he said, summoning his patience for what looked to be a long siege, "why don't you start at the beginning?"

Sloane took a deep breath. "I work for the Exler Corporation," she said, a little too carefully. "I've developed a system called the Orienteer. It's designed to locate firefighters in burning buildings."

"How?"

"It's got a microprocessor that combines global-positioning-system input with a database of building plans to locate anyone, anywhere. You want to find your team members in a burning building, you can. If they need to track their way out, it will lead them. No one will die the way they did in the Hartford packing-house fire ever again." Her voice caught, so briefly he couldn't be sure he hadn't imagined it. "We've gone through the preliminary lab qualification and breakdowns. The last step is testing in a real-life situation with firefighters."

"No way." Nick was shaking his head before she finished. "My guys aren't guinea pigs."

"I beg your pardon?"

"Not a chance." Nick knew how this went, oh, he knew it. Put on the dog for the politicians, invest precious departmental resources and when the photo ops and the elections were done, so was the funding. That was bad enough, but put his men at risk for that photo op? That was where he drew the line.

"You can't just refuse."

"First of all, it's totally impractical." That was the part that really burned him about operators like Ayre. It couldn't be something reasonable or useful. No—some babelicious Girl Scout turned up with her science project and Ayre saw only the headlines, not the lives at risk.

"Impractical?" Sloane's eyes flashed. "How can you say that when you don't know the first thing about it?"

"Where are you going to get all the blueprints?"

"We've *already* gotten them from the planning commission. The microprocessors for the test units are being loaded up with plans for every building in Boston and Cambridge."

He snorted. "Do you actually think those are up-to-date in a city like this? You really want to bank someone's life on that?"

"We're confirming layouts as we're entering them."

"Checking up on every structure? You'll never get it done," he said dismissively. "You want to be useful, get me a couple more thermal cameras, build me a better breathing mask. Something proven. Something practical."

Sloane flushed. "The equipment *is* practical. And proven. It's been completely lab tested, it just hasn't been used in a fire situation before. Both the department and Councilman Ayre's office are behind this."

"I'm sure they are. The chief and Ayre grew up on the same block."

She gave him a level stare. "What's that supposed to mean?"

He sighed. It really wasn't her fault. "Look, I'm sure you've got the best of intentions, but you don't know how the game goes around here."

"But I'm sure you'll tell me."

She looked, he thought, strung tight as a piano wire. It didn't make her any less gorgeous. "Ayre starts with the fire-safety shtick every election cycle. It gets him press, photos in front of shiny red trucks. It's all about exposure and it's nothing he'll support with funding. Trust me on that, I've been through it before." He shook his head in frustration. "Ayre just wants to make headlines. You're the tool he chose to do it with."

"What is with you? I'm talking about equipment that can help you and you're talking about conspiracies."

He bristled. "No, I'm talking politics."

"And I'm talking about saving lives," she retorted. "You've got problems with Ayre? Then vote against him next month. I don't care. All that matters to me is getting this equipment qualified."

"And you're dreaming if you think they're actually going to buy this gadget."

"It's not a gadget," she said hotly. "It's a very sophisticated system."

"A very…" He shook his head like a dog throwing off water. "Do you understand anything at all about firefighting?"

Her eyes burned for a moment; it took her a visible effort to tamp her reaction down. "Of course I do. I consulted with firefighters in Cambridge when I was designing the equipment."

"Great. Take it to them to test."

"We're not taking it to them. We've taken it to the city of

Boston and the city says you. This isn't some project of the week. This testing is critical and trust me, it is going to get done. Bill Grant in the fire chief's office wants your company to do the testing. Ayre wants it. I want it. You're way down the list, Captain Trask."

Nick didn't even attempt to quell the bright flare of anger. "That's where you're wrong. You may think that because you had a couple of nice visits downtown that you can come in here and do whatever you want." He rose, stalking toward her until she was forced to tilt her head to hold his gaze. "But this is my firehouse and I don't care what Ayre wants, I don't care what it is Grant wants and I certainly don't care what you want. I am not going to put my guys at risk so Ayre can take pictures of the two of you testing out a video game."

Sloane paled for an instant, then shot to her feet, two spots of color burning high on her cheekbones. "This equipment is going to get qualified, no matter what it takes. I don't give a damn if I'm a tool or a pawn or whatever the hell you think I am if it means that I save one person's life, just one." Her voice rose in fury. "And you are not going to stand in my way."

They faced each other, inches apart, crackling with tension. Something kinetic surged through the air between them then, something elemental that had nothing to do with firefighting and everything to do with heat.

Sloane moved away first, because she had to, because she felt the shudder of weakness in the wall of anger surrounding her. "Where's your telephone?" she demanded. "You don't want to do this, Captain Trask? I'll save you the trouble. Forget about wasting your time, testing with you would be a waste of my time." She crossed to his desk and snatched up the telephone receiver. "Where's the number for the fire chief's office?"

He studied her a moment, his brows drawn together in a frown of concentration. Then he plucked the receiver from her hand. "I'll dial it for you." He punched in the numbers rapidly and waited. "Bill Grant please. Yes, I'll hold." He handed the receiver back without a word.

Sloane waited, listening to Nick stalk out into the hallway. There was a click on the line, then a voice. "Bill Grant here."

"Hi Bill, it's Sloane Hillyard."

"Sloane, good to talk to you." The words were ever so slightly shaded with relief. "You have perfect timing. I was just trying to reach you."

"Well, you've got me now. What do you need?"

"Can you hold off contacting Ladder 67 for a day? We had a little paperwork snafu here and the memo that should have gone to them is still sitting here in my office. Give me a day to get everything set up with them and we can go ahead."

Sloane glanced out toward the hall and found her gaze pinned to Nick Trask's. He was yards away, but she felt a clutch on her chest as sure as a physical contact. The breath of a shiver that passed up her spine was composed partly of anxiety, partly of feelings she was afraid to identify. She tore her eyes away and turned back to the desk. "Too late, Bill. I'm calling you from the firehouse."

"Oh." He paused for a moment and Sloane heard the rapid, nervous tap of a finger against the phone, maybe, or the desk. "Um, is everything okay?"

"Not exactly. In fact, after talking with Captain Trask, I think it would be best for me to work with a different company."

"Let's not be hasty, Sloane. Nick Trask's one of the best men we've got." Now she heard all four fingers begin to drum the desktop in sequence. "If there's any hitch here, it's my fault. Why don't you let me talk to him and see what the problem is?"

The problem, thought Sloane, was that she didn't want to be anywhere near Nick Trask, certainly not for a period of weeks. "All right." She turned to Nick. "It's for you."

Sloane walked out into the hall where she could finally breathe. The testing couldn't be interrupted. Everything depended on getting the gear qualified. Everything.

After a moment, she looked around. To her left was the stairway that ran down to the apparatus floor. To her right, the hall ended in a T, with the dormitory on one side and probably a kitchen and rec room on the other. Without even trying she could picture the latter—worn, comfortable furniture, a TV and VCR, probably some back issues of *Fire Engineering* magazine tossed down on a table. Before she could block it, the image of a lanky, boyish-faced redhead sprawled on a firehouse couch came to her with painful clarity. Oh Mitch, she thought and grief and loss surged in for a blinding instant.

"Ms. Hillyard," Nick's voice called to her. "Grant wants to talk with you again."

She responded automatically, entering the office, reaching for the phone. "Yes?"

"Hi, Sloane," Grant answered cheerily. "I just wanted to apologize for the mixup over there. I've discussed the situation with Nick and he'll be happy to work with you on this project." Sloane glanced over to where Nick stood, staring at her again. Oh, she could see how happy he was about the project. "It's up to you, of course," Grant continued, "but it's really best. It could take quite a while to get another company lined up."

Sloane bit back a protest. Grant had her neatly cornered. The testing had to be finished in two months, when production was scheduled to begin. There could be no delays and he knew it. Sloane sighed. "All right. Let's stick with the plan."

"Wonderful." She could hear the satisfaction in Grant's

voice. "If you have any more hitches with the testing, just give me a ring and I'll take care of things, okay?"

"Sure. Anything else?"

"Actually, yes. Can you put Nick back on?"

The clamor of the alarm bells shattered the quiet of the firehouse. Sloane couldn't prevent herself from jumping.

Nick was galvanized into action instantly. "Tell him I'll call him back," he barked over his shoulder, sprinting for the fire pole in the dormitory.

"He's got…"

"I know, an explosion at the oil-tank farm. It just came in here. Sloane, thanks very much." Grant's voice was hurried as he said goodbye.

The previous atmosphere of calm had been replaced by one of controlled urgency, the air charged with tension. Even as Sloane rushed down the stairs, most of the men were on the apparatus floor pulling on turnouts, grabbing waiting helmets and gloves. A stocky firefighter turned away from the enormous district map that covered one wall and climbed into the cab of Ladder 67. "I got it, cap. Let's fly."

Sloane hurried to get clear as the last of the men vaulted aboard the gleaming apparatus. Already the motors throbbed, the station door was peeled back. She slipped outside as the ladder truck and the pumper hit the street, lights flashing and sirens shrieking.

The firefighters were on their way.

Chapter Two

If he ever won the lottery, Nick thought, he'd hire people to shop for him. Not just certain kinds of shopping—pretty much anything that involved cash registers and standing in line. Certainly anything with narrow aisles and those shiny chrome racks crammed so close together that he was perpetually bumping them with his shoulders.

"Can I help you?"

A teenaged sales clerk popped up at his elbow. The fixed, Mouseketeer smile on her face scared him a little. On the other hand, having to spend more than two more minutes in the boutique scared him more.

He looked at the piles of silky scarves and fancy handbags. "I need a birthday gift for my mother."

"Well, you've come to the right place. How about something to add a little color to her winter wardrobe?" she asked, holding up a sheer band of fabric with a twisting pattern of burgundy and gold.

The dark red brought Sloane Hillyard to mind. Not that he needed a prompt. She'd been in his thoughts since she'd come to the station two days before. Granted, she had a face that was hard to forget, but if it had only been that, he could have dismissed her as a high-tech huckster. What had made her linger with him was the way she'd looked at the end. There had been that instant that she'd paled. And the words, so impassioned she'd practically vibrated with them: *If I save one life, just one life…*

There was something driving her, that much was obvious. He couldn't help but admire her for it. There was a "Why" there and it was enough to make him wonder about the project. Of course, if his mind returned to the generous sweep of her mouth, the fire of her hair, the heat that had flashed between them in his office, he was only human, right?

Forget about the project, it was enough to make him wonder about her. And wonder where the testing might take them.

"Do you see any scarves your mother might like?"

The clerk's voice broke into his thoughts and Nick brought his focus back to the task at hand. There was plenty to think about there, too. "My mother's not much of a scarf person," he answered. At least not scarves that were more for looks than for warmth. On the other hand, why not? He'd come in with the vague idea that he wanted to get her something different, something other than a new plant or a sweater from L.L. Bean.

Something that would surprise her, maybe put the spark back in her eye, the spark that had been missing since his father had died the previous spring.

Somehow, though, a scarf didn't quite seem likely to do it.

"How about something to pamper her?" The sales clerk

was twinkling at him, he noticed uneasily. "We have some nice bath sets with body gels and lotions."

"Not sure I want to go there. How about something else?"

"A watch?" She led him from the small gift section over to the glass display cases.

"I don't think so." A watch would be unnecessary at the Trask family farm; there, you simply rose before dawn with the shrieking alarm clock and worked until long after dark. He looked at the velvet-lined cases filled with rings and bracelets of gleaming metal. Shiny and cold and all so unlike Molly Trask. He'd never actually seen her wear jewelry anyway, except for the plain band of gold his father had given her. The band of gold she still wore. "Do you have anything else?"

"Well, we've got—"

"Hold on." A warm, soft gleam caught his eye. "What's that?"

"Oh, good choice." The clerk's eyes brightened, this time in a decidedly mercenary fashion as she led him over to the far end of the case. "That's our Vintage Collection, made by a local designer out of antique and rose gold. She does some really lovely pieces."

For those prices they ought to be, Nick thought, but there was a simple grace to the necklace that had first caught his eye. "How about that one?"

She beamed. "Perfect. It's a charm necklace. The artist has made a whole collection of birthstone charms that go with it."

Perfect, indeed. "That's it," he decided, reaching back for his wallet. "Let's see...give me a charm each for October, May, January, September and December." One for her, his father, his two brothers and himself. A reminder of family around her neck all the time. She'd like that, he thought. You needed family around when times were tough.

And sudden guilt nipped at him with tiny, sharp teeth.

He hadn't left Vermont to hurt anyone. He'd left because it was the only way he could breathe. As much as he'd loved his family, he'd needed more than anything to find his own way. He'd always assumed they'd be there when he went back.

He'd never expected his father to die so young.

And yet, in its own way, firefighting was his way of honoring his father's legacy. For as long as Nick could remember growing up, Adam Trask would drop anything he was doing at the sound of the town siren and rush to join the other volunteer firefighters to beat back flames.

Nick remembered the day the siren had sounded when they'd been at the farm supply store: the exhilarating drive to the firehouse, the purposeful rush of the men as they'd leapt into the fire engine. Instructions to Nick to stay put had held only as long as it had taken the pumper to leave, then he'd jogged out into the street and down toward the scent of smoke. The mixed terror and pride of watching his father plunge into the burning building was still as fresh in memory as it had been that day. Seeing him hurry out, soot-streaked, with a young girl clutching at his neck, had filled Nick with a kind of baffled awe.

Somehow, Nick thought as he signed the charge slip for the clerk, staying on the Trask farm to make maple syrup had never even come close.

He walked outside, fishing in the pocket of his bomber jacket for his cell phone, flipping it open to punch up a number.

The line clicked. "Gabe Trask."

"You owe me two hundred bucks," Nick told his younger brother as he crossed the pavement to his Jeep.

"You don't say. You late on your car payment again?"

"Nope. You said we'd split Mom's present. That's splitting it."

There was a short silence. "I left you with responsibility of picking Mom's present?"

"Yep."

"What was I thinking?"

Nick unlocked his door and got in. "How to come out smelling like a rose with zero effort?"

"Hey, I want a shopping mall, I've got either an hour drive over to Stowe or two hours down to Concord."

"You're breaking my heart, here." Nick hooked his phone up to the hands-free cord. "Listen, I just shopped voluntarily, thanks to you."

"Now who's whining?"

"Me." Nick turned the key and the Jeep roared to life.

"So what did we buy for her?"

"A necklace." There was a short silence. "Gabe, you there?"

"Oh, yeah. Sorry, I just fell asleep from boredom for a minute there. Tell me you got something a little more original than a gold chain."

"Have some faith, will you? It's a charm necklace made out of antique gold."

"Hence, the price," Gabe said dryly.

Nick checked behind him and backed out of the parking space. "It made me think of her," he said simply. "She can wear it all the time under her clothes and it's got a charm for everyone in the family."

"That's not bad," Gabe admitted. "Let me guess. A woman helped you pick it out, right?"

An image of Sloane's face flashed into Nick's head. "Nope, not unless you count the clerk who took my money."

"Gee, my brother's evolving in the big city. So are you going to bring it up for the party?"

"I can't make it to the party," Nick said, stifling another

stab of guilt. "I've got one more week until the promotional exam. I've got to spend every minute studying that I can."

Gabe cleared his throat. "Jacob's not going to be happy."

"Now there's a surprise." There was a lot that didn't make their elder brother happy these days and most of it centered around Nick. "I've put a year into this exam. I can't drop the ball at the last minute. I'll overnight you the present and you can take it to her. She'll understand."

"I'm sure."

"Look, I'm sorry Dad died, but I can't quit my job and move home." The words were out before Nick could stop them.

"And I didn't ask you to," Gabe said carefully. "You've got something to work out with Jacob, you do it with him, okay? I gave up being the go-between when I hit puberty."

Nick pulled up to the exit of the parking lot and watched the sweep of passing traffic. "Oh, I don't know. You made out pretty well being a go-between when we were kids. In fact, I remember a couple of summers you extorted candy bars from me just about every week to smooth things over."

"*Extorted* is an ugly word," Gabe said reprovingly. "I had a gift for working with people and you wanted to show your appreciation for my efforts. Who was I to say no?"

"Particularly when you had your hand out."

"When opportunity knocks…"

Nick punched the accelerator and whipped out onto the highway. "Exactly. Still like Baby Ruths?"

Walking down the white hallway to her lab at Exler, Sloane could hear the radio before she ever neared the door. The station promo segued into a song, accompanied by her lab intern, Dave Tomlinson, an MIT engineering student assigned to her for the year. Bright and efficient, he had a quirky sense of humor and a penchant for indie rock, preferably at high decibels. And invariably he sang along. Sloane fought a smile and reached out for the doorknob.

Dave's wobbly falsetto carried out into the hall, breaking off abruptly when Sloane opened the door. "Uh-oh." His hand was already on the dial, turning down the volume. "The warden returns."

"And none too soon. Do you know they can hear you down in manufacturing? You'd better watch out or the only place you'll be playing tunes will be your dorm room."

Dave sat at the computer workstation and grinned. "You say that, but I don't think it really bugs you. Deep down inside, I think you got a soft spot for me."

"Quite an imagination you've got. You should have gone to Berklee College to be a rock star instead of MIT," she said, flicking a glance at the list of chords and lyrics he'd scribbled on the lab white board.

"But then you'd have some boring goob of an intern instead of a talented, charismatic young guy you liked."

"What I like is interns who get their jobs done." Her tone would have carried more authority if humor hadn't hovered just beneath the surface.

"Yeah, that was what you said when you tutored me in thermo."

That had been when she'd known she was in trouble. Her ice look, the one that had always kept her assistants at a respectful distance, had never worked on Dave.

Now, he squinted unrepentantly at the computer and tapped the keys. "Hey, I get something done now and then. Did you notice these?" With a flourish he indicated the Orienteer modules and user manuals stacked neatly at one end of the lab bench. "All of them loaded up with software and calibrated, ready to go live. I'm running a simulation on the last one now."

"Very nice." Sloane admired them. "Fast work. How did you get all this done? You were only just starting when I left for my meeting."

He shrugged, clicking his mouse. "I kind of skipped lunch."

"What?" She frowned at him. "You're too skinny as it is, Dave." She didn't recognize herself playing the role of older sister because she'd never been one. "Go eat and I'll finish qualifying the last one. Go," she shooed as he hesitated. "Now."

Dave stood up and grabbed his sunglasses off his desk. "Okay, mem sahib, your wish is my command." He walked jauntily out into the hall. A moment later the door opened again and his head popped back inside. "Hey, boss?"

"Yes?"

"You really think I could be a rock star?"

Sloane tried to keep a straight face. "Truth?"

"Truth."

"Don't quit your day job," she advised.

The door to the lab clicked closed on his whistle and Sloane got to work monitoring the simulations. Her good humor slid into humming concentration as she ran the Orienteer module through scenario after scenario. When the phone rang, she picked it up absently. "Sloane Hillyard."

"Nick Trask, Ladder 67."

She would have recognized his voice even without the introduction. It was unsettling how clearly she could imagine the lines of his face. Still, no one was going to distract her from getting the gear qualified, no matter how good-looking he was. Too much was at stake.

She made herself speak coolly, impersonally. "Captain Trask. How are you?"

"Good enough. How about you?"

"Fine, thanks. I saw the fire at the tank farm on the news. It looked bad."

"For a while. We held onto it, though. Chief Douglass is a good firefighter." It was the highest praise a firefighter could give.

"I'm glad everything worked out all right." Sloane took a deep breath. "So what can I do for you, captain?"

"You could call me Nick, for starters. I only get called Captain Trask when I'm visiting schools or getting chewed out by the chief."

She blinked. "Why?"

"Why do I get chewed out?"

"Why should I call you Nick?"

"We're going to be working together, right? It might make things a little more friendly."

"You didn't seem too happy about the situation the other day. Why the sudden change of pace?"

"Call it an experiment. I know Ayre's an operator, but you were right the other day, I don't know you at all. I figure you deserve the benefit of the doubt."

Oh, nice wasn't fair, she thought with a little twist of alarm. Nice could be dangerous. Nice could be just the start of far more than she could handle. She paused. "So what can I do for you…Nick?"

"I thought it was the other way around. That was the gist of our conversation yesterday, wasn't it?"

"It was." Sloane drew a precise pattern of interlocking diamonds on her desk blotter, trying to ignore the quick flutter in her stomach. "You made it pretty clear you wanted nothing to do with pandering to the politicos." And she wanted nothing to do with any man who could make her stomach flutter. Especially if he was a firefighter.

"You hold a grudge?"

"No, but I need cooperation. Nick."

"Well, my opinion of the situation hasn't changed, but as you pointed out, it isn't up to me. So if I can help you out—safely—then I'll do it."

The stiff note in his voice let her relax a bit. "Start with an open mind."

"Done. If the equipment's good, you'll have my support. Just don't expect it to go any further than the testing. The day the department has the money to buy pricey electronics like you're peddling is the day I'll be driving to work in a Rolls."

Sloane took a deep breath. "I don't know what you drive, but I do know this equipment is going to be an important tool, as common in firehouses as thermal cameras."

"No doubt."

"No, there isn't," she said shortly. There couldn't be, not after all she'd been through. "Now is there something else, Captain Trask?"

"Nick. And yeah, there is. I need to know what you want to do about the testing. How many men you want, when, what kind of apparatus, all that. You might find an engine company better suited to your needs, by the way."

Sloane shook her head, forgetting that he couldn't see her. "No, it has to be a truck company. I've got five Orienteers to test, plus the master unit that I'll be using to monitor. I'd like to keep it to the same group of men."

"We can do that if you schedule carefully."

"Good. What I had in mind was a session or two at the training facility, where we'll have control. Once I'm sure the kinks are all out of it, you can start taking it onto fire grounds.

I need a minimum of three fire situations over and above the training facility sessions to get meaningful statistics."

"Okay. Let's set up some dates."

It didn't take long, when it came down to it, and she entered the dates in her computer with satisfaction. "We're all set, then. I'll see you at the Quincy facility on Saturday."

"All right." Nick paused. "You know, Bill Grant backed you when I talked to him. Despite his unfortunate tendency to cooperate with Ayre, he's a good man. Don't let him down."

Sloane hung up the telephone. *Don't let him down.* The words echoed in her mind as she stared at the computer screen. She wasn't seeing the data, though. She was seeing a red-headed boy hanging around the local firehouse, wiping down the engine and listening to the stories of courage and glory. *Don't let him down.* She saw him on the edge of manhood, wearing the blue of the Hartford fire service, his lieutenant's badge gleaming on his chest, pride gleaming in his eyes. She saw him at the altar, uncomfortable in his tuxedo and unmindful of the discomfort as he looked at the glowing woman who had just become his wife. *Don't let him down.* She saw his casket being lowered into the ground.

The fire had been in an abandoned warehouse honeycombed with cold-storage lockers, decrepit and way below code. Two of Mitch's guys had been searching a tangle of rooms for victims when the smoke had thickened and they'd gotten lost. Mitch had plunged in to find them. And had never come out.

How quickly had he passed out from the fumes after his air had run out? Sloane wondered for the thousandth time. Seconds? Heartbeats? Before or after he heard the voices of the firefighters on the other side of the wall, the firefighters who couldn't find him?

Before or after the whole room flashed over into merciless, killing flame?

Officially, the cause of death had been the smoke inhalation, but the real culprit had been the labyrinthine building and the lack of orientation equipment. It could happen to any firefighter at any time. It had been Mitch's bad luck it had happened to him. Even five years later, remembering made her tighten with the fury of senseless waste, struggle against the tearing loss.

Don't let him down.

She wouldn't let him down, Sloane thought now, staring around her lab, nor any of the people who staked their lives on the quality of their equipment. And she wouldn't let down their families. She remembered what it was like to lose someone. She remembered too well....

Chapter Three

It was visible as she drove in, an improbable, eccentric structure that looked as though a committee of quarrelsome architects had built it out of giant-sized Tinkertoys. The closer Sloane came, the more bizarre it looked, meticulously executed building segments arbitrarily slapped together into a four-story monstrosity, the whole considerably less than the sum of the parts. Depending on the side of approach, the structure looked like an apartment house, an industrial building, a parking structure or a tract house on stilts.

It was the showpiece of the Boston fire-training facility and every inch of it had been carefully planned. It would never win any beauty contests, Sloane conceded ruefully as she parked her car and got out, but its sheer quirkiness appealed to her.

Or perhaps it appealed to her because it was where she was going to get a chance to see what her gear could really do.

Anticipation sharpened her awareness of everything

around her, the early-morning tang in the air, the lines of the putty-colored tower silhouetted against the brilliant blue sky. Nerves knotted her stomach as they had since she'd awoken that morning. There was no need to worry, she told herself for the hundredth time as she got out of her car. Everything was going to go fine.

Ladder 67's truck was already parked on the wide concrete apron surrounding the tower, its aerial ladder stretched out to the top of the building. Nearby was a pumper, hoses trailing out toward the tower. From a distance, they looked like Tonka toys. In fact, the whole scene looked like nothing so much as a child's play area after its owner had gone for milk and cookies. A mind-boggling array of fireplugs poked out of the concrete at intervals. Sloane skirted one, heading toward where the ladder truck waited in the slanting shadow of the tower.

Why did it have to be Ladder 67? she wondered, glancing at the group gathered around the truck. Things would have been so much easier if Bill Grant had let her change to another company. She had enough to worry without having to contend with Nick Trask. Not that she was about to let a man distract her from her job, but she'd have far more peace of mind with a captain who was oh, say, pushing sixty, with the start of a paunch and a couple of grandkids on the way.

She wouldn't have felt so much at risk.

Still, Nick Trask was far from the first challenge she'd faced in bringing the Orienteer this far. She'd deal with him, just as she'd dealt with everything else. The important thing was to keep focused on what really mattered.

Making her brother's death mean something.

She recognized Nick immediately. He stood out from the other men, even though they were all dressed in their department T-shirts and dark trousers. Cockiness, Sloane thought immediately, but intrinsic honesty forced her to admit that it wasn't. Instead, it was confidence, complete confidence in his ability to deal with any fire that might arise and a man who could walk into an inferno without flinching wasn't daunted by much else. He turned to look at her from where he leaned against the side of the truck and against her will she felt the spurt of adrenaline in her veins. Oh, yes, the legions of women who probably fell at his feet had to have had something to do with that confidence, as well. Willfully ignoring the sardonic curve of his mouth, Sloane squared her shoulders and kept walking.

When she drew near, Nick pushed away from the side of the ladder truck. "What, is Councilman Ayre running late for his photo op?"

"No Councilman Ayre, sorry to disappoint you."

He studied her a moment. "Who said I was disappointed?"

No man should be allowed to have such long eyelashes, she thought. "Just a guess. It's good equipment. It can save lives, including yours." Pulling a neat pair of files out of the battered leather satchel at her feet, she stacked them on her clipboard. "After Hartford, I can't see any department giving up equipment like this."

"You're obviously new to Boston, or at least the politics."

"Hardly. I've been here three years."

He laughed. Sloane stared at him, her cheeks tinting. "What?"

"No wonder you're such an optimist." The high color that stained the edges of her cheekbones suited her, Nick thought. And it was definitely personal with her.

Sloane frowned. "If Boston's such a useless place and you hate it so much, why do you stay?"

"Loving the city doesn't mean I have to agree with the agenda of the people running it."

"I suppose, but why choose a job that's subject to the whims of the politicians?"

"I didn't. It chose me."

For a moment, she just stared back at him. She looked a little like a Hollywood femme fatale, Nick thought, in her black turtleneck and tan jacket, dark glasses hiding her eyes. Her hair caught the light like a shower of sparks. Her skin was milk-pale and flawless.

He wondered abruptly how it tasted.

Concentrate on the job, Trask. "So what's the plan?"

"First let's go over how the equipment works, then get some smoke going and let them take the Orienteer through its paces."

"You want smoke, we've got it. Come on, I'll show you."

A change came over her as she faced the burn tower, a tenseness he wouldn't have noticed if he hadn't been so aware of her. For a moment something in her stance suggested wariness, perhaps dread. It was there and gone in a flash. There was a story there, he thought again.

Sooner or later, he was going to find out what it was.

He led her into the cool of the burn tower's shadow. At close range, the cinder block walls were scarred by watermarks and black flares of soot.

"What do they use for the fire?" Sloane asked.

"Bales of hay, wood pallets. It depends on whether we want smoke or heat." Nick led her to stairs that threaded up the outside of the tower. He stood back to let her go first. He'd given the tour plenty of times. Funny, he'd never noticed the narrowness of the stairway before, even when it had been crowded with a dozen people.

They stopped at the first landing, in front of a discolored steel door that led to the interior of the building. Nick pulled it open. The metal groaned in complaint. Fire was never easy on anything. "Here's the first burn room, in through here."

Coming in from the bright sunlight, it took Sloane's eyes a moment to adjust to dimness as she shoved her sunglasses up onto her head. The air felt dank and close. In the mix of odors that assaulted her nose there was the stench of stale smoke, drowned char, of burned concrete and gasoline. Their footsteps echoed as though they were in a cave.

Nick stepped in behind her. The back of her neck prickled in sudden awareness. Then the room became shrouded in shadow as he closed the door. Sloane forced her attention to the space in front of her, away from the soft sound of his breath.

She blinked, then blinked again.

The scene in front of her was weirdly disorienting, like a surrealist painting or a scene from a psycho movie. There was much that was familiar, but the context bewildered. The space looked like an ordinary living room, if one discounted the fact that the walls and furniture were completely encrusted with soot. There were the familiar shapes of a couch and a coffee table, but instead of rugs, the center of the floor was piled high with gasoline-soaked wood. It was like something out of an arsonist's daydream—or a firefighter's nightmare.

"Well, the color scheme's simple enough," she said dryly. "Black on black."

Nick stood motionless by the door, watching her as she moved about the room. "The training people like to simulate a real-life situation as much as possible," he murmured. "The furniture's heavy-gauge sheet steel. Watch yourself, by the way. This stuff is coated with soot an inch thick."

The furniture was absolutely matte black, sucking up all the available light, baffling the eye. It looked both soft as velvet and absolutely solid. Sloane couldn't resist touching it with her fingertip. She gave a surprised laugh when her finger sank in to the second knuckle, sending soot cascading down in small avalanches.

"I warned you," Nick pointed out mildly.

"Empirical method." Sloane tried unobtrusively to shake the soot off her fingers. "I have to experiment and observe. I'm a scientist, it's part of my profession." She caught the quick gleam of teeth as he smiled.

Nick pulled a rag from his back pocket and tossed it to her. "Good thing you wore a black sweater. You ought to do a study sometime of the migration and breeding patterns of soot. You'd be amazed at how much of your clothing that little bit will cover."

Sloane gave a scrub or two to her hands and handed it back to him. "Maybe I'll turn into one of those people who write fan letters to the detergent companies."

"Maybe." He frowned and stepped forward with the cloth. Before she knew what he was about, he'd touched it to her cheekbone.

Sloane jerked back.

"Hold still for a minute. You've got soot on your face. You don't want to look like Tom Brady on game day, do you?"

She felt the touch of the fabric, the heat of his finger beneath. The heat of his body. He was too near, she thought, too solid, too hard to ignore. "Are you done yet?" She glanced up and locked eyes with him and the words caught in her throat. His gaze was intent, as if he were trying to see through her skin. His eyes looked hot and dark.

The silence stretched out. "Well, that's all we can do here. Come on," he said abruptly, moving to the far side of the room. "If you like interior design, there's more to see."

It was time to get out of this close, dark room. She didn't want to react to his presence so strongly, Sloane thought as they started down the interior stairs.

She didn't seem to be able to help it.

In the stairwell, sunlight spilled through an open door high above. Light and shadow, bright and dark. They climbed the stairs in sync, shoulder to shoulder in silence broken only by the hollow ring of footsteps echoing off the cinder block walls, the whisper of hands sliding on the railings, the almost imperceptible rhythm of breath.

"Is this the first time you've been in one of these?"

Sloane jumped at Nick's voice. "Yes. I didn't expect it to be like this."

"Are things usually the way you expect?"

You're not. "Often enough."

They came to a landing and stepped through a door into another burn room. Light streamed in through the empty window cutout and Sloane breathed a sigh of relief. There would be no repeat of the shadowed intimacy of the room downstairs, no repeat of the closeness of the stairwell. It should have helped.

It didn't, especially when she saw the furniture. "The master bedroom, of course." Her voice sounded stilted and strange in her own ears. Her mouth was dry. Silly.

"Not much sleeping goes on in here."

Sloane walked to the window to lean out of the open cutout, immensely conscious of every movement, every breath. "I didn't realize we were so high up," she murmured. "The tower doesn't look that big from the ground."

"It's a lot higher when you're hanging off it on a rope."

"No thanks. I hate heights." Sloane started to turn away from the window, then gasped and jerked backward, knocking into Nick. His hands caught her shoulders automatically; he released her a moment later.

But not before she absorbed the feel of his palms.

Deep in her belly something clenched like a fist.

Adrenaline, she told herself, that was all it was. Whether it was from Nick's touch or the thing she'd seen, she couldn't tell. Because she didn't want to find out, she stared instead at the figure wedged between the bed and the wall. "What in God's name is that?"

"That?" Nick grinned. "That's Harvey."

It lay flat on the concrete, dressed in turnouts and steel-toed boots, one arm stretched out plaintively toward her ankle. It was ridiculously thin and even in its reclining position was tall enough to have been instantly drafted by the NBA, had it only been alive. "Harvey?"

Nick seemed to relax. "Our search-and-rescue dummy. They stash him and his wife, Gladys, in here somewhere before they start the fires. When we send the crew in to search, they'd better come out with both of them. Harvey's set up to weigh about as much as the average man. Feel."

Nick reached past her to pick up the outstretched arm. He was near enough that she could catch the scent of male, near enough that she could see the play of muscle through his T-shirt as he bent over. She moved to step away but a stray piece of wood from the fire pile caught her heel and she stumbled backward, arms out to brace against the wall behind her.

And in a surge of terror felt only empty space.

There were moments of absolute clarity in life. One minute Nick was bending down over Harvey, glad of something to do, the next, Sloane's cry was ringing in his ears. There was no pause for thought, no time for horror. Operating only on reflex, he surged up toward the window cutout even as Sloane's feet left the floor. Pulling her back in to safety took a flicker of a second. For an instant there was only adrenaline. Then he swept her to him, holding her tightly.

"There was nothing there." Sloane's voice wavered. "I just backed up and there was nothing there."

Four stories. Four stories down. His mind repeated it like a litany of horror. And at the bottom, solid concrete. "It's all right," Nick whispered, as much to himself as her. "I caught you. You're safe now. You're safe."

He'd saved lives before. The amazement and rush were familiar, but no close call had ever shaken him this much. All the fragrant luxuries of her, the precious individuality, so fragile and so very nearly snuffed out. She was alive now, though, wondrously, completely alive.

He'd had no idea how right she would feel in his arms, close enough that he could feel her heart beating against his chest. For a moment, there was only the soft feathering of her breath over his neck, the silkiness of her hair against his cheek. He heard her sigh, then her body seemed to melt into his.

There was a shout and the sound of footsteps clattering up the stairs. Nick pulled away, staring at Sloane, who looked as shaken as he felt. Then O'Hanlan and Knapp burst into the room.

"My God, are you all right?" O'Hanlan turned to Nick. "Jesus, Trask, what happened? We turned around and there she was hanging half out the window."

Sloane sounded calm, looked calm unless you noticed how rigidly she'd clasped her hands together. "I tripped."

"Good thing Nick was here." O'Hanlan studied her with concerned eyes. "You're sure you're okay? You scared the life out of us."

"I nearly scared the life out of myself." Sloane glanced over at Nick, as though unable to help herself.

He knew how she felt. He hadn't caught up with what had just happened himself, knew only that it had started something, a drumbeat in his head that made the idea of professional detachment toward her a joke. "Let's get downstairs," he said brusquely.

It replayed in her mind over and over as they descended the tower. The whole thing had taken a matter of seconds. Shadow, then harsh sunlight, then a glimpse of blue sky as she'd rocked outside the building. And there had been terror, blinding terror. It had seemed like hours before her heart had begun beating again.

The solid ground under her feet came as a relief. Sloane couldn't understand why it was only then that she started to tremble, first her hands, then her whole body. The men milled about nearby, talking idly, staring over at her. She took a deep breath and willed the shakes away. If she just ignored it, she thought with a tinge of desperation, maybe she could manage.

Nick walked up and looked at her carefully. "Do you need some time to get calmed down?" he asked.

To her utter horror she felt tears threaten. For a ridiculous instant, she wanted only to be held by him again. Instead, she laced her fingers together to still their trembling and took a deep breath. "I'm fine." She attempted to smile. "Let's get started. The gear's in my trunk."

Nick studied her and shook his head decisively. "Give me your keys and go sit down for a couple of minutes," he instructed.

"Don't order me around," she returned. "I'm—"

"Look, don't argue," Nick said sharply. "I don't care how tough you are, anyone would need a couple of minutes to recover from a scare like that." His voice softened. "We've got plenty of time. I'll get a couple of the guys to bring the gear over and then we can go to it. Now sit." He paused. "Please?"

Sloane perched on the step of the ladder truck and gradually the wobbliness went out of her muscles. It was a relief to feel like herself again and ready to get started. Before she did, though, she had something to take care of.

She stood and dusted her hands off. "Hey, Trask?" Not Nick. Nick was far too personal now. "I'm ready to get rolling."

Nick turned inquiringly and crossed over to her. "You bounce back fast."

Time to get it over with. She cleared her throat. "Listen, I want to thank you for catching me in there. You saved my life. I'm sorry if I was rude just now." She fumbled for words. "I just...thank you."

He smiled then, clear and uncomplicated. "Relax. It's in my job description. Come on, let me introduce you to the guys."

He led her over to where the crew stood. "Sloane, meet the guys from Ladder 67. This is Todd Beaulieu, Tommy Knapp, George O'Hanlan, our chauffeur, and Jim Sorensen, our probationary firefighter." Nick pointed to each of them quickly. "This is Sloane Hillyard, from Exler. She designed the gear we're testing and she's running the program, so listen up."

Sloane picked up one of the Orienteer modules. "Nice to meet you all. You've gotten the briefing on the equipment. Basically, we use data from a couple of sources to track where you are in a building, so that your commanders and colleagues always know where to find you and you always know your way out." She paused. "The equipment is easy enough to use, but I'd like to demonstrate adjustments and operation first. Volunteers?"

There was silence while the men all looked at one another. O'Hanlan nudged Sorensen. "You should do it, Red. You're the probie."

Sorensen hesitated and with a sound of exasperation, Nick stepped forward. "I'll do it."

"Great." Sloane handed him a helmet and one of the breathing masks equipped with the sugar-cube-sized display module. Then she held up a flat black package about the size of a pack of cigarettes. "This is the Orienteer data module." She slipped the webbed belt around Nick's waist and pulled it around until her fingers snugged up against the flat, ribbed muscles of his stomach. Sudden awareness rolled over her and she fumbled with the clasp. *Shadow, then harsh sunlight... then the hard feel of his body pressed to hers.*

"I'll get it," Nick said abruptly, pulling the strap from her hands. With a snick, the clasp locked. He put on the helmet and breathing mask.

"The belt pack sends a signal to a head-up display embedded in your mask so that you get a blue schematic projected on your faceplate over the background," Sloane murmured, a catch in her breath. "The belt pack also communicates with the master unit at the outside command post so whoever's running the scene can monitor locations on an LCD. The belt pack's a wireless unit, so it can go under your turnouts or even in your pocket." She found herself aware of every slight shift, every scent, every inch of his body. "The switch on top triggers a distress alarm to all of the other units. It shows up on the display here."

As she tapped the clear plastic of his breathing mask, her fingers brushed Nick's cheek. She glanced up involuntarily to find his eyes leveled straight at her. Even with the clear shell of the mask between them, the intensity of his gaze, the desire that flared for an instant stopped her words in her throat.

If the pause was too long, she couldn't tell. For just that time, she was incapable of speaking. Sloane stepped back, too hastily. "I think that's all. If anyone has any trouble with the fit, just ask me."

Nick pulled off the mask. "All right, guys. We're going to run this as a standard timed drill. Keep your mind on the gear, but let's remember that this is also a search-and-rescue exercise. Treat it like the real thing. O'Hanlan, Knapp, you guys take the top two floors, Beaulieu, Sorensen, you guys take the bottom two. By the book, guys, and let's get Harvey and Gladys while you're at it, okay?"

It was the scent she noticed first, the odor of burning wood drifting across on the breeze. Faint tendrils of smoke trickled from the top window.

Knapp rubbed his hands together. "Smell that, guys? Break out the hot dogs and marshmallows, we're ready for a party now."

With casual efficiency, the men donned the masks and modules and walked to the tower. Sloane saw them give a quick thumbs-up to Nick, then they plunged into the thick pall of smoke.

Nick pulled on his turnouts, the thick yellow garments obscuring the lines of his body, to Sloane's relief—and a tiny, sneaky sense of unease that she didn't want to admit. "Are you going in, too?"

Nick slipped on his gloves. "Part of my job. I do it in all fires, unless there's no one else to supervise." He pulled on his gloves. "Besides, I want to see what your work is worth."

In full uniform he became anonymous, one of the ones who

walked into hell. She could almost forget how he'd looked at her. She wanted to, Sloane thought as he headed toward the tower. How very much she wanted to.

There was a gut-level dread of fire in her that skittered around her already nervous stomach. It was a controlled situation, Sloane told herself, there was no need to be apprehensive. Still, where fire was involved no situation was ever really controlled. There was always the freak accident, the unexpected. Firefighting was a profession predicated on risk. And if you took enough risks, it stood to reason that sooner or later you'd pay the price.

She'd won the state science fair in high school, had graduated with honors from both college and grad school. She'd won research grants to develop the Orienteer. None of it had meant as much to her as the fact that her first live test had gone flawlessly. The crew had a suggestion or two, but overall it had been a success.

Now she just needed more.

"Trask," Sloane called as O'Hanlan brought down the ladder. Nick headed toward her, his walk loose and athletic. He'd taken off his turnouts and wore only his gray sweat-darkened department T-shirt and blue pants. It wasn't fair that they looked so good on him.

He looked at her inquiringly. "What do you need? We should get back to the station."

"I wanted to talk with you about the upcoming schedule." She had to strain to be heard over the drone of the ladder motor.

"It's too noisy out here. Let's go into the observation tower." They climbed the steps of the squat tower that sat apart from the burn structure. Nick opened the door and let her go in ahead of him.

The small room appeared to be entirely made up of windows overlooking the training ground. Water had streamed over the concrete and the tangle of hoses from the fire engine. Harvey and Gladys sprawled over behind the ladder truck, amid a pile of helmets and turnout coats, Halligan tools and six-foot-long ceiling hooks. "It looks like a battleground from here," Sloane murmured. She didn't glance away as she spoke.

"It is a battleground. All fires are. It's a matter of winning before they claim any casualties."

Sloane shook her head at the idea and turned. She wasn't prepared to find Nick so close behind her. "You're all crazy, you know." She raised her eyes to meet his. "How can you walk into a burning building knowing you'll face fire, injury, maybe even death?"

Nick shrugged. "I'm a firefighter. It's what I do."

For a moment, Sloane was reminded of a statue of a Roman centurion she'd once seen, strong, proud and utterly fearless. A quick, primitive wave of response rippled through her.

She forced herself to breathe. "I want to do one more testing session in a controlled environment. We've gotten permission to burn down a condemned two-story unit in Roxbury in a week. I'd like to run the crew through there, through a floor plan they don't know to get them used to relying on the Orienteer."

"We can't afford any more time off the street."

His words were quick and final. Sloane's chin came up. "It's not your choice, Trask. I want to be sure about this."

"And I want to keep my men from walking into a burning building if they don't have to. Why not do the second round of testing here?"

"Because after one run through the burn tower, even I could navigate it through heavy smoke." She didn't bother to hide the sarcasm. And she didn't plan to take no for an answer. "I want a better approximation to a real fire ground. I'd think you'd want that, too."

"Look, you know my concerns."

"And you know mine," she countered. "We need to do the testing, period. One or two more days won't hurt."

"It won't hurt?" His eyes were turbulent as hell smoke. "Every minute we're out of the firehouse, people are potentially at risk. Ladder 67 had eighty-two calls last week alone. If an alarm comes in for our company while we're gone, they call in a truck from the next station over." He took a step closer and he was all she could see, all she was aware of. "The next station is two miles away, five minutes under the best of conditions. Do you have any idea what a fire can do in five minutes? Do you know how long even a second is to a person who's trapped, waiting for a ladder?"

The blood drained from Sloane's face. Her eyes were on Nick but her gaze was within as she remembered talking with Mitch's crew chief. "The flashover just took a second or two. If we could have found him, we could have saved him. We got there just after the flashover, but it was too late…."

With an effort, Sloane drew herself together. "I'm sorry about departmental policy, but we need to do this testing in the safest possible way. If everything goes well with the next round, I'll release the units to you to take on a fire ground. It's my decision, though," she warned him. "We've got to be sure everything's working flawlessly and the guys really understand what they're doing." And the conversation needed to be over with, now. She brushed past him toward the door.

"Wait."

"I've said everything I had to say." She was too close to the edge, Sloane thought desperately, way too close.

"Will you just hold on a minute?" Nick pushed his hand against the door. "Stop, dammit."

"What?" Her voice was tight with tension.

"You're right, okay? I'm sorry. I was wrong. It's a fair decision." He caught Sloane's shoulder and turned her to face him.

Because she hadn't had time to compose herself, she was still pale. Her eyes were huge. Nick looked at her slowly, carefully, feeling the pull begin again. "This really matters to you, doesn't it?"

She looked as if she was holding herself together with sheer nerve. "Of course. I want my design to work."

Nick shook his head. "There's more going on than that. You care about this project too much."

"I care about doing my job," Sloane answered stiffly.

"There's something going on here that doesn't have anything to do with the job."

He was right, this wasn't about the job. It was about what had started in the tower and was moving out of her control with frightening speed. "Perhaps you just have an overactive imagination," Sloane responded, fighting to keep her voice even.

"I don't know. Let's test it. Empirical method," he told her as he leaned in, sliding his fingers along her cheek. "Experiment and observe."

"You're out of your mind, Trask."

"Nick," he corrected softly, so close she could feel his mouth form the word.

"What?"

"Call me Nick." Then his lips brushed hers.

Sloane stilled at the contact. Warm, soft and unexpectedly gentle. The sensation didn't bowl her over but simply engulfed her like an ever-rising tide, deceptively calm, relentless in its power. For years, she'd kept herself separate from everyone, for years she'd shied away from a simple human touch. Now, her nerve endings hummed with forgotten sensations. A quick brush with the tip of his tongue, a nibble to tempt her, his exploration was unhurried and exquisite. She barely noticed as he slipped past her defenses and made her yearn.

The subtle sounds of intimacy filled the small space of the tower: the whisper of skin against skin, the soft, involuntary noises of breath, of arousal. And the scent of desire rose around them.

He knew she intrigued him. He hadn't expected the taste of her to trigger an immediate hunger for more. When she gave a soft sigh, he fought the sudden drive to go deeper, to find out if she carried the passionate urgency she brought to the project to all aspects of her life.

He forced himself to go slowly instead, his touch gentle. She was like a fire smoldering in a closed room. He could sense the heat and power but couldn't find its source. The taste of her skin was maddening, her scent powerful enough to make him reel. He journeyed from the soft side of her throat back to her lips and suddenly the fire blazed as her mouth came to life under his.

Sloane didn't know where the hunger came from, knew only that she was driven to taste, to savor, to revel in sensation. For too long, she'd denied herself any contact. Now she searched for more, driven by the feel of his mouth and light brush of his hands over her skin. Desire flashed through her, hot as flame, threatening to overwhelm her entirely.

A blast from the ladder truck's air horn made them jerk apart. Sloane returned to a rapid, flashing clarity. She stared at the scene outside, unable to tell whether any of the men were looking at the observation tower. "Very funny, Trask.

Was this some kind of a show for your men?" She attempted to brush past where he stood, unmoving.

"Hardly. This tower is designed so people can't tell if they're being watched. The windows are smoked so dark you can't see in with the lights on, much less off."

"You'd be the first to point out that designs don't always work as intended," Sloane said curtly. "Now listen to me very carefully, Trask."

"Nick," he corrected.

"Just listen," Sloane snapped. It was terrifying, how easily he'd slashed his way through the barriers she'd surrounded herself with. She had to push him out. She had to escape before he knew how much she was at risk. "I am here to do a job that is entirely dependent on the cooperation of your truck company. I will not have my credibility damaged in front of your men."

"It wasn't damaged."

Her eyes flashed. "It could have been. You're interfering with my work."

"The testing was done for the day," Nick countered.

"I'm on the job as long as I'm on fire department property."

Nick reached out to finger a stray curl of her hair. "Next time I'll make sure we're off department property, then." There was a hint of danger in his smile. It frightened her, because it made her want.

"There won't be a next time," Sloane flared, pushing past him. She paused, her hand on the doorknob. "After all, I'm just a tool for Ayre, right? Try to remind yourself of that every so often."

Chapter Four

The hands of the clock on the wall moved noiselessly, counting off minutes of quiet broken only by the faint tick of pencils, the rustle of paper. Ranks of men sat at the tables, bent over sheaves of paper. Some scribbled madly, some thoughtfully, some stared blankly into space as though answers might suddenly, magically appear in the air in front of them. The second hand made its inexorable sweep about the clock face. The precious minutes marched relentlessly by.

The proctor at the front of the room cleared his throat. "Time, gentlemen. Please stop writing and bring your papers up to the front."

Nick glanced up, feeling as though he had just broken to the surface after a long dive into a deep pool. Over the past months he had packed his brain with an enormous amount of detail about firefighting, fire management, personnel management, equipment, building codes, construction, hazardous materials and department regulations. He could recite the pump pressure of the fire engine and the weight of each size of hose, both empty and filled. Without thinking he could list the flashpoints of gasoline, methanol, dry cleaning fluid and a host of other chemicals. He knew as much about Boston building codes as any building inspector.

For nearly a year it had taken over his life. The hours of study had been worth it, though. The answers had been there when he'd needed them. Now that it was over, he felt light-headed, as though the facts that had poured out onto the paper had had weight. He set his paper down on the stack at the front of the room and walked gratefully out into the quiet of the hallway at fire department headquarters, rubbing his neck to loosen the tense muscles.

All done, he thought, and tried to take it in. For the first time in months he could relax without the voice of guilt reminding him he should be studying. Punching the elevator call button, he bounced a little on the balls of his feet, light with a growing sense of freedom. Maybe he could actually go out for a change, listen to some music, drink a few beers. A bell pinged and the elevator doors opened to allow him into the car.

"Hold the elevator." A voice from the hallway interrupted his thoughts, a voice he recognized with the impact of a fist in his solar plexus.

Sloane Hillyard.

He'd thought of her in the four days since the testing, oh, he'd thought of her. Waving the ladder truck back into quarters after an alarm, sitting down to dinner with the crew, over and over he'd found her on his mind. He'd remembered her scent as he'd pored over statistics about building codes and fire standards. The memory of holding her against him had derailed his review of chemical reactions. He'd studied and he knew a thousand and one facts about firefighting strategies. He thought of Sloane Hillyard and he knew only one thing.

That he wanted her.

Sloane hurried down the hall toward the elevator, her mind on the clock and the relentless calendar. She'd just been through a morning that could have won awards for lack of productivity. She could only hope the afternoon would be better. Ahead of her, the elevator doors opened back up. A sign, she thought. Something, at least, was going right.

And then she stepped into the elevator.

"Hey." Nick smiled at her lazily, leaning against one wall of an otherwise empty car that suddenly seemed very small. He wore a leather bomber jacket over a rough-weave blue shirt and khakis. She'd gotten familiar with the look of him in his departmental T-shirt and trousers. This was the first time she'd seen him in civvies.

She wasn't at all prepared for the impact. They made him look leaner, rangier and subversively sexy.

"Going to the lobby?" Nick's hand hovered over the lighted buttons of the control panel as the car started to move. "Better decide quick."

"The lobby, please." She stood next to him, immensely conscious of his eyes on her. After their last interlude, she'd resolved to put him out of her mind, which had worked about as well as the childhood game of not thinking of elephants. Still, just because she couldn't stop thinking of the kiss didn't mean she had anything to worry about. After all, how long had it been since she'd locked lips with a guy? Of course she'd overreacted. She probably would have with anyone. It was simply a physical response to an extremely attractive man, she'd told herself. Physical hunger was something she could recognize. Physical craving was something she could ignore.

But the feelings that assaulted her when she saw him weren't simple at all.

Nick studied her for a moment. "You look a little frazzled. What's up?"

She gave him the easy answer. "Too many meetings, not enough time." The numbers over the doors lit and extinguished as the elevator dropped. "I spent half the morning in a production meeting with our head of manufacturing and the other with OSHA over at Government Center. I blasted over to Quincy for an eleven o'clock with the National Fire Protection Agency regulator, who told me he had an unavoidable conflict and could I do it this afternoon? I came over here to try and switch my three o'clock meeting with Bill Grant and his gang in research to right after lunch, because of course today of all days I left my cell phone at home. And naturally they can't switch. So far the morning has been a complete write-off and I don't have a whole lot of faith in the afternoon," she finished in frustration.

"It's kind of early to be going to the NFPA and OSHA anyway, isn't it?"

"What do you mean?" She was in no mood to take grief from anyone, Sloane thought, as the elevator slowed. Particularly Nick Trask.

"NFPA certification. I thought that all happened after testing is completed."

"We've spent a lot on R & D for the Orienteer. Exler wants to go into production as soon as the testing is signed off. That means getting as much of the paperwork out of the way now as I can. Assuming that's okay with you." The doors opened and she exited into the lobby without saying goodbye.

She got a few steps outside the door of the building before Nick caught up with her.

"Sloane."

Reluctantly, she turned to face him, expecting mockery or suspicion. And finding neither.

His eyes were steady on hers. "How about if we call a truce? You're having a rotten day, I just got out of a two-hour exam. We both could use a break." He paused. "I'll buy you lunch, but only under certain conditions: no Exler, no gear, no fire department." He stuck his hands in his pockets and gave her a disarming smile. "What do you say?"

She should have refused. If he'd been in uniform, it would have been easy. But he wasn't. For the first time they were totally away from fire department territory, no reminders in sight. For the first time, she saw him as just Nick. Just a man.

And before she quite knew what she was doing, she nodded.

It was his favorite dive, a classic railroad-style diner sandwiched in a small lot between two buildings. Maybe the weather of countless winters had taken the shine off the brushed-steel front, but the windows gleamed and the steps that led up to the door at the end were swept clean. A cheerful neon sign spelled out Ray's in red script. Good Eats flashed above the name; Always Open flashed below.

The interior was just large enough to hold a counter and a row of narrow booths. The gold and white Formica tabletops were spotless, though they'd lost some of their gleam; red vinyl, cracked in places, covered the seats. Next to the cash register hung a photo of a grinning city-league softball team in their Ray's T-shirts; a Red Sox World Series pennant dangled from a thumbtack above it.

And Sloane looked absolutely transported. "I don't believe it," she exclaimed, following Nick to the only two empty seats at the counter. "This is exactly like a place we used to go to where I grew up, only the Blue Hen had pictures of the local bowling team and Little League instead of softball." She shrugged out of her silvery blue overcoat, sighing happily as the comfortable-looking redhead behind the counter laid paper placemats and cutlery before them. "My grandfather used to take us there sometimes for breakfast or after we'd gone sledding. They had the best hot chocolate."

"Where was this?" Nick hung their coats on the nearby wall and handed Sloane a menu from the oblong condiment rack.

"Rochester."

"Land of lake-effect snow?"

"Hey, it saves you money on alarm clocks. You don't need one in winter—the snowplows wake you up every morning."

"Now there's a recommendation."

Her quick, flashing smile stopped him for a moment. He couldn't recall seeing it before. He'd have remembered, he thought, savoring the jolt to his system.

"Sometimes you gotta take what you can get," Sloane said. "It's a good town. It knows where it came from. Like Boston."

The waitress stopped in front of them. "You folks ready to order?"

Sloane took a look at the menu. "Clam chowder for me."

The waitress nodded approvingly. "Made right here, every day. And to drink?"

"Hot tea, please."

"And you, hon?" the waitress asked Nick.

He scanned the menu. "How about the open-faced turkey sandwich and a coffee?" He wasn't interested in food, he was interested in Sloane, in finally having a chance to look his fill, in finally having a chance to peel away some of the camouflage and find out what lay beneath.

Nick shifted in his seat a little to watch her. She looked around the diner, still grinning. This was how he wanted to see her, he thought, happy and carefree for once. Then she glanced at him and he felt the punch of desire.

And in his bed. He wanted to see her in his bed. "Rochester, huh? So you're east-coast born and bred?"

"Not exactly. I'm originally from San Diego. How about you?"

"I've been a New Englander all my life," he said. "Lived in the same town until I was eighteen."

That raised her eyebrows. "Really. Whereabouts?"

"Eastmont, Vermont. It's just over the border from New Hampshire. You know, apple cider, maple leaves, all that stuff?"

"I've never been up that way."

"Too bad. You just missed the best time. Vermont's spectacular in the fall."

"In your unbiased opinion."

He grinned. "Everybody says so." He could see her there, he realized, that bright hair gleaming against the backdrop of blazing color. "When the leaves turn, you get entire hillsides just covered in red and gold. It's pretty spectacular."

"It sounds nice."

"Well, there's always next year to see it. So did you move to the East Coast when you were a kid or have you just been a latecomer to sledding and hot chocolate?"

She flashed him another grin. "Second grade. I thought snow was the greatest thing in the world. Couldn't get enough of it. Snowmen, snow angels."

"Snowball fights," he added. "Remember getting a couple dozen kids together for the monster snowball fight?"

She moved her shoulders. "I didn't know that many people."

She wouldn't have, he thought. He'd never met anyone so self-contained. "It must have been tough," he commented, reaching over to take the coffee the waitress set before him. "New town, new school, new friends. Everything changes."

In her eyes, a shadow flickered. "Everything did," she said softly, looked at the thick, white ceramic mug before her. "Hey." False brightness jangled in her voice. "These are just like the mugs they used to have at the Blue Hen."

Nick watched her unwrap her tea bag and drop it into the small metal pot of hot water to steep. She was an enigma, hard as steel, brittle as glass. There was vulnerability there and a fascination in the mystery. Only a putz fell for the puzzle instead of the woman, he reminded himself, but it didn't stop him from being drawn to her. "So is your family still in Rochester?"

She stiffened, so subtly he might have missed it if he hadn't been looking for it. "No. They're gone." Something in her tone of voice told him not to ask anything more. Fair enough. He'd stop with the family.

For now.

"San Diego, Rochester, Boston. You get around."

"Connecticut, too. I went to UConn."

"For engineering?"

She shook her head. "Biology. I was going to do DNA research, cure cancer, that kind of thing."

"What brought you to Boston?"

"Cambridge, actually." Sloane poured some tea into her mug. "Grad school at MIT. I built the Orienteer for my master's project."

"That seems like kind of a long way from biology and research."

And that quickly the wall was there again, hard and solid. "Things changed." She stirred her tea, even though she hadn't added any milk or sugar.

He studied her. Beautiful? Sure. Desirable? Without a doubt, but there was more to her than that and the more he saw, the more he found himself wanting.

Sloane took a sip of her tea. "Anyway, I seem to be doing all the talking. It's your turn. Tell me about growing up in Vermont. Is Eastmont town or country?"

"Pretty much everything in Vermont is country," he said dryly, "except maybe for Burlington. I grew up on a maple sugar farm."

"Seriously?"

"You bet. Sugar house, maple groves, the whole nine yards."

She gave him a bemused look. "I didn't think people did that kind of thing anymore. I figured it was all agribusiness, like cattle and wheat."

"Not hardly. There are a lot of small farms in Vermont, a lot with history. Trasks have been farming for five generations and we've been producing maple syrup the whole time."

A corner of her mouth tugged up. "With your own two hands?"

He waggled his finger at her. "Don't laugh. I grew up working the farm. Come the spring thaw, we'd be out in the groves before it was light, even, tapping trees, emptying buckets. As soon as we got home from school, same drill."

"I'm sure that violates some kind of child labor laws."

"I didn't mind it, really. I loved being out in the groves the morning after we had a fresh snow. And the smell of wood smoke and maple in the air when we had the sap cooker fired up in the sugar house, that was spring to me." The little surge of nostalgia took him by surprise. He gave his head a shake.

Sloane watched him over her mug. "It sounds like you miss it. Why aren't you up there on the family farm drawing sap or whatever it is you do?"

Now it was time for a few walls of his own to go up. "Just like you. Things changed. Or maybe I did." The waitress was coming by with their plates, he noticed with relief, welcoming the interruption.

"It must have been hard to go from being a small-town boy to living in a city like Boston," Sloane commented, unfolding her napkin in her lap.

"Not really. I don't know why but I just took to the city right off. I like it. It feels right, somehow."

"You don't miss the country?" She sampled her soup.

"Maybe sometimes. Hot apple cider after being out in the groves. All the green in high summer. And I miss skiing every day in the winter."

"Every day?"

He grinned. "When I wasn't cleaning sap buckets or whatever it was that had to be done. We lived maybe half an hour from three or four different ski lodges. We'd head over and do the double diamond runs."

"Why am I not surprised?" She could see him as a reckless sixteen-year-old. "What is it with you adrenaline junkies, anyway? What are you after?"

"Excitement, challenge." His eyes glimmered. "I guess I wanted to lead a reckless life."

"You do," Sloane said quietly, setting down her spoon, appetite suddenly gone.

"Not really. There are safeguards," Nick answered, both of them knowing skiing was no longer the topic.

"Not enough of them."

His expression sobered. "It's the nature of the job. If it's hazardous, it's only because it deals with potentially bigger hazards."

"You act like it's nothing, putting your life on the line." Sloane's voice tightened. It was all suddenly there, the danger, the fear. Today he was sitting next to her, chatting about childhood. Tomorrow he could be engulfed in flames. It was crazy to get to know him, crazy to let any of them get under her skin. It was everything about why she had to leave.

"Sloane." He reached out and turned her chin toward him. "We had an agreement, remember? No fire department."

His touch shimmered over her skin. "I have to go." The words held an edge of desperation. "It's close to time for my appointment." She set her napkin on the counter, refusing to meet his eyes.

Nick studied her. "All right." He rose to get her coat.

It felt cozy, too cozy to have him hold it for her, to feel his hands on her shoulders when he finished. He'd snuck up on her blind side with his talk of Vermont and falling leaves. Now, her only defense was escape. "You don't need to go also. You haven't finished your lunch."

"That's okay, I'm used to it." He picked up the bill and guided her past him with his fingertips in the small of her back.

And heat radiated through her.

She stiffened. This was not the way it was supposed to go. Nick Trask belonged with work and the fire department in the special "handle with care" compartment in her life. She couldn't let his sexy eyes and persuasive voice and pretty stories get to her. And that mouth that turned her mind to mush. She had to stop it and stop it now.

Leaving him at the cash register, she pushed open the door, hoping the October air would clear her head. Outside, the sky was the crystalline blue of a New England fall. The chill breeze whisked red and gold leaves along the avenue. *Entire hillsides covered in red and gold...* Sloane resisted the urge to pound her head against the cold steel pole of a streetlight. Behind her, the door opened.

"So, where to from here?" Nick walked up to lean against the light pole, looking like something out of a magazine ad.

Sloane gave herself a mental shake. "I should get back."

"You've got, what, an hour and a half until your meeting? There's time."

She jammed her hands in her pockets. "Look, it was nice of you to take me to lunch. I enjoyed it."

"So did I."

"But I don't think it should happen again. There's a job to do here, and in the interest of professionalism, I think we should keep away from any other involvement."

His gaze roamed to her mouth, lingered at her neckline. His hands ached to touch her. "What's unprofessional about spending time together?"

"I work for a vendor, you work for the fire department. You're involved in qualifying my equipment."

He couldn't prevent the corner of his mouth from twitching. "It's pretty fine equipment."

"Stop it." Face flaming, she stared at him. "I hardly think the fire department would want us involved. *I* don't want us involved."

"Are you sure about that?" He pushed off the lamppost and took a step toward her. The wind tugged at the collar of her blouse, exposing the long, liquid column of her throat. "What about the testing center?"

"The testing center was a mistake."

"It was pretty intense for a mistake." And it had kept him up at night more than once. "Answer me this. If you're not interested, then why is it you always start trembling when I get just a little bit too close?"

Her chin came up. "I don't tremble."

"Sure you do." He traced his fingertips down her cheek. "Just like you are right now."

Sloane blinked, then shook her head briskly. "You're imagining things." She glanced at her watch. "Look, I have to get back."

"That's a cheap out. You've got time. You can't keep ducking away from this, Sloane." Nick's eyes were smoke dark, snaring hers, not letting her look away.

Awareness rippled through every muscle of her body. Her breath caught in her throat. "Stick to business, Trask," she snapped, trying to mask the edge of desperation. Distance was evaporating. She couldn't continue this much longer. "Round two of testing is tomorrow and then we'll be ready to go live."

The wind caught at his hair, tossing it over his forehead. "Fine. Anything else?"

She should have recognized the dangerously tight tone in his voice. She was too preoccupied with trying to keep her own responses damped down to notice. "No, that's all."

"Good." He bit the word off and pulled her into his arms.

It was the suddenness that took her breath away. It was the unexpectedness that made her knees go weak. It wasn't desire, she thought in panic, it couldn't be.

She didn't have a choice.

There had been no warning, just complete sensory assault that broke through the diminishing distance that she'd surrounded herself with. If it had been quick, perhaps she could have waited him out, but it wasn't. His hands roved over her back, his mouth demanded a response. There was no gentleness this time. This time he took and she gave, oh, she gave.

He broke through to the wanting, released the desire she'd tried to shut away in a flush of heat that surprised them both. She met the challenge of lips and teeth and tongue, plunging deeper into the kiss and pulling him after.

Nick felt her quake as he held her. Her strength, her fragility, her secrets combined to draw him on and in. Nothing, no one had ever been like this for him. He couldn't pull back from it, couldn't pull away from her. Nothing in him wanted to.

She was intoxicating in her desire. It didn't matter that they were on a public street in broad daylight. The dominant thought in his head was *more.* He felt her hands in his hair, shuddered as she traced fingers down his back. He ran his lips down her jaw, tasting the silky skin, and heard her soft moan.

How could she defend against this, Sloane wondered dizzily. It was as though he'd taken her over. It seemed impossible that she'd existed without this feeling for so long. Now, like a starving woman confronted with a banquet, she was incapable of holding back. Get away, she thought, even as her arms pulled him closer. Then his mouth found hers again and for that instant of time she became incapable of coherent thought. There was only seduction and pleasure, the sharp nip of teeth tantalizing her, the taste and texture of his tongue arousing.

They were in public, Nick reminded himself. Some sane portion of his mind warned him to stop before he lost control entirely.

Before he took it too far.

He dragged himself back from the edge and gathered enough strength to press her away. They stared at each other, breathing hard. Sloane's eyes were hot with fury and desire.

"What the hell do you think you're doing?" she asked in a shaking voice.

"The same thing you were doing. Are you going to tell me you didn't enjoy it?"

"No, I'm not." Her gaze was unflinching. "But it doesn't matter. I keep telling you I don't want to get involved."

He reached out and traced a finger down her throat, watching her shiver. "I think it might be a little too late for that." He gave her a friendly smile. "Come on, I'll walk you back to the department."

Home was usually a sanctuary, but not that night. Sloane prowled her flat restlessly. Cambridge was never short of distractions, but she didn't really feel like being out among people. A workout might have let her burn off the nervous tension, but she'd already been to the gym that morning. She debated a glass of wine. To relax, she told herself, but she knew that it would be partly to banish thoughts of Nick and decided against it.

He was sadly confused if he thought that something was brewing between them. It wasn't going to happen. She couldn't afford to let it. And yet, somehow it felt as if it was slipping out of her control.

The sound of the front bell made her start a little. She crossed over to the intercom. "Hello?"

"Sloane, it's Candy."

It was the last voice she'd have expected. Candy, her brother's widow. Candy, who'd been as close a friend as she'd ever had.

Candy, whom she hadn't seen in over a year and a half. Once upon a time, they'd been almost like sisters. They'd done everything together. They'd been close enough to finish one another's sentences.

Once upon a time.

And the loss that never really went away came welling up again, made vivid by the reminder of Candy's voice.

The intercom buzzed again. "Hello? Is this thing working?"

Sloane bit down on her lower lip, hard. "Sorry, I missed the button. Come on up."

The minute it took Candy to come inside gave Sloane a chance to regain her composure. By the time she met her at the top of the stairs, Sloane could give her a hug and a genuine smile. For a minute, everything was all right.

Candy had lost weight since they'd seen each other last. Her hair was a brighter gold, there was a new assurance in her movements.

"What are you doing here?"

Candy's mouth quirked. "Gee, Sloane, it's nice to see you, too."

"No, it's great to see you. I meant what brings you up from Hartford?"

"I've got a two-day marketing seminar in town. I left a message on your answering machine about a week ago, asking about dinner." She glanced over to where the machine sat blinking. "Of course, you may not have gotten it."

Sloane shifted uncomfortably. "I don't check the machine here very often. Work's the best place to get me."

A mixture of reproach and resignation flickered over Candy's face. "Checking out from the world again?"

"Not at all," Sloane said briskly, shoving the guilt away down deep. "For example, tonight I'm going to take my sister-in-law out to dinner."

"Unless your sister-in-law takes you out first," Candy replied. "Expense account, remember? Dinner's on me, tonight." She grinned. "Get your coat and let's go somewhere nice. I'm starving."

* * *

They lingered over dinner at Icarus, bathed in the warm rosy glow of the tony South End restaurant's dark wood and blush-colored walls.

"So how are things?" Sloane asked. "You look good. I like the hair."

"Thanks. I was worried it was going to come out too blond, but it seems to work."

"Very polished. You look like a fast-tracker. Is the seminar going well?"

"Good. I'm learning a lot so time goes pretty fast. How's work going for you?"

"Great. I'm keeping busy."

"A good way to keep warm this time of year. I swear it's another four or five degrees colder up here than back home."

How had it come to this? Sloane wondered. There was a time when Candy would have been her first confidante about everything. Forget about hair and weather, they'd have poured some wine and started really dishing, sharing their lives. Now, they'd been reduced to small talk.

A wave of regret washed through her. She set down her fork.

"So, it's Pete's birthday in a couple of weeks," Candy was saying. "He's going to be thirteen. We're having a little party. I thought maybe you could come down for it. It would mean a lot to him."

Come down to the house where Sloane had lived with Mitch and his wife after their grandfather had died, while she was finishing high school, going to UConn. Sloane swallowed. "I don't see how I can." She remembered her last visit to the Hartford house, the memories crowding up around her until she couldn't breathe. The memories Candy brought with her. "It's just that I'm in a critical phase of this project right now."

"You've been in a critical phase for the past four years," Candy said quietly.

"We've started testing. Now's the time that really counts."

"Now's the time with Pete, too."

"Candy, I just need to get past this," Sloane said desperately, knowing as she said it that she wasn't talking about the Orienteer project.

"I know that you do." Candy's voice was soft as she looked down at the pale-rose tablecloth. Laughter erupted at a table across the room. The waiter leaned in to clear away their entrees.

"Dinner was wonderful. You're going to have to come here for marketing seminars more often," Sloane said, trying for a change in subject.

"Hartford's not that far away, you know," Candy told Sloane as she topped off their glasses. "You could come to dinner. We miss you," she added.

"I check in with you guys," Sloane protested.

"Sure. Birthday cards, holiday cards. Shoot, not a week goes by that Pete doesn't get a postcard or a letter from you. But I bet he could walk right past you on the street and you wouldn't recognize him. It's not the same, Sloane."

It felt as though she were sinking in quicksand and her chest tightened. "I've been pretty tied up with work."

"Sure. Work."

"I'm doing something important, Candy. When it's done, I'll have more time. Hey, how's Pete doing?" she asked, trying to ignore the flash of hurt in Candy's eyes. "He doesn't write back very often."

There was a pause. "Not great," Candy said finally. "He's a good kid but he's having trouble in school. He's not concentrating well. He hasn't, really, since we lost Mitch."

Sloane's stomach tightened. "Is he still seeing the therapist?"

"Some." Candy spun her wineglass slowly by the stem. "Do you mind if I ask you a personal question?" She hesitated. "Mitch never wanted to talk much about when you lost your parents. How was it for you?"

Like the world had spun off its axis and nothing would ever be safe again. And it was just the first time she would have that feeling. "God, Candy, it's hard to go back there. I was so young."

"Eight isn't that young, Sloane." Her eyes were bleak. "Talk to me. Help me understand. How do you get past it?"

How could Sloane tell her that sometimes maybe you didn't?

"The therapist says he has to work his way through it so that he doesn't get emotionally locked in. I don't think he's ever really grieved. How did you do it?"

"I don't know. I had Mitch. I had my grandparents." She paused. "For a while, anyway."

"Pete has my parents, he's got me. Maybe he's got to get used to the fact that that's all he's got."

"I do what I can," Sloane whispered.

Candy reached across the table and took her hand. "I know."

Chapter Five

The sounds of ringing shattered the silence in the dark room. Nick jerked awake. Reflexively, he reached for his turnouts, searching blindly with his hand. And came up with a remote control. Consciousness dawned even as the ring repeated.

It wasn't an alarm, he realized, it was his phone.

"Yeah," he mumbled into the receiver, swinging groggily upright on his living-room couch. He'd stumbled into his house after working a twenty-four-hour trick, dumped his kit and flopped down on the couch intending to relax for a few minutes before he did something about dinner.

That had been ten hours before.

"I'm sorry, honey, I didn't realize you'd be asleep. I'll call you later."

It was his mother. He scrubbed a hand through his hair. "Hey. Everything okay?"

"Of course. Everything's fine, I'll let you go."

"It's okay, I'm up now." He yawned. "Talk to me. I've got to stay on a normal schedule anyway. Billy's got a rush job to frame up a couple of houses." Billy Burnett was a local contractor who threw work Nick's way when he had time. "I'm going to work for him Thursday through Saturday."

"Those are your days off."

"I need the money. I didn't do a lick of work for him the last two months because of the exam. I've got a lot of catching up to do. Renovation of this place ain't cheap, you know," he added, looking around the living room of the Methuen fixer-upper he'd bought the year before.

"I think it's criminal that the fire department doesn't pay you men a living wage. What other job forces people to kill themselves working outside jobs to make ends meet?"

Nick rose and stretched. "Feel free to write the city of Boston, but I don't think it'll change any time soon. It is what it is, Ma. Besides, I like swinging a hammer."

His mother snorted, unconvinced. "How did your exam go?"

"I think I scored pretty high but that doesn't mean anything until the rankings come out. I'm hoping I'll wind up near the top of the list. Then it's just a matter of waiting for an opening."

"How long?"

"Hard to say. Could be months, could be a couple years." He rose and headed toward the kitchen, taking the cordless phone with him. "So how was your birthday?"

"Very nice. Jacob and I drove to Gabriel's hotel and we all had dinner. That's why we weren't home when you called."

"Champagne kisses and caviar dreams?" He rummaged in the cupboard for a new coffee filter.

"It's a beautiful place. A little too snitzy for me, but Gabriel loves it and you can tell the people who work for him like him a lot."

Now is was Nick's turn to snort. "It's all an act. They live in fear of him. He's broken their spirits."

"Oh, I expect he's a very fair boss, just like you are."

"And did you like your gift?" he asked, scooping coffee into the filter.

"It's lovely." Pleasure bloomed in her voice. "Such a sweet idea. I wish I could wear it all the time."

"Why can't you?"

She laughed. "Gathering eggs in the henhouse? With my luck I'd catch it on a nail or something and break it."

"Ma, if you want to wear it, wear it. That's why we got it for you. Put it under your shirt if you're worried."

"Do you think?"

"Yeah, I think. It'll be fine."

"Then I will," she said happily.

"Glad to see you've got some sense. So how's everything else going?"

"Oh, we're well. We got about six inches of snow last night, so Jacob's been up and down in the groves making sure everything is all right."

"It's good for him. Gives him something to do." Nick focused on the coffeemaker, willing it to brew.

"I think he's happiest when he's got a to-do list a mile long and most of it involves being outside," she agreed. "He's always been the best suited of the three of you to the farm."

God knew *he* hadn't been, Nick thought. Too much quiet, not enough action. Being in the ladder truck headed to a fire in Boston, that was where he was happiest. "Everything okay with Gabe? I haven't talked with him for a while."

"Oh he's fine. A little worried, maybe. The owner of his hotel passed away and they're making rumblings about changes."

"Gabe doesn't mind changes." That would be Jacob, who always wanted things to remain the same.

"Yes, but he wants to be the one to choose them. How did I raise three such stubborn men?"

Nick grinned as he poured coffee and took a blissful sip. "Surely we couldn't have gotten it from you?"

"You know who you got it from. There wasn't a more stubborn man born than your father."

"Lucky for us. Otherwise, he wouldn't have kept after you until you married him and we wouldn't be here."

"Well, I'm glad he stuck with it, too. Anyway, I should let you go. I was mostly calling to see if you survived."

"I did, thanks. Sorry I missed your birthday. I'll try to get up there soon. I've got a lot of work in the next couple months, but I should have a few days coming after that."

"We're going to see you at Thanksgiving, aren't we?"

Guilt pricked at him. "I wish. I'm booked for day shift the day before and then night shift on Thanksgiving."

"Oh." She paused. "That's a shame. The other kids are all going to be here and I've invited the other Trasks."

"The whole clan," he said slowly. "You haven't done that in years."

"I thought it would be nice to gather for something happy for a change."

Even all these months later, the whisper of grief still lurked in her voice. And it left him with the same helpless feeling it always did. "I don't see how I can do it, Ma. The best I could do would be drive up for breakfast and head out after."

"Of course not. You'd spend more time on the road than

you would with us. I don't want you to take the chance of being tired in a fire. Stay in Boston. We'll keep."

"I really will make it up there. I swear. Look, I've got a three-day break after the holiday. I've got some cabinets being delivered for the house, but I'll try to get up for a couple of days at the end."

"Are you ever going to finish that house?"

Nick looked around the living room with its stripped walls awaiting fresh paint. "One of these days."

"And then you'll sell it and turn around and buy another. You thrive on chaos, Nicholas," she said reprovingly.

"I thrive on hard work."

"Like your brothers. I thought now that your test was out of the way, we might see you a little more."

"I'll get up there the week after the holiday, I swear."

"And you'll spend the whole time itching to install those cabinets," she said in amused resignation.

Nick shrugged. "They'll keep."

"Put in your cabinets. Come up later if you can. Are you working Christmas?"

"Christmas Day. I'm off Christmas Eve, though."

"Then you can come up then."

"Or you can come down."

"Don't you want to see your brothers?"

Nick didn't want to go there. "Look, I'll make it up there," he promised. "Soon. Tell everyone I said hello and tell Jacob to give you a big kiss for me."

The last light from the setting sun was fading as Sloane pulled her car into the little parking lot next to the fire station. It was the worst part about fall, the gradual shortening of the days. Sloane turned off her engine and let out a long breath, tapping her fingers on the wheel. A week had passed since the scene in front of the diner. A week during which she'd been completely unable to work out any rational plan when it came to dealing with Nick Trask.

Not that she had a lot of experience when it came to dealing with men in general. Oh, she'd dated in high school a few times but little more. It had been college before she'd gotten serious about anyone. She'd met Greg Bentley in a lab class junior year. He'd made her laugh, talked her into study sessions that stretched into pizza and beer at the student center. Those sessions had morphed into dates, at first occasional and then regularly. Let me in, he'd said. He'd been patient and she'd finally trusted him enough, cared for him enough to give him her innocence in a night that she still didn't regret.

Then Mitch had been killed and it was as though everything had frozen up inside of her. She couldn't let anybody in, not Candy, not Greg, not anyone—not that anyone else was left. As the months had worn on, Greg had been first understanding, then impatient, then frustrated.

Then gone.

Because she'd never been able to tell him the truth, the fear, the lesson she'd learned over and over since she'd been a child—that everybody she loved, she lost.

After that, men hadn't mattered a whole lot. She'd been too preoccupied in grad school with building the Orienteer and finding a home for it. What physical needs she had, she could gratify herself. Then again, she'd never understood what physical needs really were until Nick Trask had come along.

With an impatient noise, Sloane got out of the car. All right, so five years of celibacy was enough to make any person a little itchy. There was nothing magical about Nick. He was just a man, she reminded herself, trying to ignore the little taunting voice in her head. The best thing to do was keep her distance.

The only problem was that she hadn't a clue how.

Popping the trunk, she reached in for a small plastic bin. They were taking the tests live, which meant the end was in sight. It had helped that Nick had skipped the testing session the previous week, called away as an emergency substitution for an absent officer at another company. She'd have suffered torture before admitting she'd felt even the tiniest hint of disappointment.

All that was left to do now was drop off the units for the live tests, supervise the fire incidents and log the data. She'd found herself more than a little tempted to drop the gear off during the day, before Nick and the rest of his crew arrived for their scheduled night shift. It was precisely because she'd been tempted that she made herself wait until dusk. She wasn't about to let the job suffer for her own personal qualms. All she had to do was stop in, drop off the gear and leave. Straightforward and quick, right?

Except Nick would be there and it wouldn't be straightforward at all. With a growl of frustration, Sloane looped her satchel over her shoulder and picked up the bin. The best thing to do was get it over with.

On the apron in front of the firehouse sat the pumper, its high red sides gleaming. Behind it, the apparatus floor was dark, lit only by lightning-quick flashes that dazzled the eye. Sloane frowned. Craning her neck to see around the vehicle, she skirted it and crossed under the overhead door. Cobwebs dangling from the door traced over her cheek. Unable to repress a shudder, she wiped at her face with her free hand.

And looked ahead at a bizarre scene.

Everything looked strange, disjointed in the flickering light of the strobe. She caught a glimpse of a limp figure in white swinging ominously from the rafters. Across the way, a zombielike form materialized out of the rack of turnouts and helmets and shambled toward her, blood spilling down the front of its shirt. In the stop action of the strobe, it seemed to vault forward in fits and starts. Even as she stared, another form leapt at her from the side, arms and legs waving and what looked like an eyeball dangling down its cheek.

Sloane jumped back reflexively, bumping up against something solid and human behind her. Quick arms came around her. She gave a muffled cry of surprise.

The zombies broke into laughter. "Gotcha," the one with the dangling eyeball said in O'Hanlan's voice.

The arms released her and she turned to see Nick. "Happy Halloween."

Adrenaline surged through her system. "Halloween," she said blankly. "I forgot all about it." Just another man? She'd been out of her mind even to think it.

"It's not Halloween," O'Hanlan said with a broad grin. "We had a rescue call, got a little messy."

Knapp cackled. "O'Hanlan lost his grip on a bag of O-positive. I think it's a good look for him. Whaddya think?"

Sloane grinned. "I think you're a bunch of sick puppies is what I think."

"We figured we'd reverse the trick or treat on the neighborhood kids, see if we can get them to give us candy for a peek inside."

"Yeah. Did you bring us candy?" O'Hanlan asked, looking with interest at her bin.

"Actually, I brought something better—the gear. It's time to go live. No more playing around."

"Hear that, Trask? No more playing around."

"Yeah," Nick said slowly. "I did."

Sloane cleared her throat. "If we could get away from the strobe light, I can hand this over and we'll be all set."

"Well, then, let's take it upstairs." He looked at the costumed firefighters. "All right guys, you know the rules. Only four kids at a time and Sorensen stays with them. Alarm comes, Red, what do you do?"

"Kids go out, I put on my turnouts in the truck," Sorensen returned snappily.

Sloane smiled at the probie's earnestness. "And what about the rest of you guys?" she asked the zombies.

"Hey, we take off the masks, close up our turnout coats, and who's to know the difference?" O'Hanlan asked.

Sloane grinned. "Let's just hope you don't get a medical aid call for a heart attack victim. You show up with that eyeball hanging down your face and they may never recover."

O'Hanlan batted at the plastic ball until it was swinging. "I kind of like it. I think—"

"Trick or treat," chorused a group of small voices behind them.

Nick gave a brisk nod. "Okay, guys, go to it but remember the rules. Sloane and I need to talk about what comes next." He took the bin from her. "My office?"

She took a deep breath and squared her shoulders. "Sure."

"So." Nick kicked the door shut with one foot to shut out the Halloween music from downstairs and set the bin on his desk. "Whatcha got?"

Sloane pulled off the lid. "Five Orienteers, all qualified and calibrated and ready to go." She set the transmitters out one by one. "The guys already know how to attach the display modules to their masks. I updated the software yesterday and calibrated the hardware. You're good to go. All you have to do is call me when you get to a fire so I can monitor."

Nick leaned on the edge of his desk, looking at her until she shifted in discomfort. "Are you aware that yesterday was Sunday?" He watched the color drift into her cheeks and fought the urge to brush his fingertips across them.

"Yes. What of it? Lots of people work on Sunday." She slapped the lid on the bin with unnecessary force.

"Nothing," he shrugged, amused at the defensiveness in her tone. "I just thought you might have forgotten that it was the weekend. All work and no play…"

"Is that a polite way of telling me to get a life?"

"Well, work isn't everything, you know."

"Did I ask for your opinion?"

Now he grinned. "My mistake. I thought I remembered us having a civil conversation a few days ago. Or was that just a cease-fire?"

"Détente." Today, she was in jeans and ankle boots, topped by a suede blazer the color of rust. In her throat, the pulse beat under her translucent redhead's skin.

Her hair, as always, was twisted up in a chignon, but this time there were little strands hanging loose around her cheeks from where she'd rubbed away the phantom cobwebs as she came into the firehouse. It made him think about what she'd look like in the morning, soft and heavy eyed with sleep.

After they'd spent the night making love.

"What are you looking at?"

"I'm trying to imagine what you'd look like with your hair down. Every time I've seen you, you've had it pinned up. It's long, though, isn't it?"

"Why do you care?" she asked suspiciously.

Because she was beginning to be all he could think about?

He reached out to touch one of the tendrils that hung along her cheeks. "I'd like to see it sometime."

Sloane stepped away from him and sat in the client chair. "Look, Nick, it was good of you to take me to lunch the other day. I enjoyed it."

"Are we going to have another one of these conversations?"

"If we need to." She gave him a green-eyed stare, chin raised mutinously.

Walking away wasn't an option. But perhaps there were others.... "Okay, maybe you've got a point about keeping personal and professional separate. I'd say this is a hardly an appropriate conversation for the station."

"I'm glad you've—"

"I think we should have it somewhere else. Preferably somewhere quiet with good bourbon. Any suggestions?"

Her brows lowered. "If that's a cute way of asking me out, the answer's no."

"Trust me, when I ask you out I'll be a lot more direct. It's simple. We've got an issue to resolve that I think you'll agree has nothing to do with the work we're both paid to do."

"Yes but—"

"I'm just suggesting we take it elsewhere."

"The issue doesn't need any resolving. We're colleagues, period. There *is* nothing else."

He took a swift step toward her chair and pinned her in place with his hands on the arms before she could rise. "I could demonstrate, if you like." Holding her gaze, he leaned in, close enough to smell her scent, close enough to hear her breath.

Close enough to see her eyes darken.

"Now do you think there's nothing to talk about?"

Sloane stared at him, every atom of her being focusing on his mouth hovering just an inch away from hers. She knew it was outrageous, she knew it was a chance they had no business taking but God, she wanted him.

And she knew she couldn't avoid what was between them anymore. "Fine," she said in acceptance. When he moved away to his desk, she wasn't sure whether to feel relief or disappointment. She rose. "You're right, we need to clear the air. You're off tomorrow, right?" He nodded. "Okay, then, tomorrow night at seven."

"Where do you live?"

"We're not meeting at my apartment," she replied firmly.

Nick smiled a little. "I didn't say we were. You picked the time, I get to pick the place. I want to make it convenient."

"Harvard Square."

"That's easy, then. Kendall's, on Brattle Street."

Sloane frowned. "Never heard of it."

"You wouldn't have. It's about a block down from Algiers, on the right, below the dry cleaner's. I'll meet you outside."

"Inside," she corrected. "This is not a date, Trask." She rose. "I don't know what this is."

Tucked away on a quiet corner blocks away from the university, Kendall's was discreet to the point of being practically hidden, with only a small sign advertising its location. Sloane descended the short flight of stairs to the doorway, holding her coat tightly around her for warmth.

"Couldn't find a parking place?"

She jumped to find Nick behind her.

"I thought I told you to meet me inside."

"I'm not very good at taking directions," he told her.

"Stubborn," she muttered.

"So I've been told." He opened the door and gestured her inside.

She wasn't sure what she'd expected. Considering it was the Harvard Square neighborhood, maybe an Irish pub, or a microbrewery, a student hangout of some kind. It was none of the above. Kendall's was a neighborhood bar, no faux nostalgia décor, no trendy signs, just quiet, clean and comfortably shabby. There were no drunken undergraduates teetering on the stools, just enough regulars to make the place feel homey without being crowded. A neatly bearded bartender in a white apron lined up glasses behind the bar.

"How did you find this place?" Sloane asked, following Nick to a pair of stools at the far end of the bar, where the polished wood met the wall. "It's got a good feel to it."

He slid onto a leather-covered seat. "I was working a job near here for a couple months. The guys liked to stop in for a drink on the way home."

"You worked for the Cambridge fire department?"

"Construction. Side job," he elaborated. "I frame houses, build decks, hang drywall. Firefighting's a great job but it doesn't pay. You do it for love, not wealth."

The bartender set a couple of napkins and a dish of peanuts on the bar in front of them. "What can I get you?"

Sloane considered. "Maker's Mark on the rocks, water back."

Nick looked at the bartender. "Two of those, please." He turned a little on his stool to look at Sloane. "Looks like we have something in common."

"Don't let it go to your head."

He gave a quick smile. "Oh, I don't think that's all we have in common."

With quick competence, the bartender delivered their drinks and retreated. Nick raised his glass. "To polite conversation." He touched his glass to hers.

Sloane tasted the bite of the bourbon and felt it spread tendrils of warmth through her veins.

"See now, isn't this better?" Nick asked.

"Than what?"

"Bickering, for one." He leaned against the wall, watching her over the top of his glass. "We're always fighting over something and I can't figure out why."

Sloane stared at the bottles on the back wall. "Bad chemistry?"

"You know better."

"Yes." She moved her glass in little circles on the polished wood of the bar. "I do." Her eyes were steady on his. "And I don't know what to do about it."

"Why do you have to do something about it?"

"Because, when I'm not around you, I can think of all sorts of good reasons why we shouldn't be involved." When he reached out to tangle his fingers with hers, heat zoomed up her arm. Sloane looked at him helplessly. "And then I get around you and you do something like that."

"It's supposed to be a good thing. I'm attracted to you, you're attracted to me. Normally, that's all people need to get together."

She felt as if she were standing on a sandbar that was slowly eroding out from under her. Sloane swallowed. "I don't get together."

"Ever?"

"Not often."

His eyes were very dark in the subdued light of the bar. "Then why are you here with me now?"

"I don't know."

"And that bothers you," he said quietly.

What bothered her was that he'd gotten under her skin with his persuasive voice and addictive mouth and relentless eyes. She didn't want to want him. She wanted her life to go back to being safe and normal and solitary.

The problem was, she wasn't sure that was possible.

Sloane cleared her throat. "Look, Nick, this project is really important to me. I've been working on it a long time. I can't lose track of it here at the end."

"You think I'd do anything to endanger that?"

"Not intentionally. Then again, you don't believe in it much."

"Uh-uh, you're talking about work again. This is about us."

"Work is part of it, don't you see?"

"No, I don't. Can't it just be as simple as you and me trying this out to see what happens? You know, the kinds of things normal people do, dinner, maybe, or a concert. We could have fun."

"Why are you so hung up on this?" Sloane demanded. "There have to be plenty of other women out there you could see."

"I don't want other women. I want you."

It snatched the breath from her lungs. The bar around them receded from her consciousness. All she saw, all she was aware of was the dark gaze holding her as though he wanted to delve into her soul.

"I'm stubborn, as you've already pointed out," he said. "And I'm not going away. You might as well start getting used to the idea."

"I can't do this yet, Nick," she said desperately. The shifting sand underfoot was gone and she was in over her head, struggling to stay afloat.

Nick gave her a long look. "Then I guess we'll have to wait a little while until you can."

Chapter Six

The bedroom smelled of musk and seduction, the sheets soft and tangled against their naked bodies. Nick's mouth moved over her neck and his hands, oh those broad, warm hands possessed her. She'd forgotten how exquisite the feel of skin on skin could be. It would almost be enough to have just this, the feel of his hard, sinewy body against hers, the freedom to run her greedy hands over his shoulders, the corrugated lines of his abs.

But there was more, she knew in giddy delight.

He stroked her breasts and she sighed, searching for his mouth with hers. "Take a chance, Sloane." His words were a tease, his lips a hairbreadth away, holding out the promise of a kiss to her like candy to a child.

Her answer was a moan.

His hands curved over her hips, tracing the tops of her thighs, lingering until she gasped. Like a gourmet, he sampled the flavor of her earlobe, her cheek. Sloane moved to capture his mouth, but he evaded her, continuing his slow, exquisite torture. "Take a chance," he whispered.

The bells of an alarm box interrupted his words and she realized that they were in the firehouse dormitory. The room erupted in motion, the crew racing for the fire pole. "Everybody goes," a voice crackled above the ear-bursting alarm. "Everybody goes." The cacophony merged into the shrilling of her clock radio as Sloane came fighting up out of sleep.

Groping blindly, she finally managed to shut it off and opened her eyes to the morning sun slanting across her bed. For a moment she just blinked at the light, waiting for the disorientation to fade. It had been too vivid. She was almost surprised not to see a dip in the pillow next to hers. Her body still buzzed a little with sensation. Even the sheets against her skin felt delicious, every movement an invitation. She was half-tempted to close her eyes and see if she could slip back into the dream, and it was that thought, finally, that got her out of bed.

The warm water of the shower slid over her skin, hypnotic as a lover's touch. Turning the tap to cold scarcely made a difference. Even the impatience she felt with herself was distant, unimportant. As though it really were the morning after, she moved in a cloud of fatuous pleasure.

Sloane dried her hair and slipped into lingerie, silk and lace whispering over her skin. Nothing in her closet matched her mood, she thought, staring at the ranks of discreet, tailored suits. They all looked too confining. The day demanded something different.

The knock at the front door was first a surprise, then, as she glanced at the clock, an annoyance. Visitors at seven-thirty were not the usual order of the day. She pressed the intercom button. "Who is it?"

"Nick Trask."

She blinked. Of all the people she might have expected at her door, he'd have been the last. Granted, he'd walked her home from Kendall's, so he knew where she lived, but still…

She pressed the intercom button. "Come on up. It's the door at the top of the stairs."

Ducking into the bathroom to grab her robe, she belted it on securely. Then she headed to the door.

And opened it to see Nick coming up her stairs.

Overnight stubble blued his jaw. He wore faded jeans and his leather jacket over a white T-shirt. If she ran her hands beneath the fabric, she knew exactly how the ridges of his abs would feel under her fingertips. Her first thought was not what he was doing there, but how natural he looked framed by her doorway. It was as though she'd expected him. In the aftermath of the dream, she wondered with a thread of disquiet if she had.

He stopped in front of her. "Good morning."

He'd come by on the spur of the moment, because he wanted, no, needed, to see her. If he'd known what the image of her standing at the door in her silky robe, her hair tumbling down over her shoulders would do to him, he might have driven on by. He'd give her time, he'd said. He wasn't sure how he was going to manage it. "I brought up your newspaper," he said, pushing the plastic-wrapped bundle at her.

"Thanks." She watched him, looking, he knew, at the mileage from a rough couple of days. "No offense, but you look like hell."

He ran a fist along his jaw. "That bad, huh?"

"When was the last time you got some sleep?"

Sleep? He couldn't remember. Yesterday seemed an endless time ago. "A couple of days. Things have been busy. Can I come in?"

"Of course." Sloane stepped back from the door, gesturing him in. "That way you can sit down before you pass out in my hall and give the classics professor upstairs something to sniff at on her way out the door."

"I'm not that far gone, don't worry."

"Are you sure?"

"Positive," he said, following her into the living room.

It was a spacious, high-ceilinged room with broad moldings and wide bay windows that brought in the morning sun. A milk-glass fixture hung from a rosette medallion on the ceiling. His builder's eye saw good structure, graceful lines. Unfortunately, it appeared to be furnished in Early American garage sale, with rugs courtesy of the remnant room at Carpets-R-Us. It was tidy verging on spartan, with little sense of warmth or indeed that anyone made a home there.

Sloane shifted uncomfortably. "I haven't had a chance to do it up yet," she said.

"Lived here long?" A couple of bookshelves lined one wall. She alternated between reading engineering texts and detective novels, as near as he could tell.

"A couple of years."

"Let me guess, you've been working." The couch, he discovered, was surprisingly comfortable and he leaned back with a sigh.

Sloane frowned at him, hands on her hips. "So how exactly did you get into this kind of shape?"

"Oh, a twenty-four-hour trick, the full moon, the four-way payday, a lot of things. We've been…busy." His voice was subdued.

"How about some coffee?"

"That'd be great."

The coffee was already brewed; she had only to go to the kitchen to get it. Walking back carefully to avoid spilling, she got to the threshold of the living room before she looked over at him. And then she simply stared.

Nick sprawled carelessly on her overstuffed couch, eyes closed, jacket off, long legs stretched out under the coffee table. How was it that he was completely relaxed in her home while she was suddenly awkward? "Here you go," Sloane said briskly. She set the mugs on coasters, then settled herself on the chair at his end of the couch, resisting the urge to clutch the robe to her throat like some vaporous Victorian maiden.

His charcoal eyes opened. For a moment, he simply watched her until she wondered if her ivory silk camisole was showing. With a low sound of effort he sat up. "Thanks. At least now I'll stay awake long enough to get home."

Sloane lifted her mug, the sides of the cup heating her hands. Empty seconds dragged by. She shifted on the chair. "So."

"So?" Nick took a grateful drink of coffee.

"Um, no offense, but what are you doing here?"

"I brought you a little present." He set something on the table and reached for the coffee again. "From one of your Orienteers."

"From one of…" Sloane leaned over and picked the object up. It was one of the helmet display modules, or had been at one time. Now it was mostly a warped clump of plastic. Comprehension dawned. And the beginnings of irritation. "You had a fire last night."

"A fire?" Nick shook his head, taking a drink and setting his coffee down. "No, I don't think you could call it a fire. Conflagration is a better word, or maybe inferno." He leaned his head back on the couch wearily and winced.

"You were supposed to call me so I could be there," Sloane reminded him.

Nick let out a long breath. "There wasn't time."

Sloane set the melted display back on the table. "Nick, this testing is important. The longer we take to qualify the gear, the longer it'll take to get deployed and the longer guys will be at risk."

"That's assuming it gets deployed at all. Look, we were fighting a fire. That takes priority over everything."

"How about the evaluation sheets? Tell me you at least managed to do that much."

"Sorry." He shook his head.

"Why not?"

"We barely got back to the station by the end of shift. The last thing I wanted to do was bother the guys for feedback. I'll get it next shift."

When they'd have forgotten most of the details. "So you didn't notify me, you didn't get evaluation sheets, you melted the equipment. You do remember you're supposed to be co-operating, right?"

Nick frowned. "It was almost three in the morning. I didn't have time to wait for you to wake up and answer the phone. We caught a three-alarm fire at one of the projects in Dorchester. People were going to die if we didn't get them out." He leaned his elbows on his knees and rubbed his eyes tiredly. "Your gear worked fine. The only problem is that the clips that hold the displays to the helmets aren't as solid as they could be. This one got knocked off Knapp's helmet by his ceiling hook."

Sloane picked up the display again. "If I'd been there, I might have been able to fix the clips."

"What do you think a fire scene's about?" Nick demanded, dropping his hands. "Do you think we'd be standing around waiting for you to MacGyver our helmets? We had everything we could do just to keep it from spreading to neighboring buildings and get people evacuated. There were people trying to jump from the fourth floor just to get out. There were..." he broke off, squeezing his eyes tightly shut as if closing off a vision.

Sloane became very still. There was a hollow ring to his voice, a soul sickness that ran deeper than exhaustion. She swallowed. "Nick, stop. Please. You don't have to explain. I'm sorry."

He stared at his hands. "I found a family in an apartment on the top floor," he said slowly, tonelessly. "We didn't get to them in time. The parents were by the children's room. They must have been hit by the smoke and the fire just...the fire just swept through." The words were colorless, but his eyes saw beyond her to a fiery orange room in a building that no longer existed except as ashes. He wasn't supposed to let it hurt.

It did nothing but.

"There were two little girls, not more than a year or two old, curled up together in their crib. They went to sleep last night and they'll never wake up." His voice cracked. "They never had a chance at life." His eyes came back to hers and he looked at her bleakly. "They never had a chance."

"Oh Nick." Sloane knelt before him, taking his hands in hers. They were cold, so cold. "Think of the ones you did get out, the ones who were trying to jump." He made no response. She pressed his hands to her cheeks, kissing his knuckles, noticing for the first time the tiny burn marks left by stray embers.

Slowly, Nick bent his head down and buried his face in her hair. For a long time he only inhaled, pressing his lips to the tumble of red. He hadn't known what he was after when he'd walked up to her door. It was only now that he was here, holding her, that he understood how much she'd become a part of his world. He drew her against him and held her, just held her, absorbing comfort, warmth, the reality of a living, breathing human being.

Then she shifted against him.

Sloane didn't know where it came from, the sudden hunger, the certainty of rightness. Pushing him away made no sense, only being with him did. *Take a chance.* For the moment, fear and common sense fled. She wanted only to hold, to heal, to feel his touch. Blindly she sought his lips, first tentatively, then with confidence. "Nick," she whispered softly. "Kiss me."

With a groan he tangled his fingers in her hair and gave in to growing need. Soft and pliant, fragrant and sweet, she was a refuge from the bleakness inside him. Her avid mouth tempted him with taste, touch and texture, combining them into heat. It might have been the first kiss he'd ever had. It was his return to the land of the living. Giving was unnoticed, taking was forgotten. There was only growing pleasure, drawing him deeper, always deeper.

Sloane traced the lines of his face, memorizing them with her fingertips as she had already memorized his mouth with hers. She felt the taut line of his cheek, the rough scrape of his stubble. And his mouth, so warm, so soft. With a sigh, she wrapped her arms around his neck and pressed herself to him, half lying across his lap. And feasted on him with abandon.

Nick raised his head to look at her. Her mouth was soft and swollen from his kisses. Arousal had turned her eyes heavy lidded and dark. The vivid blue of her robe gapped open to show pale silk and lace beneath that shifted with her every gasp, and under that…

Under that, only warm skin.

It dizzied him. He had wanted her until it had become a constant drumming in his head. Now, he had only to reach out and he could sweep her robe aside, have her against him. He bent his head to taste the fragile skin of her throat and her scent rose around him. And he touched her, because he had to.

When she felt his hands parting her robe, Sloane caught her breath in anticipation. Then his hands stroked over the thin silk of her camisole and she gasped at the soft seduction of the fragile fabric sliding along her skin.

His mouth roamed down into the shallow V between her breasts. For long moments, every nerve in her body was focused on the warmth of his lips, the teasing circles of his tongue. Desire tightened in her, impatience built for more than this teasing touch, for him to go further.

The slightly rough texture of his hands made her shiver as he pushed her robe off her shoulders, slipped down the thin straps of her camisole. Then his lips journeyed back up to capture hers with a power that made her go utterly still. More… this was more than any kiss had ever been, ripe with promise, decadent with pleasure. There was no thought of running or stopping now; she couldn't have borne it. Explorations and caresses blended into compulsion. Passion and need became inextricably tangled in a Gordian lovers' knot.

Everything a man could want, Nick held in his hands now. Everything he had burned for night after sleepless night was his. When he lowered his mouth to hers again, he had some thought of gentleness, but it was lost in her soft gasp as he slid one hand up under the thin cloth of her top.

It tore at his control, feeling the warm, smooth flatness of her belly, the curve of her waist and the slight swell where her breasts began. He took his time, testing them both with rhythmic strokes, fighting the urge to plunder. When he could wait no longer, he slipped his fingertips up higher to feel the hard points of her nipples.

And felt himself turn rock hard.

Arousal vaulted through her. It was exquisite, it was tantalizing, it was almost more than Sloane could bear. And there was more, she knew there was more.

Suddenly she couldn't bear it anymore, she had to feel Nick's flesh under her palms, his bare skin against hers, the muscles of his flat belly raised up in taut relief. With impatient fingers, she dragged the fabric up over his head. And when she ran her fingers over his chest, his nipples, to tear a moan from him, she gloried in her power.

Nick slipped both hands under her camisole. Sloane's breath caught as she realized his intent, then raised her arms to assist him. The scrap of silk slipped over her fingertips and wafted gently to the floor, forgotten. As easily as if she were weightless, he shifted her around to place her beneath him on the yielding cushions of the couch. A tension began to coil in her belly as she felt the weight of him against her.

Sloane ran her hands down from his shoulders to his wrists, feeling the rippling strength of the tendons, the curves of muscle under her fingers. "Touch me, Nick," she whispered, eyes heavy lidded and hot. "Touch me everywhere."

The words dragged him to the edge of control. With every passing moment, he swore it couldn't get any more intense. With every kiss they traveled further and further from the bounds of sanity. Her skin glowed, milk-pale in the morning light; her breasts were small and perfect. Around her shoulders her hair swirled in wild disarray, gleaming like flame. He leaned down to pleasure, to possess.

In a surge of mingled desire and delight, Sloane felt his

tongue trace a line down her neck to the taut peaks of her bare breasts. The slick caress of his tongue against first one, then the other sent her twisting against him. It was exquisite, maddening. He scraped his teeth lightly against her nipples and she gasped for air, clutched at him as he ran his hand down the line of her thigh where the silky nylons whispered under his palm.

"Oh man," he muttered as he reached the top of her nylons and found bare flesh and the lacy line of her garter belt. "I might just lose it right here."

"Not yet, cowboy." Sloane slid her fingers down, reaching for the buckle of his belt, but as his hands grazed the tops of her thighs, she went boneless and weak. For a whirling moment, she felt his touch on the silky triangle of fabric and the exquisitely sensitive nubbin beneath. With a moan she clutched his shoulders, her hands sliding urgently up to his neck. And felt broken skin under her fingers.

Nick jerked back, gasping in a sudden flare of pain that overshadowed even desire.

"What is it? What's wrong?"

He shook his head, blanking it out. "Nothing." He turned back to her, but the movement had him hissing.

"It's not nothing. Let me see it." Disregarding his hands, she sat up and examined the back of his neck. An ugly strip of burned, welted skin ran along the back of his neck. Sloane inhaled rapidly, trying to ignore a quick twist of queasiness. This was no time to get faint, she ordered herself. "God, Nick, what happened?"

"A falling stringer knocked my hat off and hit my neck. The medic put a bandage on it." He shifted, trying to ease the throbbing.

"Well, it's come loose." Sloane took another look. "You've got to get that taken care of," she said decisively, reaching for her robe. Her skin felt sensitized from his touch as she belted on the silk. The fabric felt strange, foreign now against her skin.

As though he'd read her mind, Nick reached out for her. "You don't need to be in such a hurry with that," he murmured.

"Nick, you need to go to the hospital," she persisted, batting his hands away. "Why didn't you?"

He gave up and simply wound his fingers through her hair. "During the fire, we needed every hand."

"You should have gone afterward, though."

Nick stroked her neck and brushed his thumb over her lips. "I wanted to see you."

For a moment, she lost herself in the smoky depths of his eyes. In the next heartbeat her mouth was on his, seeking, finding. Her hands slipped up to pull him closer and he flinched again.

"Nick."

"Forget it, it doesn't matter," he muttered, kissing his way down the neckline of her robe.

Sloane pushed back. "It does matter. Look, I'm sure I've got some bandages and stuff. I can clean it a bit and cover it for you, then you have to go get it taken care of." She stood up, not trusting herself to stay in physical contact with him, "Relax. I'll get the peroxide."

Of course, she hadn't actually seen the peroxide in a few months, she realized as she rummaged through the medicine cabinet over her bathroom sink. What had she done with it? More to the point, what in God's name was she doing? She tried to look sternly at herself in the bathroom mirror but only managed a rather foolish grin.

Yes, it was risky. But maybe, just maybe, it was worth it. She wouldn't fall all the way, but surely partway was all right, wasn't it? Taking a chance wouldn't destroy her, but turning away from a feeling like this just might. It had been so long….

Switching to the cabinet under the sink, she pulled out a nearly full bottle of store-label ibuprofen and peered at it. She didn't see an expiration date; then again, the label was so faded perhaps it had disappeared.

Illness generally made her impatient. Her method of treatment was to ignore everything and simply sleep until it was gone. It worked splendidly with colds and flu but was probably not going to be effective on lacerations and second-degree burns. "Ah-ha," she muttered as she unearthed a small first aid kit she'd gotten one time after she'd taken a fall running. At the back of the cupboard, she finally located the peroxide. Toting her prizes triumphantly, Sloane hurried back into the living room.

"I've got enough to…" she stopped. Nick had taken her order to relax seriously. He lay back on the couch, eyes closed, chest rising and falling in the steady rhythm of sleep. His lashes made dark, feathered crescents against his skin. Stripped of cares, he looked younger, almost vulnerable. Sloane shook her head.

"Damn you, Nick Trask," she said softly, looking down on him. "And damn the fire department, too."

Afternoon sun was slanting its way across the couch by the time Nick awoke to an empty room. He sat up stiffly, remembering too late not to touch his neck. He winced as he rose.

"Hello? Sloane?"

There was no answer in the silent flat. He was about to walk to the bathroom when he glanced down at the coffee table. Peroxide and gauze sat on top of a scribbled note. "There's food in the refrigerator if you want. Let yourself out the back door and don't forget to go to the doctor. I'll be in touch." No signature, just a capital *S* scribbled at the bottom.

Nick shook his head ruefully. Of all the idiot timing, his had to take the cake. He picked up his shirt from the table, where it sat neatly folded. Falling asleep on a lady was definitely bad form. Falling asleep on a woman like Sloane was criminal. Still, she hadn't booted him out on the street, however much she might have been tempted to. He'd have to categorize that as an improvement overall.

Pulling the shirt over his head with care, Nick began to whistle.

Yep, definitely an improvement.

Chapter Seven

"She's going to what?" Nick stared at the telephone.

"Sloane's going to ride along with your shift for a while," Bill Grant told him.

"You can't be serious." Nick loosened his jaw and tried for patience. Just thinking of Sloane conjured a mix of desire and frustration. He'd tried repeatedly to reach her over the weekend, only to get her answering machine. Getting close to her was like tracking some wild animal—every time he thought he was getting near, she dashed away again.

"Look," Bill said, "when I talked with Sloane last Friday she was concerned about missing the fire the previous night. She understands why it happened but she's got certain objectives to meet. To ensure she's on site for all fire incidents, she's asked to be there in the firehouse with your shift until the testing is concluded."

Perfect. Nick could just imagine working shift after shift,

Sloane around every minute as he did his best to keep from thinking about the feel of her nearly naked body against him. "It's going to cause an incredible disruption."

"For Christ's sake." Grant's voice rose. "You've been working with the woman for nearly three weeks. Deal with it. You've never complained about ride alongs before," he managed more reasonably. "What's different now?"

What was different? Most ride alongs hadn't turned into a constant grinding in his belly, for one.

"Nick, she's mostly interested in being at the fire scenes. Otherwise, I'm sure she'll stay out of the way," Grant continued. "She shouldn't interrupt your routines."

Interrupt his routines, hell, Nick thought. Be careful what you ask for, or you will surely get it. He'd wanted more time with her, more, period. He'd never in a million years wanted it to be at work. How was he supposed to concentrate on the job when all he wanted to do was tumble her into bed for about two weeks straight? He didn't care for endless days of frustration. And he particularly didn't care for having his decisions made for him. Nick scowled. "When's this going to start?"

"She should be there now. I told her your shift started at eight."

"*Today?*" Nick bit back a curse. "Why didn't you call and let me know this earlier?" he asked finally.

"I didn't want to bother you during your time off."

Yeah, right. Nick hung up the phone and stalked out of his office. No wonder she'd laid low over the weekend. He strode purposefully down the hall, hearing the noise rise as he turned the corner to the kitchen.

And stumbled into a mob scene.

"Hey, Nick," Knapp called out from the crowd around the kitchen table, "we got ourselves another rookie."

O'Hanlan thumped his coffee mug down on the painted wood. "Hell of a lot easier on the eyes than Red is, that's for sure."

"She's too smart to hang around with you truckies," said Ken Giancoli, chauffeur for the engine crew. "She wants work with the nozzle men, that's where the real excitement is. She should ride with us on the pumper."

"Nobody in their right mind wants to ride with you, Giancoli." O'Hanlan grinned, taking a swig of coffee.

Nick approached the table.

"Hello, Nick." Sloane looked up, surrounded by firefighters. "Looks like I'm on the crew for a while."

Every time he saw her again, he was surprised anew at the impact of those eyes, that mouth. That damned voice of hers. Maybe if he could stop her from talking the entire time, he'd be okay. Nick glanced down at the handful of department announcements he held. "Okay, let's get to it," he said curtly. "Night-shift guys, take up, you're relieved. Let's run through the announcements first and then the shift work." He sat down and began. Most days, friendly insults and jokes flew, but today he was in no mood for interruptions. Speeded by caffeine, the update went quickly.

When he'd finished, Nick looked at the crew. "Okay, work-detail assignments are on the bulletin board. Don't forget to sign up for next shift. Questions?"

Giancoli raised his hand. "Yeah. We gotta have O'Hanlan cooking today? He always uses too much garlic."

"I use just enough," O'Hanlan countered. "You sure you weren't fathered by the mailman, Giancoli?"

"Fa Chrissakes, O'Hanlan, I had to do mouth-to-mouth the other night after you cooked, this little old gray-haired granny.

I revived her and she turned around and passed out again from the garlic smell."

"We been meaning to talk to you, Giancoli," Beaulieu said. "There's this invention called a toothbrush you oughtta know about."

Nick raised a hand. "Okay, enough, time to get to it, guys. Maintenance first, then drills."

Reluctant to disperse, the firefighters milled about rinsing out coffee cups and joking.

"You can come help me out, Sloane," Knapp said, tucking her hand into his arm.

"No way," O'Hanlan argued. "You're going to vacuum the dorm. I'm going to check the ladder truck. She'll learn more with me."

"Ride alongs stay with me," Nick reminded them. "Sloane, let's go to my office."

As he led the way, all Nick was aware of was her scent. Okay, maybe he could concentrate if he could stop her from wearing it. He stood aside to let her walk into his office. The walk, though, the walk was still a problem. Maybe if he could stop her from moving. Or wrap her in a muumuu. Maybe if he could…ah hell, Nick thought as he closed the door. How the hell was he ever going to get anything done with her around?

She sat in his client chair, looking up at him, so cool, so composed, as though they'd shared nothing more important than a handshake. All he wanted to do was clamp his mouth on hers and bring that wild hunger into her eyes again, just to prove to himself and to her that he could. Instead, he leaned back against the edge of his desk and folded his arms across his chest. "You've been busy, I hear."

* * *

There wasn't enough oxygen in the room, Sloane thought uneasily. Nick's eyes smoldered at her, dark and dangerous. So maybe he felt as though he'd been blindsided. After all, she hadn't warned him of her idea. Then again, she hadn't thought of it until she'd been back at work, trying to put those hot, urgent minutes on the couch out of her mind.

It all made her want to run, and yet she was slipping closer and closer to the point at which running away wasn't possible. She was too honest with herself to pretend it wasn't what she wanted anymore. That he wasn't what she wanted. It didn't make things simple, though. Before, things had at least been clear. Now, nothing was.

So she focused on what was safe and all-important—qualifying the gear. "I assume you've talked to Bill Grant."

"About ten minutes ago. You, now," he said conversationally, "I tried to talk with you over the weekend but you didn't seem to be around." An edge underlay his words.

"I'm not very good about checking my home messages." Of course, if she'd picked up the phone when she'd heard his voice coming out of the machine, she wouldn't have had to. So close, she'd come so close, but she known where it would lead, and away from the heat of the moment, she just wasn't sure she was ready. If she'd ever be ready. In the end, she'd turned away, heart thumping.

"Grant says you called him Friday about missing the fire."

"I wasn't trying to get you in hot water," she said to forestall his anger. "I told him I understood why you didn't call me and that I was okay with it. It just can't happen again. This seems like a good solution."

"A good solution? More like a permanent problem in my firehouse."

She raised an eyebrow. "*Your* firehouse?"

"You saw how things went in the morning meeting," he said, ignoring her.

"It's a new situation. Of course it gave everyone something to talk about. Give it a little while and they won't notice me anymore."

"You've got to be kidding." He gazed at her and her face warmed. "Okay, so I didn't notify you of the fire the other night. It was a screw-up, I admit it. And I told you, it won't happen again."

"How do you know?" she demanded. "You were right, Nick. I thought a lot about what you said after I went to work on Friday. You were taking care of business, saving lives, and there is no way I want to interfere with that. We can't ignore the testing, though, because that can save lives, too. It'll be easier if I'm just here all the time."

"Easier? For you, maybe. But as far as my men are concerned, you're going to be a distraction."

"Really?" she tossed back at him. "Are you sure you're not just worked up because I'm trespassing on your turf?"

"I'm not worked up." He pushed off the desk with studied deliberation and strolled slowly toward her. "Or at least I'm not the only one. For example, why the big surprise? Why didn't you tell me about this before?"

"I didn't think of it before. I decided on it once I got to the office."

"You could have called me."

"How, by calling my house?" she shot back. "Besides, I was hoping you wouldn't be there."

"Was that why you walked away and left instead of waking me up? You're getting your stories mixed, Sloane."

"Don't start on me," she snapped as her temper heated.

"I'm not the one who fell asleep." And her eyes flew open in horror. Given a knife at that moment she would have cheerfully cut out her tongue.

The smile bloomed across Nick's face. "I'm sorry about that, more than you'll know. I usually have better manners."

"It didn't matter," she muttered, rising to walk past him.

"It did to me." He caught her arm and used it to pull her to him.

She warned herself not to get in too deep even as he lowered his mouth to hers. For a moment, she held herself away from him but then her control dissolved. When he was giving her one of those mind-bending kisses that turned her bones into taffy, anything seemed possible. Being with him seemed like the only thing. For long, hazy seconds the firehouse receded.

Footsteps sounded in the hall. Sloane broke contact and twisted away. "I don't think this is the place…"

"And that's exactly why you shouldn't be here."

She raised her chin. "We're not sixteen, Nick. I think we're both professional enough to deal with our hormones."

He stared at her maddeningly. "Is that what you think it is?"

"I don't…" she fumbled. "I don't think this is the time to get into this," she finished, her voice stronger.

"But we will."

Slowly, unwillingly, she nodded. "I know."

Hot triumph filled his eyes. He brushed his lips over hers. "I still think you should have called me."

"Would you have agreed?" Even just the quick contact had her head swimming.

He considered it. "No, probably not."

"Right. And I'd have gone to Bill and the same thing would have happened. This is important, Nick. I've got to get the gear qualified. I can't trust anyone else's opinion on this. I need to see with my own eyes."

Nick crossed back to sit behind his desk again. "Why does this mean so much to you?"

"It's important to me."

"Important." He tapped his fingers on his faux wood-grain desktop. "You're not always going to be able to shut me out like this, Sloane."

"Leave it, Nick." She stared at him and for once the snap and fire was replaced by a kind of pleading.

He let it pass, but the days when she could close herself off from him were waning. He needed more than that from her, he was discovering, much more. But now was not the time. "All right," he said abruptly. "If we're going to do this, let's do it right."

They stood on the apparatus floor by the racks of helmets and turnouts. O'Hanlan rummaged under the open hood of the ladder truck.

Nick plunked a helmet on her head. "See if this one fits." It slipped forward and the rest of the garage disappeared as it covered her eyes. "Oops. Okay, I guess you wear a different size."

Sloane pushed back the black leather brim until she could see again. "You think?"

The next wasn't any better, nor the next. One after another, they tried the spares without luck.

"Last chance," Nick told her.

This time, the helmet stayed in place reasonably well. Once Nick adjusted the inside, it held even when she shook her head. "Good," he said in satisfaction. "You'll probably never need it, but I'll feel better if you've got one on at a fire scene. Now let's get you some turnouts."

It was a longer, more difficult process. The coat wasn't a problem but the bunker pants were. Granted, Sloane was taller than a lot of guys. She was also more slender. Even the smallest of the spares hung from her shoulders by the suspenders, the waistband hovering at her waist like a clown suit at the circus. Nick's lips twitched as he looked at her. "I guess this'll have to do," he said finally.

"I'm not going in a fire. I don't see why I need them at all."

"During the day, you don't. When we get a call in the middle of the night, though—and we will, believe me—you'll see. You sleep in sweats and a T-shirt. All you have to do is step into the boots, pull the pants up and throw the suspenders over your shoulders and go. It's the fastest way. Now we just need to fit you for a vest and we're all set."

"A vest?"

"Body armor."

Sloane gaped at him. "You're joking."

"No. This isn't the best area in town, in case you haven't noticed. There's an area by the projects where someone's been taking potshots." He gave a humorless smile. "I guess they don't like the noise. One of the guys on A shift got grazed by one, so now we wear the vests any time we have a call in that area. Sloane—"

"Yes."

"I don't want you to get hurt. Why won't you give this up?"

Her shoulders squared. "I'd be at the same risk if I were driving to meet you at a fire." When he only looked at her in silence, she nodded slowly. "Unless you didn't call me. Nick, you can't block me. You take risks all the time. It doesn't stop you."

"It's my job."

"Right now, it's my job, too."

They stared at each other, neither backing down, bound

by that same swirling awareness. "All right," Nick said finally. "Come on."

The bulletproof vests were near the foot of the stairs. "The police department loaned us a dozen last week. Here." He selected one by eye. "Try this one."

Sloane slipped it on over her head, the fabric of her shirt tightening across her breasts as she tugged it down over her torso. "It needs adjusting, I think," she muttered, reaching awkwardly around her sides. "Damned things...why do they make them so you can't reach the..."

"I've got it," Nick said brusquely, pushing her hands out of the way. Sloane blinked at his tone of voice. His touch was impersonal, almost rough. His head bent toward hers as he concentrated on what he was doing, close enough that she could touch him and if he looked up, close enough to kiss.

She let out a breath. He was probably right, it was a bad idea to be there. She wasn't finding it any easier to be around him than he was to be around her. She thought of the feel of his mouth on her bare breast and her stomach did a lazy flip-flop.

"There." He pulled the bottom of the vest down, keeping his hands scrupulously away from her hips. "That should fit all right."

Though she wasn't sure exactly what fit entailed for a bulletproof vest, Sloane nodded. She needed to get away from him, somewhere she could get her equilibrium. The day seemed to stretch out unbearably. She'd take it, though. She had to. Stripping off the vest, she looked at Nick. "Where do I put this?"

"Over here." He led her to the ladder truck, where the boots and turnouts and hats were piled in careful, distinct stacks. Her jacket, he hung on the side of the ladder truck. "It goes back there in the same place every time the truck backs into quarters."

"Hey, cap?"

Nick glanced over his shoulder.

It was Sorensen, the probie, with a question about his house watchman duties. It was also a chance to escape, Sloane thought as she wandered over to where O'Hanlan was crouched down by the tire of the ladder truck.

"Is something wrong with it?" she asked.

"Nope." He squinted at the pressure gauge. "We just have to check the fluid levels and tires every day. These babies have to work right every time." He rose and walked a few steps to the next tire. "Anyway, doing this is a lot more interesting than the next item on my duty list."

"Which is?"

He gave her a mournful look. "Cleaning the bathroom."

"Come on, you guys don't really have to do that."

"Maid's year off," Nick said over her shoulder. "Besides, it keeps him out of trouble."

"We should conserve our energy," O'Hanlan countered. "How else can we save the lives and property of the good citizens of Bos—" The alarm bells began to ring. Instantly, the jokes ended. "Multi-car accident, intersection of Dudley and Columbia," Sorensen called out over the loudspeaker.

"Who goes, Sorensen?" Nick called over to the little house watch office at the front of the apparatus floor where the crew took turns logging calls in the station book and announcing alarms.

"Oh, uh, sorry, cap," Sorensen said, accidentally keeping the mike button depressed. He cleared his throat. "Um, Ladder 67 goes."

"All right, Red," shouted Knapp, clapping his hands as he headed to the ladder truck for his coat.

Nick pulled on his turnout pants and boots. "Sloane, you ride up front with us."

Thankful she didn't have to wear the clumsy boots and turnout pants in the daytime, Sloane climbed up into the cab and Nick swung in beside her.

"Everybody in place?" O'Hanlan asked, looking around from behind the wheel. "Okay, boys and girls, let's roll."

Flipping the switch for the siren, Nick gave a few blasts to the air horn and O'Hanlan pulled the truck onto the road.

Urgency. It permeated the air around them as O'Hanlan unerringly choose the most effective route to the incident. Too many of the drivers on the road, however, seemed cheerfully oblivious. On Columbia, a clot of traffic blocked their way. O'Hanlan laid on the horn. "You know, I keep telling the department, put a set of monster truck tires on this baby and I'll just ride right over all these civilians. Get to the scene faster and teach 'em a lesson or two." With surprising deftness, he threaded the truck around the worst of the snarl, forcing a few drivers up onto sidewalk. Finally, they were rolling forward again.

"There it is." Nick pointed. "Up ahead."

Sloane looked and felt sick. She'd never been the type to stare at accidents on the highway, preferring instead to keep her eyes on the road and be thankful it wasn't her. In this case, driving past wasn't an option. She was still immensely glad she wasn't one of the unlucky victims involved.

A one-ton pickup truck touted in TV ads for its size and toughness had gone head-on into a compact. The truck was indeed tough—it had turned the front end of the smaller car into a twisted crush of metal. O'Hanlan pulled to a stop.

"Okay, guys," Nick said, "let's get to it."

Sloane followed him as he approached the cop who crouched by the compact. "What's the situation?" Nick asked.

The cop rose and took a few steps away. "Four inside, two in front, a couple of kids in back. Got an ambulance on the way but we're gonna need your can opener to get them out." He lowered his voice. "The driver's pretty bad off."

Nick nodded and stepped away. "O'Hanlan, Sorensen, get the jaws and the torch. Knapp, Beaulieu, check out the passengers in the back. Get them stabilized. I'll handle the driver. We've got ambulances on the way." He pulled the bulky first aid kit out of a locker and went swiftly to the front of the car.

This was a Nick Sloane hadn't seen before, decisive and in command, and she was surprised at just how sexy that was. It wasn't just the offhand skill with which he applied pressure bandages and spinal stabilizers, it was the quietly capable way he dealt with the people in the car. If she were one of the victims, trapped and hurt, she'd want to hear a calm, reassuring voice like that telling her everything was going to be all right. He said it as though there was no possibility of anything but.

Metal screeched as the jaws peeled open the car as though it was made of tinfoil. Knapp and Beaulieu helped the pair in the back get out. Nick waited to remove the driver and front passenger until the ambulances had arrived with their stretchers. More quickly than she'd expected, the victims were spirited off to the hospital and the ladder-truck crew was heading back to the vehicle.

"This is my favorite part," O'Hanlan said. "Getting to go home when the interesting work's done. That poor schlep," he jabbed a thumb toward the cop, "has to wait for the tow truck and the cleanup crew. We'll be sitting down to lunch while he's still out here, I'm betting."

"Will they be all right?" Sloane asked as they drove back to the firehouse. The front seat was designed for two, not three, and she was burningly conscious of the hard length of Nick's leg pressed against hers.

"The kids in the backseat will be home tonight," Nick told her. "The driver's going to spend time in the hospital, along with the person riding shotgun."

"Don't you ever wonder what happens to them?"

"You kidding?" O'Hanlan asked. "This one calls the hospital and checks sometimes."

Nick shifted in his seat and looked out the window. "I just want to make sure we're taking care of people."

"You are," Sloane said softly. "You are."

Chapter Eight

Nick stood in the courtyard of the fire station, watching Sorensen and the Engine 58 probie go through rope-tying drills. He'd left Sloane in the firehouse talking into her cell phone, computer open on her lap as she dialed into a meeting. She was out of sight. She should have been out of mind.

And he should have been a lottery winner. He knew she was there. He couldn't stop thinking about her.

He couldn't stop wanting her.

His cell phone rang. He flipped it open. "Yo."

"Nick, Jacob."

In a different era, Jacob would have been a trapper who lived in the wilderness and only came into a remote trading post every three or four months. Brusque and uncomfortable in conversation, he never seemed quite to know what to make of people, even his own family.

Which had never stopped him from trying to be the big

brother and telling Nick what he should do. And Nick had a pretty good idea that was what he was calling for right now.

"Hey, Jacob, what's going on?"

"I hear you're not coming to Thanksgiving," he said without preamble.

Other brothers who hadn't talked for months might have made small talk for a little while, Nick reflected. Jacob just got right to business. "Yeah. I'm working the night shift."

"You're an officer. Why can't you trade days and get it off?"

"What's your point, Jacob?"

"Look, you want to stay down in Boston it doesn't matter to me. I know you don't want to come back to the farm. It matters to Ma, though."

"She never mentioned it to me. It kind of sounds like I'm supposed to drop everything, haul in favors and get the day off because you think I should?" He knew it was surly; somehow Jacob always managed to bring it out of him.

"Is it really too damned much to ask, Nick? You know how hard these eight months have been for her? Or maybe you don't. It's not like you're ever around."

And here they were again, at the core issue that inevitably came up whenever they talked—Jacob's reminder, spoken and unspoken, that he was the only one living on the farm, that Nick should somehow find a way to do more. "Thanksgiving is two weeks away. How am I supposed to get anyone to trade their holiday?"

"You're off the day after, though."

"Sure, at 8:00 a.m. the day after, and I'm due back twenty-four hours later. I'd barely get up to the farm before I'd have to come back."

"So what you're saying is that you can't be bothered."

"No, I'm saying that it's not going to be a lot of quality time.

I'd rather wait and come up when I've got a three-day break, spend more time. Mom knows that. We've talked about it."

"Do you think she cares if it's a short visit? She just wants to see everyone here."

"Funny, she didn't seem to mind when I talked with her. It sounds like the only one who has a problem with it is you."

Jacob snorted. "Like she's going to say anything."

The guilt bit deep. "Cut with the big-brother stuff, Jacob," Nick snapped. "I'm not going to make it, okay?" He glanced up to see that Sorensen had finished his drill and was walking over, out of breath. "Look, I've gotta go."

"Funny how that works," Jacob said. "You always do."

Rescue calls, medical aid calls, inspections, even a false alarm; the day spun out in ongoing variety. And each time Sloane saw Nick walk up and quietly, capably take control of a scene, something scurried around in her stomach. She saw him lifting equipment and found herself remembering the feel of his hard hands on her body. She stared at his unsmiling, intent face and thought of the way he'd looked as she'd stroked her fingers down his belly. She watched him at work and she wanted him more than ever.

When they returned from their third medical aid call, O'Hanlan stopped the truck on the apron. "Hey, cap, I'm going to run up the ladder, give her a check." Outside, he stood at the control panel and pushed a switch to release the white supports that stabilized the truck when the ladder was extended.

Nick stood by, balanced and easy.

When Sloane had arranged the ride along, she'd never thought that being around him would be a challenge. The danger, she'd assumed, lay in his hands, in those persuasive kisses. Who'd have guessed that he'd have slid so easily under her skin without ever a touch?

He glanced over and caught her looking. He raised a questioning eyebrow.

Sloane cleared her throat. "So is this a typical day?"

Nick smiled faintly. "I'm not sure there is such a thing. You never know when you come in what's going to happen. Keeps life interesting."

"Is that what you like about it?"

"I like everything about it. The people, the variety, the fact that it's not something that everyone can do."

"You don't shy away from challenges."

His eyes locked on hers with the power of a punch. "Not when it's something I really want."

For just that instant, she couldn't breathe. Desire thudded through her. It seemed impossible to be this close and not have him.

Sloane swallowed. "And what you want is firefighting?"

"It's one thing. I like going up against a fire, head to head."

"Head to head?" she repeated, relaxing enough for amusement. "You make it sound as if it's alive."

"It seems it is when you're in the middle of it. It's fast, it's tricky and it keeps coming at you. I like beating it. And I like having a chance to make a difference," he added thoughtfully, watching O'Hanlan extend the ladder. "I like going to work knowing that maybe I'll have a chance to save someone's life today."

She remembered the awards in his office. "You already have, right?"

"I got lucky a couple of times." He shrugged. "Right place, right time."

He'd be uncomfortable with being called a hero, she

thought, even though he was. "It didn't sound as if it was just luck to me. It sounded as though you made it happen. What's it like?"

The corners of his mouth tugged and suddenly his smile was a mile wide. "It's the greatest feeling in the world. I was psyched for weeks, especially the last time, with the two kids."

"What happened?"

"It was a fire in a triple-decker about five blocks from here."

"Is that all you ever get around here, fires in triple-deckers?"

"Seems like it, doesn't it?" he agreed. "The same house, over and over and over, most of them in their second century, overcrowded, undermaintained. Wiring wears out, people start fires with space heaters, candles."

"Dangerous," Sloane commented.

He nodded. "It keeps us hopping. Anyway, this little girl was babysitting her brother on the top story. She was just a kid herself. Smart, though. She'd moved them both to the floor by a window. I got lucky."

"Sounds like she did, too."

"The fire came up the hall after me. The hose company hadn't gotten up that high yet and the far side of the room was starting to go up. They had the stick up outside but I figured if I opened the window to get to it, the oxygen would pull the fire that way. I wasn't sure I'd have enough time to get them out."

"What did you do?"

He shrugged. "Went for it. Handed the boy to the guy on the ladder, grabbed the girl and got on the windowsill. I figured I'd wait until they cleared the top of the ladder, but the fire was coming too fast. So I held the kid tight and got on the underside of the ladder. Surprised the hell out of the truckie who had the boy."

"But you saved the girl and yourself."

"Not by much. The fire chased after us pretty fast. We had O'Hanlan running the ladder. He was on his toes and got us out of there."

"I can't imagine what it's like to be that high up on a ladder."

Nick gave her a sidelong glance. "Want to find out?"

"You mean now?"

"Why not?" Before she could respond, he whistled to Beaulieu, who was standing house watch. "Hey, Todd, radio in an out-of-service for ten minutes. O'Hanlan, leave the outriggers deployed. Sloane's going to go up on the stick."

It was too good a show for the rest of the crew. In ones and twos they trailed out of the firehouse to watch. Perfect. Just what she needed—an audience. She'd never been particularly fond of heights, Sloane thought uneasily. "How high is the ladder, again?"

"Eighty feet," O'Hanlan said cheerfully. "Don't worry, she slides up smooth as silk."

"Okay, put on your helmet and turnouts," Nick directed.

"The pants don't fit."

"Put them on anyway. We need the belt clip. You can leave off the turnout coat if you want."

She felt a little like a clown in the oversized trousers and garish red suspenders. Knapp whistled. "Now you're styling."

"Lookin' like a firefighter," Beaulieu added.

"Fireman, fireman, save my child," O'Hanlan cried in a reedy falsetto, hands clasped in front of his chest.

In a few moves, Nick was on top of the ladder truck. "Okay, come on up," he directed, holding out a hand to grab her.

Atop the ladder truck, the ground was already far enough away for her, but no way was she going to back down. She'd get through it, Sloane told herself grimly. If they could do it, so could she.

The telescoped white ladder lay flat on the truck. "O'Hanlan, bring it up," Nick directed. Motors whirred as the layered bulk of the ladder tilted up to a seventy degree angle. The rungs for all of the telescoped sections were in line with one another, she saw. "Okay," Nick told her, "it's a piece of cake. I'm going to be right behind you the whole time, so you've got nothing to worry about. You're going to do great." He spoke in the same calm, reassuring tone she'd heard at the accident scene and bit by bit she began to relax. "Now climb up about five rungs up and stop. The ladder's going to unfold and take us the rest of the way up."

The metal vibrated against her palms as Nick stepped on, standing just below her. Holding onto a rung with one hand, he reached the other around in front of her to attach a carabiner from the waist of her turnouts to a rung of the ladder. "Safety line, just in case." He put both hands on the rungs, his body just behind hers, his breath feathering over her neck.

"Check your toes. Make sure you're stepping on just the rung for this section," Nick directed her and then raised his voice. "Okay, O'Hanlan, put 'er up slow."

The engines rumbled. "Going up," O'Hanlan called. "Top floor, ladies' hats, gloves and finer dresses." Smoothly, the white ladder began to rise into the air section by section. The movement didn't seem particularly fast, but the ground fell away all too rapidly.

Sloane gulped.

"Okay," Nick said, "you can move your feet more onto the rungs now, our section's untelescoped. Don't be tense. You're perfectly safe, trust me."

Trust me. Sloane concentrated on the calm words. Nick

would never put her, or anyone, at risk. She focused on the comforting feel of his chest against her back. She'd be okay, he was there.

"Take a good grip, now," he said in that same easy tone. "We're going to jerk a little when we hit the top."

The jolt had her looking down. Far below them, the truck was a small red square surrounded by tiny figures. Sloane closed her eyes and tried not to hyperventilate.

"Hey, you can look at the ground any time," Nick said. "Don't stare down. Look around you, at the city."

Sloane raised her head and clenching her hands on the rungs, opened her eyes. "Oh!"

She was, purely and simply, captivated.

"Prettier from up here, isn't it?"

She'd never realized there were so many trees in the city. Gold, red, glorious orange, everywhere she looked it blazed with autumn color. Boston had draped itself in its fall finery and it was all laid out for her enjoyment. To her left, she caught a glimpse of Boston Common and the Public Garden. The spires of the financial district appeared level with her eyes. A small blue slice of the Atlantic glittered far to the right. Dirt, crime, traffic, all the evils of city life were far away. "It's gorgeous," she breathed.

"Like magic, isn't it?" Nick murmured in her ear. Up this high, the engine was far away and Sloane could hear everything he said, even the rhythmic sound of his breath. His arms were around her, his body next to hers in what was almost a lovers' embrace, she realized abruptly.

"Look over there, you can see the Charles River." He reached over her shoulder to point.

Sloane searched the horizon, seeing only buildings.

"No." He gently turned her head. "Over there."

It was the first time they'd touched all day. His fingertips pressed little coins of heat against her jaw. A slow curl of desire awoke inside of her.

"I see it," she fibbed hastily. "What's back behind us?" She turned her head.

It put both of them at risk. It brought his mouth much too near. Dangling from a ladder, eighty feet above the ground was no time for her palms to get damp, no time for the want to start flowing through her. She took a shuddering breath.

"Seen enough?" Nick asked.

Not trusting her voice, Sloane nodded.

"Okay, hold on. The ladder might jump a little bit when it starts down." Nick made an arm motion and they headed back toward the ground. She felt a little twinge of disappointment as they dropped away from the view.

It was a bit like landing in a jetliner. At first the ground was unimaginably far away and exotic, then closer, then near enough to be mundane. Finally, the ladder stopped and they stepped down.

The crew broke out in applause and whistles. Sloane bowed to her audience from the top of the ladder truck, waving modestly. Behind them, a sedan pulled into the lot.

Laughing and breathless, she let herself be helped off the ladder truck. The men surrounded her, clapping her on the back, slapping the top of her helmet.

"Speech, speech," hooted Knapp.

"How'd ya like it?" O'Hanlan asked.

"Oh, it's gorgeous. I loved it."

"Well, you make it worth my while, I'll send you up again. I take brownies, ice cream sundaes or American Express," he told her.

Sloane tucked her tongue in her cheek. "I think you're an operator, O'Hanlan."

"To know me is to love me."

"Well, Sloane, you certainly seem to be diving into things," said a voice behind them.

And Sloane turned to see Councilman Ayre and his entourage.

It was a coincidence, Nick had to believe that. He saw the shock and dismay chase across Sloane's face. He wanted to believe she hadn't concocted the ride along as part of a cheap publicity stunt for Ayre, but one hand washed the other and the timing was eerily perfect.

Ayre walked up to her as though he owned the place, Nick thought furiously. As though he owned her. "Well, I see you've wasted no time getting to work. Glad we've got a go-getter like you on the job." Standing next to her, Ayre pasted on a toothy smile for the photographer who trailed him.

The photo op was everything, of course. It was the whole reason he was stopping by, to use them for a little campaign boost.

"I'm happy to see that you're so involved in monitoring the testing," he told Sloane, pumping her hand. "I'm even more impressed than I was before. We're really behind this equipment. I'm very excited about it."

"That's great," Nick heard himself saying. "Given the fact that you've voted for departmental budget cuts for each of the last seven years. Kind of hard to figure out how that's going to help us buy this fancy new equipment you're flogging."

For an instant, Ayre looked absolutely furious. Then his expression relaxed into an affable smile. "And you are?"

"Trask. Nick Trask, registered voter."

"Well, Firefighter Trask, I'm sure you realize developing

a budget is a matter of compromise," he said warmly, reaching out to clasp Nick's hand and give it a brisk shake.

"Captain Trask," Nick corrected. A flashbulb popped. Ayre held on. Another photo op, Nick realized in annoyance.

And when the camera was down, Ayre started to turn away.

"We'll be looking for that funding boost," Nick persisted.

Ayre swung back toward him, all of his caps showing. "I'm completely behind this project," he answered. "I'll be going to go to the mat for you guys, just like I always do." A young, slick-looking guy in hair gel and a fancy suit stepped up to murmur in Ayre's ear. The politician looked at his watch. "Well, looks like I've got to run to another appearance across town. It was a pleasure to meet you all," he said smoothly. "Don't forget to get out and vote tomorrow." He walked toward the waiting sedan.

Sloane stood frozen, staring at the car as it drove away. Just then, a red truck drove up and parked in the lot. The first of the night shift, coming in early. "Was that who I thought it was?" a burly, mustachioed firefighter asked incredulously.

"Sure was," O'Hanlan told him. "Nicky's never going to wash his hand again, are you?"

"As quickly as possible," Nick said shortly. "Todd, call us in as active again." He turned and walked back into the firehouse.

Chapter Nine

Sloane slipped out of the turnouts and helmet and hustled after him. “Nick, wait.” She caught him on the stairs. “I wasn’t a part of that.”

He turned and flicked her a cynical glance. “Of course you’re part of it. We’re all part of it.”

Anger whisked through her. “I didn’t know they were coming.”

“Oh no? I did. It’s just that with everything else going on I kind of forgot.” He turned to go the rest of the way up the stairs. “That was the payoff for the whole project, Sloane. He pushes your system, you give him the pre-election photo op.”

“Did it ever occur to you that someone in the department might have tipped him off that I was here?” she demanded, on his heels. “They probably figured it was good for the department.”

"No, it's good for Ayre. And it doesn't matter who tipped him off, it's the only reason you're here."

"I'm here to test the equipment and get it into the field."

Nick reached the top of the stairs and turned to Sloane as she joined him. "Look, I don't doubt your sincerity. I know this project means a lot to you, so it's probably more unfair to you than it is to us, but if you think that Ayre has considered buying your equipment for one minute…"

"I'm not working with him. I'm working for you," she returned hotly.

"Sloane, you're dreaming. Ayre's the one who controls the future of this thing. Why don't you just accept that this equipment is not going to make it in Boston no matter how good it is?"

Stung, she glared at him. "Aren't you sick of saying that, Nick? Because I'm sure as hell sick of hearing it. I'm going to get this equipment qualified, whether I've got your support or not."

"My support doesn't matter. It's not going to happen."

"It has to," she burst out passionately. "Firefighters can't keep dying. It has to *stop*."

A moment went by in silence. Nick looked at her. "Who was it, Sloane?" he asked softly. "Who did you lose?"

She couldn't swallow, couldn't breathe for the knot in her throat. "My brother," she whispered, fighting the urge to scream at the unbearable truth.

And downstairs, alarm bells began to ring.

The wind of the raw November night blew down Nick's collar as he stood on Sloane's front stoop and pressed the bell. He stepped back and squinted up at her windows. There was faint light there, but he couldn't tell if anyone was home. He jammed his hands into his pockets. All he could do was hope.

The alarm—a medical aid call—had stopped their conversation cold. By the time they'd returned, the night shift had arrived. One minute, he'd been talking with the night captain, watching Sloane hang up her turnouts. The next time he'd glanced over, she'd been gone without a word. Intentionally, he was sure.

That didn't mean he planned to let it end there. It was time to talk. He looked at the bell, considering giving it another push.

And then the door swung open and she was there, looking at him with wariness but no surprise. "Hello."

"You disappeared," he said, his breath making puffs of white condensation in the chill air.

She was barefoot, in a baggy green sweater and jeans, wrapping her arms around herself to keep warm. "I thought I'd get out of the way. You were busy and everything was finished."

"Not everything. Not our conversation, for one."

She shivered at little. "I thought we'd said everything that needed to be said."

"Not by half, but it's kind of cold to be going into it out here." He could hear the tension in her voice, see the shadows in her eyes. And he knew, because he knew her now, that she'd fight like hell to try to keep the barriers up. It wasn't going to happen this time, though. This time, she was going to let him in. "Do you want to go somewhere, get dinner or a drink?"

She hesitated and then let out a breath of acceptance and stepped back. "Why don't you come in?"

Upstairs, the flat was as tidy as it had been the first time he'd seen it, and as bare. No photographs of family sat around on any of the walls or surfaces, he noticed now. It was as though she existed in her own universe.

And maybe now he understood a little more why.

She stood at the living-room door, watching as he hung his jacket on the coat rack. "I'm having a drink. Can I get you something?"

He looked at her glass. "If that's bourbon, you can give me one of those, too."

"No ice," she told him. "Water? Straight up?"

"Straight up."

He walked over to the windows and looked out at the night. So it had come down to this, the whole possibility of anything happening with them came down to this conversation and what she'd been through. If he could get her to open up, lance the wound, then maybe they had a chance together.

He heard her come back into the room and turned to take his glass from her. When he saw the smudges under her eyes, he felt the tug of responsibility.

"So." She chose the isolation of the chair. "You wanted to talk?"

"Apologize, first, for getting you upset about Ayre." He took a swallow of the bourbon and sat on the couch. "I know you're not pandering to him. He just got to me. He always gets to me."

She nodded. "I'm trying to do something good here, Nick."

"I know. It's just that I don't believe you know what you're up against."

"And I don't believe in worrying about that. You just put your head down and get the job done."

"Kind of like the way you go through life?"

She gave him a sharp look. "You said apology, not five-minute analysis."

"Tell me about your brother," he said, his voice gentle.

She rose. "It's private."

He stood as well. "It's there in the room every time we're

together. It's here now." He reached out and closed his hand over hers. Trusting to the contact, he pulled her toward the couch. "Tell me."

She stared and moistened her lips. Finally, she sat in a corner of the sofa, her knees drawn up, her arms wrapped around them. "He was a firefighter." She swallowed. "In Hartford."

And he knew. It made the hairs on the back of his neck stand on end. "The packing-house fire."

She nodded.

It was infamous, a hellish conflagration in an almost entirely windowless building full of thick walls and sealed rooms. Firefighters searching the structure had gotten lost in the maze and the blinding, toxic smoke. And their would-be rescuers had been lost as well, in a hideous chain of events that left five men dead.

Among them, apparently, Sloane's brother.

"Mitch had always wanted to be a firefighter. When we were kids, he used to go down to the local station and hang around, wipe the truck, do whatever they'd let him. He was a lieutenant by the time of the fire, a veteran.

"They were in on the first alarm and the first pair of guys lost were from his company." She moved her head in blind misery. "Mitch went after them. It would never have occurred to him not to. I don't know if they ever even got close. The last thing they heard from him was over the radio, saying he was lost and running out of air." Her voice shook with the unbearable, imagining him moving in blind circles in the choking black smoke, methodically searching for escape.

She blinked back the quick sting of tears. "It haunts me, you know? You read about those pilots in falling airplanes who try all the different drills, right down to the point of impact. That was Mitch. He was a by-the-book guy. He'd have kept looking and when he found himself lost, he'd have kept trying to work his way out." Hoping for a miracle and trying to ignore the rising bubble of horror. "They said his voice at the end was perfectly calm," she whispered.

"So you built the Orienteer."

She swiped at her cheek. "I built the Orienteer because no one, no one should be in that spot ever again. No one's brother, no one's wife, no one's father or sister. And if I have to make nice with Ayre for that to happen, then I do it. It doesn't matter a hell of a lot to me, do you understand?" She gave him a searching gaze. "All I care about is the gear." She glanced down. "Anyway, now you know why I can't be involved with you."

"Because of your brother?"

"I can't do it, Nick."

He shook his head. "But Sloane, we *are* involved. You can't make it go away by pretending it's not there." And he had no intention of letting her.

Her eyes were hot and angry. "Don't push me into a corner."

"I'm not. I'm just sick of chasing after you."

"Then stop. It's easy enough."

He took her hand. "No, it's not, and you know that. Stop running, Sloane. You're too gutsy for it."

"I'm not running," she flared.

"Oh yeah? What would you call it?"

Self-preservation, but it was too late for that and she knew it. Rising, Sloane crossed to the windows and looked out at the bending trees in the street below as the wind stripped them of their leaves. "I don't know what to do about you, Nick," she said finally. She turned to find him behind her.

He smiled faintly. "I haven't known what to do about you from the beginning."

"Then why pursue it?"

"Because you don't turn away from things just because they're hard."

"You just don't know…"

"Yes I do. Take a chance with me, Sloane," he urged softly. "Take a chance and see where we go." And he slid her into his arms.

At first, all she felt was measureless comfort. For a moment, she curled against him, feeling his warmth, his solidity. And for that moment, he was a shield against all of her fears, that calm, quiet voice reassuring her that everything would be all right.

Nick pressed a kiss on her hair. Her breath eased out in a sigh as he lowered his mouth to hers. It was a gentle touch, so soft it was barely there. Intended to sooth rather than arouse, the exploration lulled her into trust, into comfort. He smoothed his hands down her back, over the curve of her hips.

And the slow pulse of the blood in her veins began to speed.

This time when her mouth met his, her lips parted to taste, to touch, to feel the tempting stroke of his tongue. For once, he wasn't dragging her into an embrace. She went willingly, eagerly, and the power of it shocked them both. Tomorrow, she would deal with the aftermath; tonight was for savoring, tonight was for taking chances.

It was like bringing a match to gasoline, comfort flaming into urgency. For too long he'd held back, for too long they'd waited. Now it was all released at once.

His hands raced over her, sliding down her hips, curving over her breasts, seeking the long, lean lines of her body under the bulky sweater. Impatient, he slipped his hands under the cotton weave to feel her, only her, springy and taut and fevered. Her skin was silky smooth and when he moved his hand up to feel the curve of her breast under his palm, Sloane gasped against him.

It wasn't enough, he thought as he tugged the sweater off over her head. It still wasn't enough. He wanted her, opening up to him physically as she'd opened up to him emotionally. He pulled off her sweater even as she tugged at his shirt with eager hands. Pulse hammering, he pulled her to him, body to body, skin to skin. And the feel of her half-naked against his chest dragged him into a hot arousal where nothing was certain except desire, silk and flesh in his hands.

Sloane couldn't hold back a moan, even with Nick's mouth covering hers. It was as though every nerve in her body were on edge, every fiber of her focused on the heat and pressure of his bare chest against hers. She felt his breath, his heartbeat. But she wanted to feel even more. And with eager hands, she tore at the waistband of his jeans.

Making a noise of impatience, he lifted her in his arms and walked to the doorway of the living room.

"Bedroom?" he rasped.

"Across the hall," she murmured, her lips against his throat.

Nick nudged the door open with his shoulder, stepping into her bedroom with a sort of exhilarated anticipation. The room was as spare as the rest of her home, the sole notes of femininity and indulgence injected by the pile of pillows at the head of the bed and the vivid turquoise of the silk robe hanging on the open closet door. The weak light cast by the lamp on the bureau made her skin gleam.

He laid her down on the bed, pressing her against the pillows. Seeing her breasts, pale and luminous, only made him want to see her fully naked, to feel her fully naked. She'd dropped the barriers earlier that night; he wanted the final barrier of clothing gone.

Sloane stared at him, watched his eyes darken to jet. Giddy expectation surged through her. She felt him unbutton her jeans. The air was cool on her skin as he slipped the denim down. She raised her hips to help him and felt the helpless surge of arousal at the motion. Molten desire burst through her. Then she was naked before him but for the scrap of silk and lace at her hips.

With a quick, impatient movement he stripped off his shoes and jeans. His body in the dim light was all lean lines and hard rises of muscle. She caught her breath as he stepped to the side of the bed, reached for him but he pressed her back against the pillows.

Gaze locked on hers, he reached out to touch her with his fingertip. Heat burst through her. Every fiber of her being focused on that burning spot. Then he slid his finger down, over her shoulder, into the dip above her collar bone, along the slight rise of her breast to the sensitive tip. She caught her breath there but he didn't linger, moving down the smooth flat of her belly to the point where the black silk blocked his way. He edged his finger under it until she moaned and moved against him.

His teeth gleamed. "Black lace, Sloane? I like that." And then he hooked his fingers in the sides and dragged it down her legs, tossing it aside. "I like it even better off."

He eased onto the bed beside her to press his body against her and she had to moan again because it had been so long and it felt so, so good. And because she knew there was more.

With a kind of delirious joy Nick ran his tongue down the slender column of her throat and then lower, to where her breasts began with their fragile skin and their exquisite sensitivity. Sloane moved against him but he took his time, sampling, tasting every inch until his lips were against the stiffened flesh of her nipples. He ran his tongue over each hardened nub in turn, feeling her body quake, hearing her shocked gasp as he bit gently.

The quick whisk of pain made the arousal more intense and she felt the tightness coiling in her body, at the apex of her legs where all sensation met. Each squeeze of her nipples had her catching her breath and arching toward him. It had never been like this for her. Never had she moved without volition, moaned without thought, ached to be filled. Her body, which she'd thought she'd known intimately, was his entirely and he was showing her just how much control he had.

He did things, bewitching things with his hands, stroking the dip of her sides, the long muscles of her thighs, coming closer to where she yearned, burned to be touched. He didn't, though, just kept stretching it out, tempting her until she couldn't hold back. The feel of his muscles under her fingers, the groans of his own arousal as she trailed her fingertips down his belly made her giddy with desire.

It wasn't enough to make love, Nick thought feverishly. The need inside him was a grinding ache. He didn't just want her to submit, he wanted her twisting against him in abandon. He wanted to take her to where no other man had brought her, a place where she couldn't regret, she couldn't second-guess, she couldn't hold back.

A place where she was his.

He stroked his hand up the inside of her thigh and she quivered against him. When he brought just two fingertips higher, he could feel the goose bumps on her skin. And then he went higher still, to find her already slick and hot.

It nearly undid him to know that she was so aroused. It took him even closer to hear her helpless moan, to feel her hips move against his hand. He wanted more, though, much more before he was going to let himself go. And when he went, they were going to go together.

He moved down between her legs, then, teasing her with

his tongue, first the flat of her belly, then the long lines of her inner thighs. Even here, she was exquisitely sensitive. He traveled lower to press a kiss on the fragile skin, to her mons and felt her twist feverishly against him.

"Please, Nick, please." She couldn't bear any more, Sloane thought as he took her to a higher pitch of excitement. The heat of his tongue slid down lower. His breath was warm on her skin, dragging a moan from her. And then his mouth was pressed against her there, finally, and all the waiting and arousal and temptation coalesced into that one shivering point.

Sloane flung her head back against the pillow in shock, trying to force air into her lungs. He drove her relentlessly, with pressure and liquid strokes, curving his hands around her thighs to pull her to him. She clutched at his shoulders, felt his hair beneath her fingers. Never, she'd never experienced anything like this, hadn't known it was possible for her body to be electrified, half-mad, shuddering with arousal. She was strung wire tight, everything in her drawing down to that one point under the heat of his mouth, the tension rising, drawing in, contracting until it exploded outward, rushing through her to the tips of her fingers, sending her writhing against him for endless minutes until she finally crested and drifted down.

But his hands were already driving her up again. This time, the path was known and she raced up it, straining at his touch, knowing she wanted more. "I need you in me," she whispered, dragging at his shoulders.

He moved up until she could reach down to find him shuddering and hard against her fingers. When she would have moved her hand, he stilled it, sliding his body over hers, his breath uneven, his face taut with the battle for control. She felt the velvety soft tip of him brush the entrance where she was already slick and ready. "Look at me," he murmured. "Look at me when I go inside you."

And with a thrust of his hips he buried himself in her.

It ripped a cry from her. He filled her utterly, pressed in to the hilt. For that moment, there were no evasions, there was no escape. And when he began to move, his back muscles flexing under her fingers, it was as though they were one being, the sensations that started in his body ending in hers.

Each stroke, each slick caress brought her to a new pitch of pleasure. If she'd thought she'd experienced what he had to offer before, she'd been mistaken. It was incomplete, gratification without substance. Now, with his body intimately connected with hers, everything tied together.

Deep inside her slick heat, Nick fought to hold on, to prolong the feeling. Sloane twisted beneath him like a wanton. Eyes fevered with excitement, silken legs wrapped around him, she cried out each time he drove himself into her. It dragged him to the edge, knowing he could bring her to this, knowing that at this moment she was utterly abandoned to it, to him.

To what they made together.

She stared at him, her eyes widening in sudden shock and then she was jolting under him, clenching around him, crying out her pleasure as the orgasm broke through.

And it was that, finally, that tore away his control so that he surged once, twice and spilled himself.

They lay motionless, still intimately twined together as their hearts gradually slowed. Nick kissed Sloane's shoulder, utterly overwhelmed. If he told her he'd never experienced anything like it would she believe him? Would she understand? She'd given herself to him, maybe with reservations at first, but wholly and completely by the end.

How was it he only wanted more?

Sloane made a move to pull up the sheet and he stilled her hand. "Hey, what do you think you're doing?"

She flushed. "Covering up."

"Don't. I like looking at you. When I see you in clothes again, it'll give me something to tide me over until the next time."

"The next time?"

He stroked a hand down her waist. "Yeah, the next time. I'm planning on a lot of them."

She did twist loose then to sit on the edge of the bed. "Nick, just because this happened doesn't mean…"

"Doesn't mean what?"

"It doesn't mean we're having an affair."

"You don't strike me as the one-night-stand type, Sloane."

"Yes, well—"

She yelped in surprise as he snaked out an arm and tumbled her back against him.

"So I guess we've got to be something," he said, gathering her to him.

She rolled on top of him, leaning on his chest. "I don't like somethings. Somethings make me nervous."

"Then don't think about it."

"We have to think about it," she protested. "We can't just barge into something—"

He kissed the tip of her nose. "There you go, worrying about somethings again. How about this—let's try it out, see where it goes. Maybe you can have some fun for a change, God forbid. There is life outside of work, you know."

"The project is important to me."

"I know. And I also know you'll do a better job at it if you give yourself a break once in a while." He stroked her back, enjoying the feel of the firm rise of muscle below. "You know, laugh a little, maybe see a movie or actually get out of Boston."

Sloane sighed. "You understand, Nick, I can't let this become too much. You can call it whatever you want—"

"Or not."

"Or not," she agreed. "But it has to stay contained."

It was the classic guys' dream—sex with a beautiful woman, no commitment. So why did it bug him? "Limits, Sloane?"

Vulnerability flickered in her eyes. "Only one. No promises. Let's enjoy what's here right now. Okay?"

It wasn't okay. It was very far from okay, just how far, he was tempted to tell her. But he knew already that it would take very little to make her take flight. It was still too soon. He'd known there was passion in her, had glimpsed it briefly, but nothing had prepared him for the fire, the generosity, the wantonness of her lovemaking.

And he had no intention of letting her walk away. He'd go along with her conditions. For now.

Nick kissed her lightly. "All right."

Sloane let out a sigh of relief, then she sighed again, in reaction. "Mmm, what are you doing?"

"Well, if this is only going to be a brief, meaningless non-something, we'd better get the most we can out of it, hadn't we?"

"You might be right," she said, pressing herself against him.

"Bet on it."

Chapter Ten

Nick sat at his kitchen table reading a *Globe* article on the latest Big Dig fiasco and savoring the morning quiet. Some people liked day shifts. He'd take a night tour anytime. So he got dragged out of bed a few times. Having a nice leisurely start to the day more than made up for it.

It would have been better if he'd been sharing coffee and orange juice with Sloane, but so far he hadn't been able to convince her to spend the night. It was early days, he reminded himself and tried to find patience.

His cell phone burbled. He checked the display and flipped open the phone with a grin. "Whadda you want?"

"Get up on the wrong side of the bed again today?" Gabe asked. "You'd never survive in the hospitality industry, bud."

"Who said I wanted to?" Nick asked.

"I figured you'd be tired of getting cats out of trees and vacuuming the firehouse floor."

"You're the vacuuming guy, with that antique you run."

"That national historic landmark, you mean."

"You hoteliers are so touchy." Nick went to the refrigerator to pull out the carton of orange juice.

"All I gotta say is don't expect the family discount next time you want to bring a woman up here to impress her," Gabe told him. "Not that any woman would be misguided enough to get involved with you, of course."

Nick picked up his orange juice glass. "Did you call to talk about my personal life?

"Not after I've just eaten. Actually, I just called to see what's happening over the holiday. You going to be up?"

"Not this year. I'm scheduled for a night shift on Thanksgiving."

"Yeah, I heard that."

He could just imagine. "Let me guess. You've been talking to Jacob. Did he tell you to give me a lecture, too?"

"There are other ways to deal with you. Did I tell you I've taken up tae kwon do?"

Nick grinned. "You think that will help?"

"Just keep it in mind. You're only a couple of hours away, you know," Gabe said mildly.

"Three."

"That's in range. Close enough for me to come down and kick your ass."

"On your day off, you mean?"

"On a workday, if it's important enough." Gabe's voice sounded amused.

"If I keep one arm tied behind my back, maybe." The grin on Nick's face faded. "So why are you doing Jacob's errands, Gabe?"

"I'm not. I was over at the farm for dinner last night and Thanksgiving came up."

"Gee, now there's a surprise." Nick leaned back in his chair. "What did Jacob have to say? Or do I have to ask?"

There was a pause. "Actually, it wasn't Jacob, it was Ma."

Nick blinked. "No kidding. What did she say?"

"It wasn't what she said."

"Are you trying to learn mind reading in your tae kwon do?"

"No," Gabe said quietly. "I'm just trying to make my mother stop hurting so much. Look, Nick, you got problems with Jacob, take them out on him, okay? Not Ma."

Gabe always had known how to deliver an effective sucker punch, Nick reflected. Especially when he was right. "Gabe, I've been through this with Jacob already. Even if I leave as soon as shift ends the day before Thanksgiving, I won't hit the farm until nine or ten at night. And I'd have to peel out by noon the day of to make it back in time for start of shift. There's no way to make it work. I'd hardly be there before I'd have to go."

"You've done it other years. Work isn't the reason you don't want to come."

"Really? What is the reason, Great Swami?"

"I don't know. I'd like to think you've got some babe that you can't tear yourself away from. Of course, you and Jacob always seem pissed off at each other these days, so it could be that you just don't want to deal with him." Gabe paused. "Or it could be that you don't want to come up because it'll make you miss Dad too much and feel guilty that you're never around."

Jacob bludgeoned and was no match for Nick's stubbornness. Quick, clever Gabe whipped in quickly to poke weak spots Nick didn't know he had.

The silence stretched out.

"Nick, you there?"

"Yeah." He shifted. "I'm here."

"Look, I'm not trying to play pop psychologist and I'm not playing Jacob's errand boy. I just thought you should know that it matters to Ma, even if she wouldn't tell you so. It's your call, bro. She's not going to blame you for not coming. She'll understand. But it might make it a little easier for her to get through the day with you there. Jacob and I are always around. You being there will make it special." He cleared his throat. "For her, anyway."

Nick blew out a breath and accepted the inevitable. "All right. I've taken a couple of shifts lately for a guy. I'll see if I can call in the favor, get the night off. Maybe even a couple of days."

"Don't go overboard," Gabe said. "There's only so much of you we can take."

"Hey, Gabe?"

"Yeah?"

"Practice that tae kwon do," Nick suggested. "Practice hard."

Half an hour later he hung up from his mother, the warm pleasure in her voice still resonating in his ears. Gabe had been right. Bitter as it was to admit, Jacob had been right. It was too easy, sometimes, far away from the farm, to forget what it had to be like for her to live with the daily reminders.

To go to sleep at night in an empty bed.

In the months after Adam Trask had died, family duty had whispered to Nick that he should take a leave of absence, return to the farm to help out. Yet that meant days under Jacob's thumb and nagging concern about the guys at the firehouse. Responsibility—loyalty—pulled him in two directions at once. The only easy answer was avoidance. Maybe Sloane wasn't the only one who hid behind a job.

Sloane… He'd held her less than eight hours before. He'd see her in another eight.

It seemed unimaginably distant. Tapping the phone, he punched the speed dial for her number and listened to it ring.

Sloane sat in her office typing an e-mail to the production manager for the Orienteer project. She clicked Send just as a calendar reminder flashed up on the screen. Pete's birthday Saturday, buy present.

The party, she remembered. There was a time when she wouldn't have missed it. Not now, though. Because of work, she told herself and tried to ignore the fact that it felt like an excuse. A gift, though—she wanted to get him something he'd like, something to let him know she was thinking of him.

The phone rang and she picked it up absently. "Sloane Hillyard."

"A fine thing, as far as I'm concerned."

"Nick." It felt good to hear his voice, dangerously good. "How are you?"

"Not nearly as good as I'd be if you were around. How are you?"

"I'm fine. Trying to get some work done." Of course, she'd have had more success if she hadn't repeatedly found herself staring into space and thinking of him. Not good, she told herself. It was supposed to be a simple fling. It wasn't supposed to get in the way of what was important. It wasn't supposed to *be* important.

"So what are you doing at work? Don't forget, my crew's on night shift tonight."

She opened her Web browser and began searching for gift

ideas. "Business doesn't just shut down because I'm not here. I've missed two days this week while I was at the firehouse."

"But you've always got your laptop on."

"That's just to keep my head above water."

"A very fetching head, by the way."

She couldn't help the smile. "My, what a smooth talker."

"Aren't I, though? So, you have lunch plans? I thought I could come by and take you out. I don't have to be at the firehouse until five."

The little buzz of pleasure hit before she could block it. *Keep it contained, Hillyard.* "I can't make lunch."

"Meeting?"

"I've got to run an errand. My nephew's birthday is tomorrow and I completely forgot about it. I've got to go get him something and stick it in overnight delivery."

"Where does he live?"

"Hartford."

"It's not that far. You could drive it down."

No, she couldn't. Sloane hesitated. "It's complicated."

"Your brother's son?"

"Yeah. It's just too hard to get away right now."

Nick thought of his conversation with Gabe. "Yeah, that's a pretty easy thing to tell yourself."

She bristled. "I don't recall asking you to sort out my life."

The seconds stretched out in silence. "I guess I deserved that," Nick acknowledged finally.

"I'm sorry I jumped on you. I know you're only trying to help. It's just not the time. Anyway, I'm stressed out. I've got to get a present, get it packed and mailed and still make it to my two o'clock."

"So let me help. We can find your nephew—has he got a name, by the way?"

"Pete."

"We can find Pete a present and I'll take care of getting it boxed up and mailed."

"You don't have to do that. I'll see you tonight at the firehouse, okay?" Tonight, when she could keep her distance while she figured out just how she felt about the affair she'd blundered into. Because for all that they avoided labels, they were having an affair.

"Tonight is too far away," Nick responded. "I want to see you before then. Look at it as a time-management issue—if you don't have to take time to mail the package, you can spare a little while to have lunch with me."

Lunch. That had been when she'd started losing her footing with him and she'd been tumbling ever since.

"So do we have a deal?"

"Deal," Sloane sighed.

Voices and footsteps echoed off the tiled floors of the Prudential Center as they walked past the ranks of stores and kiosks. There was too much to go through. It left her feeling simultaneously harried and overwhelmed.

Nick caught her hand in his. "So what do you want to get him? A Red Sox jersey, maybe?"

"No way. He's a Mets fan."

Nick looked at her dumbfounded. "A Mets fan? He lives in Hartford. Close enough for all right-thinking people to be Sox fans."

"I see." She fought a grin. "Well, his daddy grew up in Rochester, so he was brainwashed from a young age."

"Tragedy. I suppose everyone has their story. So what are you going to get him?"

It was the question she'd been asking herself all day. "That's the problem. I haven't got a clue."

Nick looked at her a long moment. "Don't see them very much, huh?"

"Not anymore," she said, her voice barely audible. "Not for a long time. I used to live with them back when I was going to UConn. Since Mitch died, though..." She spread out her hands helplessly.

Nick reached out and brushed his fingertips across her hair. "It's okay. We'll find something. How old is he?"

"Thirteen. Maybe I can just get him a gift certificate he can use for music or video games or something. Kids like that, don't they?"

"Nothing says I couldn't be bothered to think about you like a gift certificate. There's got to be a better choice."

"Don't rub it in. I already feel bad enough as it is."

They stood near the end of the mall, staring back at all the stores. With all the possibilities, it seemed impossible. It would have to be the gift certificate, whatever Nick thought.

A woman walked past them toward the Prudential Center stop on the Boston subway. She opened the door to walk inside and the strains of a street musician floated out into the air.

Nick snapped his fingers and turned to Sloane. "Got it."

"What?"

"Do you have a price limit?" he asked quickly. "Could you go a hundred?"

She considered. "Maybe. It'd have to be a pretty great gift. What are you thinking?"

"It'd make you look goo-ood," he wheedled.

"Spill it, Trask," she ordered.

He pointed through the glass doors of the mall to the music store across the street. "A guitar."

* * *

"So you wound up ahead," Nick said, unwrapping his sub. "The ultimate cool present, the store takes care of shipping and you come off smelling like a rose."

"Maybe not a rose," Sloane said, wishing it were that easy. "It's a good present, though. I think he's going to like it. It sounds like he's been having trouble lately. A guitar will give him an outlet and a focus."

"Happy to be of help."

They sat at the food court, the only way to manage a quick lunch under the circumstances. Sloane had picked out an acoustic guitar in glossy golden wood that the clerk had assured her would take abuse and see Pete from novice to proficient player. The offer to ship was a pleasant surprise. She should have gone straight back to work. The fact that she couldn't make herself leave without a bit more time with Nick gave her pause.

"So how long's it been since you've seen Pete?" he asked casually.

Sloane toyed with her baked potato. "Do we have to talk about this?"

"Maybe I'm curious."

"What am I, your lab experiment?"

"No, you're someone I care about. I'd like to know about what's bothering you."

It stopped her for a moment. Slowly, she nodded. "What makes you so sure this is?"

"The fact that you don't want to talk about it?" He gave her a level stare. "Would it help if I said I might have some idea how it is for you?"

Hot protest bubbled to her lips but then she looked at his face and saw that he wasn't patting her on the head. "Tell me."

"Last March I lost my father. He had a heart attack in the groves during the spring sap run."

"I'm sorry."

He gave her a half smile. "So am I. I never thought it would be so hard to go home. I walk around the farm, the house, and I see him everywhere."

Sloane looked away.

"And I've been staying away, just like you have." Nick hesitated. "Sometimes the easy thing isn't the right thing. I've been staying down in Boston for all the good reasons—work, side job, fixing up my house. And I've been trying like hell to avoid thinking about what my mom's been going through."

The same way she'd been avoiding thinking about Candy and Pete. "So you think I should go down there?"

"I don't think it's for me to say. I'm still trying to figure out my own life. I will tell you that I was going to stay away for Thanksgiving this year. My brothers talked me into coming. I'm glad they did."

"You're going back to the farm."

"Yeah," he said, shifting a little. "I don't know what it's going to be like, but it feels like the right thing to do. So," he focused in on her, "got plans for the holiday?"

She gave him a suspicious look. "I'm working, at least part of it. You're on a night tour on Thanksgiving, remember?"

"Yeah, that was my excuse," he said. "Not anymore. I traded with the B-shift captain. I'm going to head up to the farm as soon as we get off the day before."

"Vermont, right?"

"Maple syrup." He finished his sandwich. "I don't suppose you'd want to go with me?"

Sloane blinked. "I can't go with you to Thanksgiving."

"Why not?"

Where did she begin? "It's a family holiday. It's where you bring someone that you've got a *thing* with."

"A thing sounds suspiciously like *something*. Off-limits, remember?"

"You know what I mean. Someone you're serious about."

"Not necessarily. I've brought friends along before and so have my brothers. My younger brother," he amended. "I'm not sure Jacob even *has* any friends. Anyway, back up. If we're not having a thing, then it shouldn't matter to you what my family thinks. After all, by that standard you won't be seeing them again."

"And in the meantime I get grilled as Nick's potential squeeze." She stared balefully at the Chick-fil-A stand. "Anyway, I don't need to be your charity invite."

"What's that supposed to mean?"

"I get it fairly regularly around the holidays. People ask what I'm doing, I say hanging, and there's this awkward silence and then presto, an invitation. People don't like the thought of me being alone. It makes them uncomfortable."

"Maybe they just want your company."

Her response was a snort.

Nick leaned forward. "You've been getting a lot of practice at pushing people away, Sloane. Why don't you try something different? Get out of town for a change. Meet some friendly people. Eat too much turkey and just kick back for a couple of days. Bathe in maple syrup."

"A couple of days?"

"A day and a half. Wednesday night to Friday afternoon.

You can tour the farm. Hell, you can hang out with Jacob. He'll be no threat to you. He's more antisocial than you are."

"And what are you going to say to them about your guest?"

He crumpled up his sandwich wrapper. "The truth. That we're seeing each other and I think you're good company."

She raised an eyebrow. "I'm good company?"

"Well, my usual rule is to invite people I don't like a lick, but I'm making an exception with you. Don't make a federal case out of it."

She scowled, tossing her napkin down on the tray. "I'm not making a federal case."

"You said you'd never been to Vermont. Come with me." He paused. "Unless the idea of meeting a few Trasks scares you."

"I'm not afraid to meet anyone," she retorted, knowing he was baiting her but powerless to keep from reacting.

"Well, then, it's easy. Come with me. Or am I going to have to mud wrestle with you over it?"

"You can get that idea right out of your head."

"Come with me, Sloane." He looked at her, the fun ebbing out of his eyes. "It'll be easier for me to get through it with you there."

And what could she do but say yes?

Chapter Eleven

Night shift on the apparatus floor and the air was filled with controlled urgency. The ladder crew hurried to don their breathing gear, slipping the harnesses on over their turnouts, pressing their masks against their faces. Breathing the compressed air, they stood ready to do battle with the flames.

Nick clicked his stopwatch and clapped. "Forty-five seconds, guys. Not bad. Okay, pop quiz. Sorensen, when your mask starts vibrating for your low-air warning, how much time do you have left?"

Sorensen took off his mask and considered. "Four or five minutes." He gave a quick grin. "Except for a blowhard like O'Hanlan. He might get thirty seconds if he's lucky."

There was a moment of surprised silence and then the group broke out into guffaws.

"I think that was the first time I've ever heard you make a joke, Sorensen," O'Hanlan said.

"Hard to get a word in edgewise with you around, O'Hanlan," Sorensen told him.

"You got that right, probie," Knapp said.

"Come December, he's not going to be a probie anymore," Nick said.

"Red as a grown-up firefighter?" O'Hanlan asked. "You know what that means, Knapp."

Knapp nodded vigorously. "He cooks us all a steak dinner. I like rib eye, Sorensen, in case you want to plan ahead."

"I'll be sure to stop at Burger King on my way to work that day."

"You hearing this, Nick?" O'Hanlan demanded. "He's getting mouthy now that he's almost earned his badge."

"Around you, O'Hanlan, it's self-defense," Nick said. He scanned his drill sheet and decided to have mercy on the crew. "Okay, we've pretty well done our hour. Let's call it good."

There was a general exodus. Nick was gathering together his notes when he realized that Sorensen was still hanging around.

He glanced up. "You need something, Sorensen?"

"I was hoping I could talk with you."

"Sure."

The probie looked at the corners of the room and cleared his throat. "I'm coming to the end of my probationary period, cap. Outside of overhauling and ventilating, I've only done searches in four fires. I want to work on one of the rescue squads eventually. When am I going to start really going on search detail?"

"When you've got a little more experience."

"How can I get more experience without going into fires?"

It was a logical question, Nick thought. He'd been slow to send Sorensen in for search and rescue, mostly because the kid looked so young. He wasn't a kid, though, he was a man.

Maybe it was time to start giving him the kinds of chances he was looking for.

Nick nodded. "No guarantees but I'll start trying to give you some more fire time. Keep working on your drills, do a good job inside and when it comes time I'll try to give you a recommendation for the rescue company."

"No kidding?"

"If you get it, it'll be because you've earned it. Fair enough?"

"Fair enough."

Nick glanced over Sorensen's shoulder to see Sloane walking up the stairs, her hips swaying. And that quickly, desire twisted through him.

Maybe she'd worked six shifts without seeing an honest-to-God fire but the ride alongs had given Sloane an appreciation for life in a firehouse. Including the experience of having yet another dinner interrupted by the bells. Not a medical aid call, this time, but a trash fire on a corner with a vacant lot. They'd put it out using the tank on the pumper and the ladder crew stumbled around on the heap to dig out the last sparks.

Now, they were back in the firehouse. Nick walked around the truck in his turnout pants, cleaning up. He'd shrugged off his red suspenders to dangle jauntily around his hips. His gray T-shirt stretched across his chest.

Was it any wonder that every woman she knew harbored a secret affection for firefighters? He looked her way and something twisted sweetly inside her. They didn't have a thing, she reminded herself. It was nothing serious, but, oh, it stretched a smile across her face.

Nick glanced over at her and stopped. For a long minute he just looked at her. Then, as though he couldn't help it, he walked straight over to her and brushed a hand over her hair.

She raised her brows. "Is that wise, Captain Trask?"

"What, you missed the general stampede for the kitchen? I can assure you, everyone's inside lining up at the microwave."

"What about you, aren't you hungry?"

His gaze was steady. "Oh, yeah."

"What do you suggest we do about it?"

He rested a hand against the ladder truck and leaned toward her. "I've got a few ideas we could try out. For example, we could—"

"Hey, you guys are missing out on warmed-over pork chops up here," Beaulieu's voice hollered down from the stairs. "Everything's all set."

Nick's eyes closed for a moment. "On our way," he called and gave Sloane a resigned shrug. "Life on the clock."

Sloane turned toward the stairs, tugging him after her. "Come on, I could use some dinner, anyway."

His lips twitched. "You are kind of skinny."

Sloane gave a sniff. "Junkyard dogs are skinny. I am not skinny. The term is *willowy,* Trask." They mounted the stairs.

He traced one finger down the center of her back, almost making her lose her footing. "Deliciously willowy, Hillyard," he murmured. "I'd be happy to show my appreciation at an appropriate time."

The warmed over pork chops, she had to admit, were not half-bad.

The dormitory was black as pitch. Nick rolled onto his back and stared up into the darkness at the invisible ceiling. He could hear Sloane's soft breathing in the darkness, felt the deep curl of need. She was only feet away, so close he could almost touch her.

Almost, but not quite.

Dinner had given way to a movie that he barely remembered. He'd sat in the darkened lounge, staring at the screen and conscious only of Sloane sitting in the chair next to him.

At this hour, it was as though the entire world were lost in slumber and only he lay awake. Wondering. Wondering if she slept, wondering if she dreamed, wondering if she lay awake staring into the darkness, wanting the way he wanted. If they'd been alone, he'd have gone to her. Nothing would have stopped him. He could imagine the feel of her sleek body, the silken spill of her hair against his cheek, the taste of her mouth, avid and hungry under his.

The seconds dragged by, stretched to minutes in the almost imperceptible march to morning.

There was a deep creak as someone rolled over and O'Hanlan's unmistakable grinding snore filled the air. Nick sighed. He reached beside his bed, feeling for the beanbag he kept there, as they all did. With unerring aim that spoke of night after night of practice, he lobbed it toward the source of the noise. There was a soft "oof" in the darkness and the snoring stopped.

And the seconds returned to dragging torturously by.

How long could a night last? Sloane wondered with a small stab of desperation. She shifted slightly on the mattress trying to find some position that would let her drift off. All around her there was only sleep. In her there was only awareness.

She wanted him. There was nothing to distract her from that knowledge. No battle, no sparring, only the thought that he lay so near and absolutely unreachable. She turned, but sleep remained stubbornly elusive.

Finally, she flipped back the covers and rose to pad noiselessly across the dormitory to the doorway. Maybe she couldn't sleep, she thought, easing the door shut behind her, but she shouldn't have to lie awake thirsty. A glass of water first and then maybe she'd distract herself with work or a book.

Her stockinged feet were quiet on the floor as she walked down the hall to the kitchen. She didn't need to switch on a light to see her way. Moonlight shone through the window across the floor, a broad swath of it, ghostly and serene. Sloane went to the window and looked out at the trees outside. The entire world had gone silent, hypnotic and washed clean in the pale light.

She thought afterward that she'd known he would come. The small sound didn't make her jump, but rather turn in expectation. His eyes were silver, his mouth intent. In silence, he came to her and in silence she flowed into his arms.

The moonlight spilled over her face, silvering her lashes, bringing her skin the pale translucence of marble. She looked, Nick thought, ethereal, fragile. In his arms she felt warm and alive. For a long time it was simply enough to hold her, browsing over her face with soft, nibbling kisses, feeling her heat.

"I want you," he murmured softly. Her response was to pull his face to hers. Her answer was on her lips. All heat and temptation, the kiss lured and aroused. For every desire it satisfied, it ignited a dozen more. Every touch made him want, every taste made him hunger. Desperation colored every move; there could never be enough.

Down the hall and behind the doors, a dozen men slumbered. Here, in this shadowy room, there were only the two of them.

The lights went up and the abrupt sound of the alarm bells shattered the stillness. They broke apart, breathing hard. Nick turned toward the dormitory. The others were just rising. Yawning, they stepped to the fire pole to slide down to the apparatus floor, taking no notice when Sloane trailed in after Nick.

Downstairs, the firefighters pulled on their turnouts. Sloane frowned at the stiff canvas. "They're the quickest way," Nick advised. "Step in and go."

Sloane dragged up the pants and threw the suspenders over her shoulders. The canvas was stiff, the boots awkward and heavy as she climbed up into the cab of the truck. So why was it she could still feel that wanton sense of arousal? Every inch of her was piercingly aware of Nick beside her. She didn't trust herself enough to look at him as the truck drove out of the lighted garage into the darkness of the streets.

"What I want to know is why these people always pick the middle of the night to have these fires," O'Hanlan groused. "I was having this great dream. I won the lottery and was sailing down the bay in Florida on this great big yacht. How people set their houses on fire at 2:00 a.m. is something I'll never figure."

"Nineteen-twenties' wiring and insulation, probably." Nick gestured at the dilapidated triple-decker ahead of them, smoke already seeping out of its second-floor windows. "Look at the place."

They pulled to the front of the building, by the knot of neighbors and the spectators who always seemed to have some sixth sense about fires. Ahead of them, the pumper had dropped hose by the hydrant ahead of the house and driven forward to give the ladder truck room. Already, the engine crew was stretching lines from the pumper to the hydrant.

Nick tapped Beaulieu on the shoulder. "See if you can find out anything about who might be inside." He turned to flag down Giancoli of Engine 58. "What's the word on occupants?" Nick asked as he tightened the harness on his breathing mask.

"Three apartments, one on each level."

Nick glanced over to Sloane. She stood staring at the fire like Joan of Arc facing the armies of France. He wished he could go to her. He didn't have that luxury. As ranking officer, he ran the scene until the district chief showed up.

Beaulieu hurried over. "Everybody's already out," he said, gesturing toward a small clutch of stunned-looking adults and crying children, shivering in the night cold.

That made it easier, though they still needed to run through the building just in case. "Let's get a one-and-a-half inch line in there," Nick directed. He turned to the ladder crew. "Beaulieu, Knapp, I want you on the roof ventilating. O'Hanlan, run the stick up over at the corner where the A wall meets the B wall, away from the smoke. Sorensen?" He looked at him. "You and I are on inside detail."

Excitement leapt in the probie's eyes. "I'm on it, cap."

It might have been nearly three in the morning, but people were straggling out of their houses, awakened by the noise. Unfortunately, the police hadn't shown up yet for crowd control, Nick thought in annoyance. Without the other companies on the alarm, who had yet to appear, he couldn't spare the time.

The sound of gasoline-powered saws sounded from the roof where Beaulieu and Knapp were cutting holes to let out hot gases and smoke. Once they'd ventilated the fire, the inside teams would have an easier time.

Suddenly, one of the children in the knot of occupants began to wail. A women crouched down to talk with him, but he shook her off and came pelting over to the firefighters.

"T.O.'s still up there," he burst out, even as a man who might have been his father hurried over to scoop him up.

"Don't bug the firemen, Jamal. They're busy." Behind them, a pair of enginemen hauled a hose line through the front door.

The boy twisted his in father's hands. "What's gonna happen to T.O.?"

Nick crouched down in front of him. "Is there someone still inside?"

"T.O.," the boy cried. "I want T.O."

"His hamster," the father said apologetically.

All of his problems should be so easily handled. "Okay. Where is it?"

"On the second floor, back bedroom, against the window."

Nick grinned. "Hey Sorensen, want to go rescue a hamster?"

The probie hefted his six-foot-long ceiling hook. "I got a nose for hamsters, cap."

"You mean a nose *like* a hamster," O'Hanlan heckled him as he headed toward the front door.

It wasn't much of a fire, Sloane reassured herself. White smoke streamed toward the sky from the hole the roof team had cut. White smoke was good. White smoke meant the fire was out, so why was she still riven with anxiety? To take her mind off it all, she turned toward the spectators. "Okay, everyone, move back," she said with the authority the turnouts gave her. "Let's leave the crews room to work." Repeatedly, she glanced over at the building, searching for an indicator of progress.

"Miss?" Sloane turned to see an older woman behind her. "Can you tell me how bad it is? I live on the top floor." Her face was worn, her eyes worried. Although she twisted her hands together in unconscious tension, her shoulders were squared and resolute beneath her shabby robe.

Anxiety was forgotten in a rush of sympathy. Sloane caught at the woman's hands. They were icy cold. "What's your name?"

"Latrice Winston."

"I'm Sloane. You're out safely, that's what matters."

"Everything I own is in there." Her voice wobbled for an instant, but she raised her chin. "I got to know what's happened."

It wrung her heart. "Here, sit." Sloane drew her down to the running board of the ladder truck. "I don't know the status, but I promise you I'll do everything I can to find out for you. Let me get you something to keep you warm first, though."

After she'd draped a red firehouse blanket around the woman's shoulders, Sloane turned to the house in time to see Sorenson and Nick emerge with a small cage.

"T.O.," a little boy shrieked and raced over to him. Grinning, Sorenson handed him the cage. Inside, a furry chestnut-colored ball stirred and unrolled to inspect them with beady black eyes.

"Here you go, one special-delivery hamster."

The boy clutched the cage to his chest. "T.O., you made it, buddy."

And Nick had made it, Sloane thought with a surge of relief. He was out of the house, away from the fire.

Safe.

She walked up behind him. "Hamster search and rescue?"

"I'm one of the best."

"I'm sure there's no one I'd trust more. How's the fire?"

"History. It wasn't much to begin with." He shook his head. "Looked like a candle tipped over in one of the second-floor units, caught the sofa and the curtains and a little bit of the wall. We'll spend an hour or so here overhauling to be sure there aren't any little pockets of embers, but the excitement's over."

And finally the iron clutch on her stomach could ease entirely. Then she remembered her mission. "How's the third floor? Any damage?"

"Clean. We're going to have to go into the walls to see if anything's involved up there, but unless we find that the fire's spread, we won't bring in water."

Sloane glanced over at Latrice and gave her the thumbs-up. "That's great. I have to go pass the message along."

"Who was doing crowd control?"

"I was."

"You?"

She shrugged. "It was a way I could help. Nothing's harder than watching."

"I know." He stared at her and she felt the buzz begin again. It wasn't what she'd choose, but choice had become irrelevant. He wasn't what she wanted but he was who she had to have. Silver-gray, his gaze delved into hers until it was inside her.

Nick took a step back and gave a brief smile. "Well, we've still got work to do here. Get comfortable, because we're going to be awhile. We've got business to finish."

And when the overhauling was done and they were back in quarters, she and Nick would finish the business between them.

Bright lights, loud thumps and voices. Dragged up from sleep, Sloane opened her eyes, staring groggily out into the dorm at men who rose slowly, stumbling to the bathroom in the hope that a splash of cold water might make them feel more human. She fumbled for her watch on the little bedside ledge. Six in the morning. They'd pulled back in to the station, she recalled, a whopping hour and a half before. An hour and a half of sleep.

It wasn't enough.

She rolled over, away from the light. And with her cheek to the pillow, she locked eyes with Nick.

He'd been awake for long moments watching her sleep, her hair like a pale cloud of fire against the white of the pillowcase. When she rolled over to face him, he quite simply lost his breath. Less than a yard of space stretched out between them but it was spanned by the heat that sprang up instantly, demanding satisfaction. Only the sounds of the fire crew stopped her from going to him. Only the knowledge that others were in the room prevented him from reaching for her.

They stirred and rose at the same time, keeping their distance from one another. Perhaps no one else would have noticed, but the certainty was there, in their eyes. When she rubbed her arms, he felt her skin. When he stretched, her hands knew the feeling of muscles flexing beneath them. The boundary between imagination and reality, awareness and experience thinned dangerously. They stared at each other, neither wanting to leave the room, to leave the other's sight.

The scent of coffee drifted into the dormitory, drawing the others. Sloane turned into the women's bathroom. Her reflection looked back at her from the mirror, eyes huge, mouth soft. She started to pull her hair back and then on second thought left it loose to tumble down over her shoulders. The soft cotton of her shirt feathered over her skin like a caress.

And when she stepped back into the hall, she saw Nick walking from his office to the kitchen.

It wasn't that she stopped, simply that her muscles no longer accepted the command to move. He was taut, lean in jeans and a fresh T-shirt. He hadn't taken time to shave away the dark overnight shadow on his jaw. His hair was damp, slicked back, but already loose strands hung down over his forehead.

Sexuality. It vibrated around him until she thought she could almost see the air wavering with it. Her heart slammed against her ribs in a violent tattoo.

To want this much was terrifying.

Nick saw the rise of Sloane's breasts as she caught her

breath. Desire wrapped around him until he wanted to groan with the need. It was like the moments before flashover, heat rising, coming closer to the instant when everything would spontaneously combust. She was so close. Just a few steps would take him to her. He watched.

She waited.

The edge of control sharpened.

"Hey, Trask, if you want any of this coffee you'd better finish up and get in here." The voice broke them free just as Nick approached the point where nothing mattered but touching her. He had to move away while he still could.

"We'd better…"

Sloane nodded, walking the few steps into the kitchen, trying to stay as far from Nick as possible. If they brushed against each other she didn't know what she would do.

Her every movement felt distinct, underlined with importance, with the certainty that he watched. She took the last empty seat at the table, dimly aware that the room had filled with the next crew, the hubbub of conversation filled with descriptions of the fire. Nick leaned against a cupboard. Their eyes locked.

Arousal hummed through her entire body, saturating the air between them. She wondered that it wasn't visible, like the rising, crackling sparks of a Jacob's ladder. The minutes ticked by unbearably. She waited for release.

O'Hanlan looked at his watch. "Well, boys," he said, clapping one of the day crew on the shoulder. "Looks like it's that time again. I can't think of better hands to leave the gig to. I'm outta here." He grabbed his shoulder bag and headed for the door. The rest of the shift began to trickle out.

In the parking lot, Sloane started her car. She pulled out to the driveway and paused. He would follow. She knew it.

The streets stirred with early-morning activity. Everything seemed unbearably vivid, unbearably clear. She didn't look for the red truck behind her.

She didn't have to.

The drive seemed endless, yet in a surprisingly short time she was parking in the small lot behind her house, turning off the ignition. Her feet made hollow thumps on the porch boards.

With a throbbing roar, Nick's car pulled in behind hers. At her back door, Sloane stopped and turned. His eyes were turbulent. Her satchel dropped from suddenly nerveless fingers. Swift, intent, he walked straight to her and wordlessly dragged her against him.

The kiss was explosive, as though a spring that had been coiled to the strain point, then coiled just a bit more had been suddenly, violently released. His mouth savaged hers and she gloried in it. Her fingers clawed at his back and desire pulsed in her. When they broke away they were both breathless, speechless, knowing only what they wanted from each other.

Sloane's fingers shook as she fit the key into the lock. It took an unbearably long time to get upstairs to her flat. And when she'd unlocked it, they fell inside, their mouths fused together, stoking up the heat, higher and higher.

Her lips moved hot and eager under his, her hands dragged at his shirt. He shrugged out of his jacket and pressed her toward the couch. The bedroom was way too far.

They'd made love night after night, but never like this. This time, desire owned them. They were swift and impatient to strip off every scrap of clothing. Naked, he would have slowed, but she drove him more quickly, her need egging him on. Tangled together, they fell to the couch, their mouths and hands frenzied.

Nick's mouth raced down her neck to feast on her breasts,

his tongue flicking over the nipples, the faint nip of his teeth making her cry out. The tug of desire started an answering throb lower down. Pleasure pressed itself to the point where it blurred into pain, intensity overwhelming the nerves' ability to discern the difference.

Never like this, all flame, possession and plunder. She discovered her power in a blaze of passion. The brush of her hands over his chest, his nipples, made his breath hiss out, made him jolt. When she followed the path of her fingers with her lips, she tore a groan from him. She ranged across his chest, dropping lower to nibble over his belly, then lower still.

And with her lips and her tongue she saw how far she could take him from civilized man.

His body arched, caught in a shudder of pleasure. He rode it almost to the point of no return, then reached down to pull her up to him again. When their mouths met, hers could have been made for him alone.

She surrounded him, the sleekness of her body, the softness of her skin. The dark taste of her threatened to overwhelm his senses. His hands ranged over her body, searching for hidden sensitivity, driving her, always driving her higher. When his fingers slid up the inside of her thighs she gasped. She arched as she felt his touch.

Then he took her up again, more intensely than she'd ever known, her body rising, rising to a crescendo. When he sensed she was teetering on the edge he shifted. Their cries melded as he plunged into her, then they drove each other to that final precipice and tumbled off, together.

Chapter Twelve

Sloane stared at the dark ribbon of pavement unrolling in the car's headlights. If it had been daylight, she could have been distracted by the Vermont countryside they were driving through. Instead, she could only focus on the visit that lay ahead. At least it was getting late. They'd left as soon as possible after the end of shift, but holiday traffic had conspired to delay them. Now, it was pushing ten-thirty.

The later the better, as far as she was concerned. With every minute that passed, her misgivings mounted. She'd been out of her mind to agree to come up for the holiday. Small talk wasn't her forte at the best of times, and certainly being grilled by family who saw her as a serious girlfriend—or threat—was far from the best of times. Maybe everyone would be in bed when they'd arrive and she'd get an overnight reprieve.

The headlights picked out a large sign painted in the vivid

colors of fall foliage. "Trask Family Farm and Sugar House" it read, with an arrow pointing toward a branch road.

"Almost there," Nick said.

Sloane felt the clutch of nerves in her stomach. "I don't belong here. Why don't you drop me off at that inn we passed a couple miles back and have your weekend with your family?"

The dash lights of the car showed the gleam of his smile. "Because I want you here with me."

Ahead, high-wattage arc lights created bright pools in the parking lot of what she assumed was the Trask farm. "If you really cared about me, you'd take me somewhere else," she said, only half joking as the car slowed.

"It's because I care about you that I'm not. Stop trying to get out of it. They're not going to bite." He turned in and headed to the far right of the lot, searching out a narrow lane that threaded its way past the sugar house and gift shop. Behind loomed the dark bulk of a farmhouse; a yellow light on the side porch gleamed in welcome.

Nick's family might not bite but she had a pretty good idea they were going to be very curious about Nick's friend. "What did you tell them about me?"

He flashed a grin as he stopped on the broad parking apron and turned off the ignition. "I told them you were in the witness protection program and they couldn't ask you any questions. Oh, and that you've already taught me a dozen new sexual positions."

Amused despite herself, Sloane gathered up her purse and opened the door. "A dozen, huh?"

He popped the trunk. "I didn't think they were ready for the real number."

Around them, the woods stretched out dark and silent. In

Cambridge and Boston, there was always light, always noise. Here, the chill night was its own presence. Sloane shivered.

"Come on, let's get inside," Nick said, grabbing the bags and leading her up the steps of the little porch. He opened the door without knocking and walked inside.

There was no place she could walk into like that, Sloane realized in an instant of painful clarity as she followed him into the mudroom. What was it Frost had said, "Home is the place that, when you have to go there, They have to take you in"? The only home she had was the one she paid for herself.

Nick walked through the mudroom and stopped at the door to the inside of the house. "Come on, what are you waiting for?"

Sloane shook back her hair and followed him.

The kitchen was warm, fragrant and welcoming after the raw November night. It probably looked just about the way it had a century before, with a broad planked floor and butter-colored wainscoting. On one wall, a granite fireplace big enough to stand in held an enormous copper kettle. Pots and pans dangled from an overhead beam. A swinging door led to what she assumed was a dining room; another empty threshold presumably led to the rest of the house.

In the center of the room sat a thick oak table with massive turned legs. On it, checkered dishtowels covered cooling pies. A half-dozen of them. Just how many people was Molly Trask expecting to feed? Sloane wondered a little desperately.

On the stove, onions and celery sizzled quietly. A spoon in the spoon rest and a pot holder tossed down on the counter gave clues that the cook was nearby.

"Hey, Ma," Nick called, walking over to turn off the burner. "You planning to burn the house down?"

"Nicholas?" Wiping her hands on her apron, a wiry-looking woman walked into the kitchen from the inside of the house.

Nick grinned and swept her into a bear hug.

"I can't believe your timing," she scolded when they were done. "I sit here all night waiting for you and the one minute I take to use the restroom you show up."

"We got a call a couple of weeks ago for a fire started by someone who'd left a pan on the stove unattended."

"I know, I know," she said with a flush. "I promise I won't do it again. Now introduce me to your friend."

"Sloane Hillyard, this is my mother. Ma, this is Sloane."

"Welcome." Blue eyes set like Nick's looked at Sloane in amusement. "My name's Molly, in case you want an actual name."

Sloane grinned. "Thanks."

She'd given Nick his good looks, but Molly Trask appeared to have other things to worry about than vanity. She wore an apron over jeans and a flannel shirt. Her iron-gray hair swung down to her jaw. Her skin might have shown signs of weathering, but it showed more signs of laughter. Crossing to the stove, she stirred the onions. "Can I get you coffee or tea or something?"

"Just some water for me, thanks," Sloane said. "No coffee at this hour or I'll never sleep."

"I'll take coffee, but I'll make it myself," Nick said.

"Like his father, this one," Molly said fondly as she scraped the cooked onions and celery into a bowl. "He'd drink coffee at midnight and still go out like a light. Same thing with Jacob," she added, nodding toward the sudden noise in the mudroom.

"Jacob what?" The kitchen door opened and a bear of a man walked in, all black beard and bulk in his parka, stamping the snow off his boots.

"Jacob's here to meet our guests," Molly filled in.

Vivid blue, his eyes flickered over Sloane before fastening on Nick. "You're parked in a soft patch."

"A soft patch?"

Jacob looked around. "Yeah. I need to get the whole apron rolled. They're predicting rain tonight and if it doesn't freeze, you're going to have a mess."

"I guess I'd better move it, then," Nick replied.

"Hello, Jacob. Oh, hello, Nick. Haven't seen you in a while. That's right, it's been since spring." Molly spread plastic wrap over the bowl and put it in the refrigerator. "Honestly, you could at least say hello, you two."

A corner of Nick's mouth twitched. "Hey, J.T."

Jacob stuck his hand out in resignation. "Nick."

No hugs, no shoulder pounding, Sloane noticed. An awkward current of tension ran through the room, something not quite comfortable.

"Jacob, this is Sloane Hillyard. Sloane, this is Jacob, my older brother."

She found her hand enveloped in Jacob's. She could see the resemblance now that she looked, but in contrast to Nick's ease, Jacob seemed awkward, too big for the kitchen. He belonged outdoors, she thought.

"Nice to meet you," he muttered. "Well, I just came in to tell you. The back door's open. I'll see you tomorrow."

Molly stifled a yawn as Jacob disappeared. "It's probably time for me to go to bed, too." She walked over to kiss Nick and squeezed Sloane's shoulder. "The guest room is made up."

The bedroom could have been in a B and B, with colonial blue walls and scatter rugs covering the wide-planked hardwood floor. She caught the scent of freesia from the vase of fresh flowers that sat on a maple bureau that had been polished until it glowed. The bed was a spindle-topped four-poster, with an intricate quilt laid over the top of the double-sized mattress.

Sloane cleared her throat. "We're not staying in here, are we?"

"You don't like it?"

"With your mother in the house? It doesn't quite seem right."

The corners of Nick's mouth turned up. "Old-school. I like that."

"I'm not a prude," she muttered, blushing furiously. "It just...well, it feels disrespectful."

Nick leaned in to kiss her. "God, I adore you. You didn't let me finish. You're staying in the guest room, alone. I'll be bunking in Jacob's house, out back."

"Well, you don't need to go to a whole 'nother building," she protested.

His eyes crinkled with humor. "I'm old-school, too. Relax. I'll come over in the morning and make you coffee."

She smelled it before she even opened her eyes. Sloane took a blissful sniff. Any man who would be up and making coffee for her at six-thirty in the morning was her hero.

Or heroine, she discovered a few minutes later as she walked into the kitchen to find Molly Trask wrestling with the turkey and cursing a blue streak.

Sloane stopped in the doorway. "Need some help?"

Molly glanced ruefully over her shoulder. "Yes, actually. If you could just hold the drumsticks together so I can get them tied, we'll be all set. They keep slipping out of the string."

It was about the biggest turkey she'd ever seen, Sloane thought as she washed her hands. "Just how many people are you expecting today?" She pulled the ends of the legs together so Molly could tie them securely.

"I think we're up to sixteen now, give or take a grandniece or -nephew," Molly said, snipping the ends of the string with kitchen shears. "The boys, you, my in-laws, their three kids and their families and a neighboring couple who have known us forever." She ticked them off on her fingers. "Now if you could just help me get the bird into the roaster, we'll be all set. I'll lift him up and you slide the roaster under," she directed. "Ready? One, two, *three.*"

The turkey safely transferred, Molly wiped off her hands and leaned against the counter. "If you want coffee, there are mugs in that cabinet over there. Tea, too."

"Coffee's perfect," Sloane assured her.

"Well, how about if you pour us a couple of cups while I get old Tom in the oven?"

Sloane searched out a pair of pretty blue ceramic mugs. "These are nice."

"Nick got those for me one year for Christmas. He said they reminded him of my eyes. Always did have a romantic streak, that boy."

"Really?"

Molly picked up a dish of melted butter. "Well, he could hardly be a firefighter without it, could he? I mean, a lot of it is hard work, but a lot of it is making a difference, maybe saving a life. That takes being a romantic, doesn't it?"

And romantics didn't agree to relationships that had no future, Sloane thought uneasily.

Molly basted the turkey. "I hope butter doesn't alarm you. Nick's brother Gabriel brought home a girl one year who wouldn't eat a thing once she saw I was cooking with butter. Honestly, it's Thanksgiving, for heaven's sakes. Every now and then you throw out the rules." She shut the oven door briskly. "I'm a stickler for basting a turkey."

"My sister-in-law used to swear by cooking the turkey upside down until the last hour and then flipping it."

"Your sister-in-law?"

Sloane hesitated. "My brother's widow, I mean."

Molly's gaze softened. "Nick mentioned that you'd lost your brother. I'm sorry. It must be hard."

"It is," Sloane said simply. And to her surprise the sympathy was easy to accept for once, rather than embarrassing. Few people she knew were aware of her loss, a loss she kept fiercely private. Perhaps it was easier with Molly Trask because they had loss in common. Sloane looked at her. "Nick told me about your husband, too. I hope you're getting along all right."

"I keep thinking it will get easier. Does it?" For an instant, Molly's eyes held a glint of pleading.

She deserved frankness, Sloane thought. "Maybe. It's always there waiting for you when you least expect it. After a while, though, you stop getting ambushed so often."

"How long has it been since your brother passed away?"

She thought for a moment. "Five years." And it still seemed like yesterday.

"I can't believe it'll be a year in spring for us. It still takes me by surprise. Something will happen and I'll think, oh, I have to tell Adam and then I remember that I can't. When does that stop?"

"I don't know. For a long time I thought it never would. It's gotten easier lately, though." When had that happened, she wondered. Since she'd been so busy with the gear? Or since Nick? "I try to focus on other things, go on about life. Get past it." But who was she kidding? She hadn't gone forward at all.

Molly drew in a breath and gave an uneven laugh. "Well, now's not the time to talk about this, not with a house full of people coming."

"What can I do to help?" Sloane asked.

"Sit and drink your coffee. You're company. You don't need to do anything."

"I want to. I'll be more at home if you put me to work."

"Shy around strangers?" Molly's eyes were sympathetic. "Well, then, you can start by helping me fix breakfast."

Breakfast was a memory and the scent of roasting meat was beginning to perfume the house. Sloane stood slicing sweet potatoes, watching Jacob and Nick through the kitchen window as they repaired the soft spot in the parking apron. Being put to work was soothing; to her surprise, she was actually beginning to relax.

As she reached for the baking dish that Molly had set out she knocked over the box of brown sugar, sending it cascading onto the floor. "Oh hell," she murmured. The goal was to help, not make a sticky mess.

Sloane set aside the sweet potatoes and hurried over to the broom closet. Molly was out of the room ironing a tablecloth. With luck, Sloane could have everything cleaned up before she returned. Knowing how sugar migrated, she swept the better part of the floor before she finally had a small pile near the stove. All she needed was a dustpan and she'd be all set.

As she reached into the closet to pull the dustpan off its hanger, the hook flipped out of the wall to land in the back of the closet with a metallic tink. Perfect. Come for the holiday and tear the house apart. With a muttered curse, she groped in the corner for the hook, bending down to search with one hand.

And someone swatted her on the behind.

Halfway inside the closet, she jerked upright so quickly she thumped her head on the bottom shelf and came up cursing.

"Funny, Nick."

She reached back for help getting out of the closet. When she turned, though, she realized the hand wasn't Nick's. It belonged to a complete stranger.

"Oh hell," the man said, his wide grin dissolving into consternation, discomfiture and the beginnings of amusement. "I thought you were my cousin."

"You always greet your cousin that way?" she asked.

"When she deserves it, which is most of the time." The smile was back as he stuck out a hand. "I'm Gabe, Nick's brother. I take it you're his guest?"

"Gabriel!" Molly bustled into the room and gave him a quick hug. "You know Sloane?"

"We've met," he agreed, face straight.

"Hey, bro." Nick stood at the edge of the mudroom, stamping his feet. There was none of the uneasiness with Gabe that there'd been with Jacob, Sloane saw as the two men came together and thumped each other on the back.

Molly beamed at them. "Such good-looking boys."

It was true, Sloane saw. Gabe was perhaps more polished than Nick, his features and style more refined. Nick wore a chunky olive sweater and khakis. Gabe wore a black blazer over an untucked white tuxedo shirt and jeans, with loafers. She could see him wining and dining a lady at a five-star restaurant rather than taking her to a neighborhood tavern. And if Sloane found Nick's slightly rough-hewn, casual look more appealing, she was sure that Gabe had his choice of female companionship.

"You're the one who runs the hotel," Sloane said, thankful for Nick's briefing on the way up.

"Not just any hotel," Molly said, brushing his arm affectionately. "He manages the Hotel Mount Jefferson." The phone rang, adding to the cacophony. "You should see it." Molly walked over to answer the telephone. "It's gorgeous. Like the old hotel in that movie where Christopher Reeve goes back in time." She picked up the receiver.

"Or like *The Shining,*" Nick added with a wicked smile. "Redrum, redddd rummmmm." He tattooed his fingers up Sloane's sides. "This isn't really Gabe, he's been taken over by the spirit of the hotel so that all he can do is walk around doing the white-glove test."

"You're just jealous of my organizational skills."

"We're going to need them," Molly said from across the room as she hung up the phone. "That was the Demmings. Their daughter Marta just showed up with a new fiancé in tow, so we're going to have two more for dinner."

"That'll be interesting," Nick observed. "Any ideas?"

Molly pushed open the swinging door to stare into the dining room at the crowded table, already stretching near to the French doors at the far end.

Gabe looked thoughtfully over her shoulder.

Molly frowned. "There's just no room, not with the French doors there. We can put a couple of the kids at the kitchen table, I suppose."

"Nope." Gabe stepped forward. "Now we come into my area of expertise. You've got a card table, right Ma?"

"Sure, but we can hardly fit another table."

"We'll take care of that. Jacob, do you still have those sheets of plywood left over from fixing up the sugar house?"

Jacob nodded.

"Perfect. Let's get one of them in here. And your toolbox."

"What do you have planned?" Molly demanded suspiciously.

Gabe grinned. "Trust me, you're going to love it."

Chapter Thirteen

The clink of serving spoons on china. The scent of roast turkey and stuffing perfuming the air. The murmur of conversation, the boisterous noises of children and above all, the sound of laughter. The place and faces might have been different, but the sights, sounds and scents of Thanksgiving never changed.

All things considered, Sloane thought, the table looked wonderful. Under Gabe's direction, Nick and Jacob had taken down the French doors between the dining room and living room and extended the dining-room table courtesy of the plywood and the card table. Molly and Sloane had done some last-minute juggling with place settings and table linens, and if everything wasn't a perfect match, the crowd around the table scarcely cared. What mattered was food and company.

And it felt way too good, she thought with a sudden twinge. Somewhere along the line, shyness had slipped away. There was no room in the Trask world for strangers, and the teasing, joking and sense of purpose had carried her along. This wasn't her family, though, she had to remember that. It wouldn't do to get used to the warmth and easiness. Sure, it looked great from the outside but everything ended.

She knew from firsthand experience.

Next to her, Nick reached out to squeeze her hand. "You okay?" he murmured.

Sloane glanced at him, startled that he'd known. "Sure, I'm fine." She gave him a smile. "Would you pass the turkey?"

Another thing that never changed about Thanksgiving was the dishes. Sloane set a stack of plates on the kitchen counter and looked around. They'd managed to convince Molly to take a break and let others handle the cleanup. Now they had to do it.

Jacob pushed through the swinging door that led to the dining room, his hands dwarfing the serving dishes he carried. Now that she saw him in his neat corduroys and pine-colored twill shirt, she realized that her impression of bulk the night before had been mostly a factor of his parka and unruly hair. True, he topped Nick by a couple of inches but he wasn't fat, not even remotely. Instead, he was solid with muscle built over years of manual labor.

She took the dishes from him and, with a nod, he left.

"Just set that over here," Lainie, Nick's cousin, directed. Sleeves pushed up and apron on, she was ready to work.

"Let me help," Sloane said. If she didn't wash dishes, she'd find herself facing the dreaded living-room conversation with the rest of the family. Better to pitch in.

Lainie grinned. "You want to work, you'll get no arguments here. You want to wash or dry?"

"I like washing."

"Hmm. I do, too." She considered. "Okay, rock, paper, scissors," she said briskly, making a fist.

Sloane considered. "All right. One, two, *three.*"

They both held out scissors. "Again," Lainie commanded, clenching her fingers together again.

This one took a bit more thought. Sloane bounced her fist three times and poked out two fingers in scissors.

And glanced over to see that Lainie had done the same thing. They locked eyes and burst into laughter. "Great minds," Lainie said.

"Two out of three?" Sloane suggested.

Lainie shook her head. "Nope, we think too much alike. We'd probably wind up in another tie. You're the guest. I'll sacrifice myself and dry."

Sloane slipped her hands into the warm wash water. "So your father is Nick's uncle?"

"Yep, more Trasks. We grew up just the other side of the ridge, but my parents live in Burlington now." She took the plate Sloane handed her and began to wipe it dry.

"Where are you?"

"Down in Salem, Mass."

Sloane set a stack of plates in the dishwater. "Oh, you're the witch cousin."

Lainie rolled her eyes. "Let me guess, Nick's been briefing you. I'm not actually a Wiccan, you know. I just run the museum." She took another clean plate from where they'd begun to stack up by Sloane.

"It sounds like a fun job."

"It has its perks. I got to meet Daniel Day-Lewis when they were filming *The Crucible* in town." She sighed.

"Nice?"

"Beautiful. *And* nice. If there's a reason I'm single, it's because he ruined me for mortal men."

Sloane gave her a dubious look before submerging the caramel-encrusted sweet-potato dish. "I don't know, do you have to have a reason at our age?"

Lainie snorted. "When you come from my family and all your other sibs are married off? You bet."

Sloane scrubbed at the baked-on caramel. "Looks like you're stuck, kiddo."

"Tell me about it." She lapsed into silence for a few seconds, then cheered up. "So have you known Nick long?" she asked casually.

Here it came, Sloane thought. "Not really. A month or so. I'm sort of working with him."

"You don't look like a firefighter."

"I'm not." She rinsed the sweet-potato dish and handed it to Lainie. "My company's built some fire equipment. Nick's testing it for us, seeing if it works."

"Seeing you, too, right? Is it serious?" Lainie's eyes were bright with speculation.

"Are you grilling me?"

"Hell, yeah." Lainie laughed. "I figure if everyone's worried about you and Nick, the heat's off me. Come on," she begged, "just one thing I can tell my mom."

Sloane raised a brow. "He knows how to handle his hose?"

Lainie just snickered.

Nick and Jacob carried the plywood sheet toward the work shed behind the house, the same way they'd carried loads together as kids. It was harder now to time their steps so that they were in sync, though. Each of them was so solidly set in his ways, maybe, that there was no longer room for compromise.

Around them gamboled Murphy, Jacob's big black hound who looked like a cross between a black Lab and a small horse. Dried leaves crunched underfoot. "The groves look good," Nick commented, looking out at the solemn silver ranks of trees.

"Thanks," Jacob said. "I'm trying to figure out whether to cull that stand over by the creek, plant some new stock. It's still producing but it's been falling off for three years running. We won't be able to tap them for thirty years but we've got to plan for the future."

Nick shrugged as best he could. "You're the expert."

"I guess it's not your problem anymore, is it?" Jacob fell silent and kept walking.

Nick felt the same stirring of irritation he always felt with Jacob. Only this time, he'd had enough. "Nobody made you stay here, Jacob. I thought you liked it. I thought it was what you wanted to do."

"It is."

"Then why do you always give me guff about leaving?"

Jacob stopped before the door to the shed, holding the plywood with one hand and opening the door with the other. "I don't."

"Yeah, you do. It's getting old." And it was time, long past time to have this out.

"Yeah, well it's getting old that you think you can just walk away and not have any responsibility to any of us." He set the wood down and turned to face Nick then. "You're still a part of this family."

"And you think I should come home and do my duty?"

Jacob frowned. "Here? To live? No way."

"Oh, come on." Nick rounded on him. "You hint at it every time we talk."

"I like working the property. It's a big job and I'm not quite sure what I'm going to do when the sap run starts in the spring, but that's my problem."

"When you talk about it, it becomes mine, too." And it made him feel like he should come up with an answer.

"For Chrissakes," Jacob snapped, "can't I ever talk with you about the stuff that's bugging me? Do I have to pretend that everything's perfect? Yeah, it's hard work and yeah, I'm a little concerned about the spring, but I'll figure out a way to make it work." He stalked over to the grimy window that looked out at the groves. "It's all of our property but guess who's responsible for it succeeding? Five generations, Nick, five, and it all comes down to how I manage it today." He swung back to face Nick. "Did you ever stop to think that maybe I just want you and Gabe to know what's going on? Did it ever occur to you that sometimes I just want to talk about it?"

"You never just want to talk about anything," Nick said, with a try for flippancy.

"And maybe you don't want to listen," Jacob retorted.

There was something in his voice, Nick realized, something he'd never heard before. A tiny, miniscule hint of self-doubt. Self-doubt? Jacob, the big brother? Jacob, the one who'd always known how it was supposed to be and rammed it down Nick's throat, whether he wanted it or not? Jacob, stubborn, opinionated Jacob, suddenly turning human?

Or Nick, maybe, finally opening his eyes.

And now he didn't know what to say. "Look, we never meant to throw everything on you. If you want to unload the property, we can—"

"Sell the farm? What are you, nuts? There's no way. You want out, fine, I'll buy you out, but this is what I do. It's what I am. I don't want out of the farm, but I'd like to be able to talk about it without you getting pissed or thinking that it's a jab at you. I'm not a big talker, you know that. So, God, cut me some slack when I do," he finished in disgust.

A second or two went by. "I think that's the longest speech I've ever heard you give," Nick said finally.

"Try me again sometime, if you can do it without getting pissed and stomping off. Nick, you're the only one who thinks you should come home, okay? You've got your life. I'm happy here alone. You moved back, we'd kill each other inside of a week."

He had a point, Nick had to agree. Still… "Look, you're right about it being a big job and I don't want Ma out there killing herself to pitch in. I could take a week or two of vacation during the sap run if it would help."

"If I need a hand, I'll tell you. But only if you don't hassle me about it."

"I won't hassle you about it." Nick held out his hand. Jacob stared at it a moment and then reached out and shook it. "Okay," Nick said briskly. "Now can we put this damned wood away? I'm freezing my tail off here."

A stealthy shake to Sloane's shoulder woke her the next morning before it was light. She opened her eyes to see Nick. He gave her a quick kiss. "Get up," he said softly. "We got new snow overnight. Come out and see."

They crept out of the house, their breath forming white plumes in the chill air. Above the ridge to the east, the sky was rosy with the light of the still-hidden sun. Nick caught at Sloane's hand. The path led around Jacob's house and to the trail that led into the maple groves.

It was magical, she thought as they walked out into the

frozen landscape. Soft, white and absolutely smooth, snow stretched out into the trees untouched in all directions. It was as though they were the first people to walk there, ever. The maples stood at regular intervals, silent sentinels in the pristine whiteness. The air was still and quiet.

"Wait a minute," Nick said, "Let me see something a minute." He stopped and looked around, then gave a brisk nod. "Yep, it definitely looks better with you in it."

She laughed and they resumed walking. "So how's it been, being back? Everything okay?"

"Yeah. Yeah, things are good. I got some things hashed out with Jacob." He scrubbed his free hand through his hair. "Things haven't been that great with us lately."

"I noticed when we got here." Sloane glanced at him. "Was that why you wanted me to come along? To dilute things?"

He considered. "I don't know, maybe at first. Mostly, I wanted you to meet my family because I thought you'd like them. I was pretty sure they'd like you. And they do."

"How do you know that? Have you guys been sneaking off and comparing notes?"

A corner of his mouth quirked. "Lainie and Gabe wanted to know why you're having anything to do with me. That's usually a good sign."

She grinned. "I'm glad I could measure—"

"Shh." He stopped and touched her shoulder. "Deer," he said, turning her a little.

It took her a moment but then she saw their soft reddish coats in the distance. "Oh," she breathed. Stiff-legged and graceful, they walked along in a line, threading their way through the maples in the hush of dawn. The sun just peeked over the nearby ridge then, sending a ray of warm gold light through the grove, gilding the deer from afar. Sloane caught her breath. "It's so perfect," she murmured and turned to Nick.

"You're perfect." And in the first glow of the rising sun, he kissed her gently.

Morning slipped into afternoon in a whirl of activity: snowshoeing, exploring the sugar house, blind-tasting maple syrup. Getting on the road took longer than they expected. By the time they reached Nick's house north of Boston, it was pushing eleven.

Yawning, Sloane stood on the sidewalk near her car. "This is where I wish I could just snap my fingers and go instantly across town to my bed."

"I can offer you the next best thing. Stay here tonight."

She gave him an amused look. "And get up at four to have time to get to my house before start of shift at the firehouse?"

"Not necessarily. You've got clothes with you, right? We can throw your clothes in the wash. Tomorrow, we just get up and drive straight to the firehouse."

It was tempting, especially after the numbing drive. She was more tired than she wanted to admit. Spending another forty-five minutes behind the wheel was the last thing she wanted.

"What do you say?" Nick watched her closely.

Sloane found herself yawning again.

"I'll take that as a yes," Nick said and picked up her overnight bag.

He was all efficiency, getting the bags inside, stopping in the laundry room, going upstairs. At the threshold of his bedroom, though, he stopped her with his hands on her shoulders.

"What?" Sloane asked.

Appreciation bloomed in his eyes. "This'll be the first time we've stayed together. I'm just savoring it."

It made her flush. "Yes, well, it's just the best way to get some sleep, that's all," she muttered.

Nick ran his hands up her spine, fusing the two of them together. "So tell me how I can miss you when I spent the last two days with you," he murmured and held her, just held her, for long moments.

"It's not the amount of time, it's the quality," Sloane returned.

"And it *is* quality," he murmured, tipping her face toward him with his fingertips. Softly, he kissed her so that pleasure dripped through her like warm honey. Without breaking apart, they moved into the bedroom and sank down on the bed.

His touch made her shiver. The heat of his body made her moan. When she would have quickened, Nick put his hand over hers. "Slow down," he whispered, kissing her eyelids closed. "We've got all night."

The gentle smoothing of a hand over bare skin. The soft exhalation of breath. She'd thought that passion meant flash and fire. It was a revelation that it could also be slow and sweet.

They undressed, but afterward she couldn't recall quite how. It wasn't the usual fever of tearing at each other's clothing but leisurely, deliberate, every inch of skin revealed all the more arousing. Naked, they came together in comfort and in quiet.

They touched, they tasted, they took each other up. Nerve endings that usually crackled with the flash and spark of a live fuse now radiated a deep, powerful heat. When he covered her body with his, she caught her breath softly. When he slid inside her, it was as though the barrier of skin no longer existed. Instead, they melded. The measured strokes, the bunch and flow of muscle sent desire flowing through them, one to the other. She felt suspended in pleasure, weightless and liquid.

And when they slipped over the edge they did it together, floating down softly and so, to sleep.

Sloane woke at first light nestled against Nick, his arm wrapped around her from behind. Her initial haze of bemusement morphed to consternation and then steadily increasing dismay. Resisting the urge to groan out loud, she slipped from under his arm and escaped to the bathroom.

She sat on the edge of the tub, her head in her hands. Trouble, big-time trouble. She'd made the rules. She'd set down the conditions. Lighthearted fun, no commitments. Nothing serious.

Yeah, right.

It would be easy to blame the night before on exhaustion but she knew it wasn't so. Just as she knew they hadn't had sex—they'd made love.

Panic lodged in her throat. How much of an idiot could a person be? The whole time she'd been going blithely along, telling herself she had it all under control, she'd been getting in deeper and deeper. She hadn't paid attention. She hadn't kept herself protected and now her heart was very much at risk. That was what happened when you let people into your life, she reminded herself, thinking of Nick, thinking of his family. You loved people and you lost them.

Not that she'd let herself fall in love with Nick, of course. She hadn't let it go that far. It was only a matter of time, though, if she kept on seeing him. Which was why she had to get out now.

Holding her breath, Sloane opened the door and slipped back out into the bedroom. Nick lay on his side, still out to the world, the depth of his sleep making up for the firehouse nights that consisted of little more than a series of catnaps.

For a moment, she stood helplessly and just watched him. Then she shook herself.

Escape first and deal with the fallout later. The fact that it was hard to walk away was exactly why she had to. He might be disappointed but he'd understand. It would be okay.

She bent to gather her clothes and tried desperately to believe it.

Chapter Fourteen

Nick was staring at the annual employee-evaluation paperwork in front of him, searching for the right mix of positive reinforcement and constructive criticism when a shout came from the direction of the kitchen. Impatiently he rose and strode down to the kitchen, only to stumble into a circle of noise and activity. It centered about the kitchen table, where O'Hanlan and Knapp arm wrestled while Beaulieu took the bets from the rest of the cheering crew.

"Why don't you give it up, Tommy, me lad?" O'Hanlan said between clenched teeth as Knapp pushed his knuckles back toward the table. "I'm just playin' with you."

"Looks more like work to me," Knapp replied, huffing a bit as he pushed O'Hanlan's hand down. "You're getting soft running the ladder, O'Hanlan."

"I'll show you soft," O'Hanlan gritted and thumped Knapp's hand over and down. He rose to cheers and slaps on the back. "There now, have I convinced you all or do I need to take on someone else?"

"You want to do anything else to impress me while I'm writing up your evals?" Nick snapped.

They gaped at him in sudden and surprised silence.

"If anyone wants me, I'll be in my office."

"Someone's in a bad mood," O'Hanlan observed as Nick walked out.

Someone was, Nick thought. He'd been out of sorts all day, from the moment after he'd opened his eyes.

And awakened in an empty bed.

Things happened, he knew that. Plans changed. It was just possible that Sloane had remembered something important she had to be home for. He had a harder time understanding why she'd sneaked out on him. That she hadn't wanted to wake him was the reason she'd given in her note. That she hadn't wanted to face questions was more likely.

She was hiding out, he was certain of it. Somehow, some way she'd gotten spooked and now she was backing out. And it surprised him just how much that stung. It didn't matter that they'd spent two solid days together at the farm, he missed her. It was hard to admit how disappointed he'd been to wake alone.

Only if they didn't get serious, she'd said, only then would she get involved with him. Only if they didn't let themselves care for each other. And that was bull, he thought in sudden fury. It was what made relationships work, the caring. Otherwise, it was just friction and hormones.

Frustration surged through him. He was allowed to get close, but not too close. He was supposed to keep his distance, pretend he didn't feel what he felt when he knew it, he'd known it for days.

He was in love with her.

* * *

Sloane sat in her living room, staring at the walls. She couldn't avoid Nick forever. He wouldn't let her, for one thing. More than that, he deserved better. She might not be able to give him her heart, but she could at least offer him honesty. Breaking it off like an adult was the only way to go. She owed it to him to be up front. And she would.

As soon as she could do it without falling apart.

It would be all right, she told herself. After all, he surely wasn't expecting happily ever after. A light fling, they'd said, nothing more. A light fling with an exit clause and she was invoking it.

So why was she sitting on the couch and shaking?

When her phone rang she jumped, heart hammering against her ribs. She couldn't talk to him yet, not yet. Another day and then she'd be able to go forward.

The machine clicked and the speaker buzzed a little. "Sloane?" said a voice.

The relief was only momentary. It wasn't Nick, it was Candy. Candy, whose life was the sum of all Sloane's fears. Candy, who'd lost the man she loved. Candy, who'd sat on the couch beside her in the nightmare hours after they'd heard the news that firefighters were missing, clutching Sloane's hand so tightly that her fingers went numb. And they'd waited with dread for the knock at the door.

The knock that had put the final blow to Sloane's world.

She reached out and picked up the phone. "Hi, Candy."

"Happy late Thanksgiving. How are you?"

Terrified. Desperate. Falling apart. "I'm okay."

"You don't sound so great. Something going on?"

She wanted so much to pour it all out, but how could she? To tell the woman who'd lost her husband that she was breaking up with a firefighter because she feared the same thing? Candy's face, her voice, conjured up the ghosts that haunted Sloane. Candy was a reminder of the worst that could happen. A reminder of why she had to walk away. "Nothing's going on," she said aloud. "Just working a lot."

"You didn't work over the holiday, did you?"

"No, I took a couple of days off. I'm paying for it now though." She was paying for it, all right. Sloane swallowed. "So how was your holiday?"

"It was nice. We went to my brother's house. I missed you, though."

And I miss you. "Maybe next year."

"Hey, Pete loves his guitar, by the way."

Sloane grabbed at the news like a drowning person snatching at a rope. "Does he really?"

"It's perfect. What made you think of it?"

Nick, she thought, and tried to push it away. "A friend suggested it."

"It's been like a miracle, Sloane. He's finally got an outlet. He's been pouring himself into it, playing nonstop. You'll have to get down here sometime and listen to him."

"I'd like that."

"Great," Candy said, "how about Christmas?"

"What?"

"Please come, Sloane. It would mean so much to have you here."

There, in the house where every turn reminded her of Mitch. Of what she could lose when she got involved, when she let herself care. "Oh, Candy, I don't—"

"Now don't worry that it's going to be a mob scene," Candy hurried on. "Mom and Dad will be coming, but that will be it. Dan and Rob are spending the holiday with their wives' families."

Sloane groped for a way out. "It's a lovely invitation."

"It'll be fun. We can hang out like we used to on the holiday, do jigsaw puzzles, maybe even ski if the snow holds out." Enthusiasm bubbled in her voice. "I've got a soup recipe I've been itching to try. It'll be like the old days."

Like the old days. "I'd like to but…"

"But you can't." Candy's voice went flat. "Of course. Do you have plans already?"

"No. I just…"

"You just don't want the reminder."

Sloane's throat tightened. "It's not you."

"I know." Candy gave a brittle laugh. "That makes it worse, doesn't it? God, you know it's been five years and not an hour goes by that I don't think of him. There's a hole there that's never going to be filled, but you go on." Her voice caught, shot through with pain. "You don't just keep your life empty, Sloane. You don't cut everyone off."

"I haven't cut you off."

"No. You just avoid us. Cards and presents don't do it. It's not about money and time, it's about you. That's all we want, the person we used to know."

"I've got responsibilities right now."

"Sure you do, and when that's done you'll find some other way to hide."

She felt backed into a corner. "What do you want from me, Candy?" she cried out.

"I want my friend back." The words shivered in the silence. "I didn't just lose Mitch that night. I lost you, too. God, Sloane, we were like sisters. It killed me to lose him, but then you were gone, too."

Sloane blinked back the sting of tears.

"We used to know every detail about each other's life. Now you're like a stranger. I know something's wrong and I can't help because you won't let me. There was a time you'd have told me instead of lying and saying everything's fine." She paused. "I loved him, too, Sloane, you know? We all did. But you've got to get past it and live your life. He'd have wanted that."

"It hurts too much, Candy," Sloane whispered.

"It hurt to lose Mitch, it hurts me every single day, but you know what? That's being alive. Try, Sloane," her voice caught on tears. "Just try. We need you."

"It's too hard."

"Hard? You want to talk to me about hard?" Sudden bright anger filled her words. "Tell me what I'm supposed to say to Pete when he asks about whether you're coming to Christmas, just like he asked about his birthday. You could help him, Sloane, you could help him figure this out. Maybe we could help each other. But instead you'd rather hide out in your little bunker."

"I can't!" It was as though for years she'd held herself together with string and packing tape and bare will, terrified to let loose for even a moment, terrified of what might happen. Suddenly, it was all threatening to fly apart.

And she didn't know how she'd survive if it did.

Seconds dragged by during which she didn't speak over the ache in her throat. She couldn't.

"All right, then," Candy said finally.

Sloane's hand tightened around the telephone receiver.

"You know, I keep thinking if I try one more time I'll get through to you, that you'll let it all out and go back to the person you used to be. I miss her so much. You have no idea."

Don't leave me.

Candy sighed. "Maybe it doesn't matter. Maybe you're happiest where you are. I hope so." Her voice was empty now of both anger and tears. "Happy holidays, Sloane."

Then the line clicked and she was gone.

And finally, finally the tears began to fall.

Sloane drove into the station parking lot the next evening, dreading the moment she'd have to turn off her key and go in. The night before she'd walked for hours, trying to clear her head, trying to make herself believe that things were okay. But they weren't okay and she knew it.

She just had to figure out a way to live with that.

Push it away. Don't think about it. That had been the way she'd always coped.

Somehow it didn't seem to be working anymore.

As for sleep, it had been nearly impossible. The only upside was that so far, at least, so far she'd managed to avoid Nick. She had to talk with him, she knew that. Just not now, not while she was holding on by a thread. She rested her forehead for a brief moment against the steering wheel.

Then she steeled herself and headed into the station.

The door to the apparatus floor was open and Ladder 67 was gone. A little surge of relief went through her. They were out on a call. Not a fire, she diagnosed rapidly by the presence of Engine 58. Just a rescue call. And if she hoped for it to be a nice, time-consuming rescue call, that didn't make her a coward, did it?

It was later, much later, when she heard the rumble of the approaching ladder truck. When it stopped on the apron, all the rest of the crew piled off.

"Hey, you missed out, Sloane," Knapp called as he waved. "We had a jumper all ready to go. Guy sittin' out on the ledge, threatening to take a header if we brought up a ladder. We had the nets out and everything."

"Did he go?"

Beaulieu snorted. "Do they ever? The ones who really want to off themselves do it quietly. Guys like this, they're not serious."

"Maybe he just wanted help and didn't know how to ask for it," Sorensen said. "It can happen, you know," he defended against the hoots and the eye rolls.

"Just as long as we're not sitting around for a time-waster like that when someone in a burning building really needs help," O'Hanlan said. "Guy like that needs to go to a crisis center."

Maybe that was what she needed, a crisis center. And then she glanced up and saw Nick.

He stood back, just watching her while the rest of the crew made their way inside. He took his time, waiting until O'Hanlan was backing the truck into quarters before he walked up.

"Hey." He tapped a fist lightly against her shoulder. "You're late."

"I was here at six. I must have just missed you. Something came up."

Something flickered in his eyes. "There's been a lot of that lately, hasn't there? I tried to reach you yesterday."

She should have known he'd brook no evasions. "I was—"

"And today," he continued, not allowing her any. "I left messages. I even dropped by. You weren't around."

"I've been busy."

"I guess. Look, we need to talk. Something's going on with you and I'd like to hear what it is." He locked eyes with her without blinking. "I don't want to walk away from this, Sloane."

"This isn't the place or the time, Nick."

"Then name the time and the place. Don't just disappear on me, Sloane. You've got more guts than that."

Once again, she found herself pushed into a corner. "You seem to think you know a lot about me."

"I want to know a whole lot more than you'll let me, that's for sure. I—" He broke off and raised his head.

"What?" Sloane stared at him.

"Smoke," he said slowly, walking out onto the apron and searching the sky. "There's a fire."

At the same moment she smelled it, the bells sounded. "Thirty-three Ramsey Street," Knapp, on house watch, read out over the PA system. "Abandoned building, fire showing. Everybody goes."

They didn't need to check the map. They didn't need help finding it as they pulled out of the station, siren blaring. They had only to drive toward the twisting column of black smoke that blocked the lights of downtown.

Streamers of smoke drifted past them as they turned toward it. Nick pulled on his gloves. He knew this building. He knew its history.

And it was trouble.

The four-story brick structure had started out more than a century before as a furniture factory that had been converted to a recording studio, then a gentlemen's club. Nick had inspected it a couple of times and knew that above the nightclub level on the ground floor was a warren of private rooms, and above that a maze of sound-baffled recording rooms, still coated with foams and plastics. When fire hit them, they'd create an inferno and release every toxic chemical under the sun.

As they drove up, flames shot around the edges of the plywood that covered the few windows on the third floor. It had blown the glass in places. At least it was partially vented, Nick thought, although all the airflow had done was strengthen the burn. Flame streamed fluidly up into roiling smoke, the crimson-streaked black churning like the fires of hell.

"First in." O'Hanlan pulled the ladder truck to a stop in front of the warehouse. "All the fun for us."

"Looks like there's going to be enough fire for everyone," Nick told him. "I'm calling in a second alarm. In the meantime, get the stick up."

O'Hanlan nodded and the rest of the crew hit the pavement. Gone were the jokes as they pulled equipment out of lockers. Now it was all about focus and efficiency. This was going to be a bad one and everyone knew it.

"Am I going to go inside, cap?" It was Sorensen, raising his voice over the sounds of the motors, the approaching sirens, the roar of the flames.

Nick looked at him. He wasn't doing the probie any good by protecting him. It was time for Nick to back off from being the big brother and let Sorensen take a few steps on his own. "Stand by for directions. You might get your chance."

With a whoop of sirens, Deputy Chief McMillan's red Expedition pulled up. They'd need the chief to coordinate something this big, Nick thought as he walked over. Seven engines, four ladder trucks, a rescue company and a tower company to drown the fire from on high. They had a crowd coming.

McMillan finished talking on his radio and got out of the truck, reaching in the backseat for his turnouts. "Trask, what's the situation?"

"It's abandoned and boarded up. Looks like it's fully involved. We've got some partial venting on the third story and one of my team reported flames showing in the back. Must be a mess inside. We're getting our stick up to vent it."

McMillan nodded. "I just called in another alarm. I don't like the looks of this building."

"It's one tricky mother inside. Used to have a strip club on the bottom two floors and a recording studio up above that. Floor two has all these private rooms with back hallways for the club people and floor three still has most of the sound-proofing materials in the sound studios. Lots of flammables and toxins in the walls there. We've inspected it a couple of times over the past five years." He hesitated. "It's a maze, sir. We've gotten turned around each time." Without the smoke, the heat, the pounding risk of a fire.

"You found your way out, though, right?"

"Yes."

"Then we need your company inside leading. You'll split the job with the rescue company. They should be here soon. Brief them before you go in."

Nick nodded and turned to go.

"Hey, Trask?" McMillan called.

"Yeah?"

"Watch your guys."

Sloane stared at the fire. This was nothing like the harmless blaze at the triple-decker. This was a ravenous beast, unleashed and ready to devour. Its red glow flickered over the faces of the men. Like gladiators, they girded up, snapping closed turn-out coats, pulling on air packs, picking up their tools.

Hands shaking, she pulled out her master Orienteer unit and turned it on, staring down at the LCD display. When she'd hoped for a chance to test the units, she'd never wanted the men to be put in harm's way, she'd never wanted a fire like this.

A fire like the one that had killed Mitch.

A sudden scream made her look up. A teenage girl fought to get past Beaulieu and Knapp, her beaded braids flying wildly as she struggled toward the building. "Dontrell!" she shrieked. "Dontrell's in there."

Sloane ran over to her. "What's going on?"

Hysteria had her gasping. "My man's in there. The Dudley Street Doggs pulled him in there and torched it. They going to burn him up." Her voice rose again in a shriek and she twisted to get out of their arms. *"Dontrell!"*

Sloane's eyes widened in alarm. "Nick," she cried.

"I heard." His face was grim as he turned to the deputy chief behind him.

McMillan raised his voice. "Okay, we can't wait for the rescue company. Trask, you get your men inside along with Ladder 61. I want three hose teams stretching two-and-a-half-inch lines, one to each of the three involved floors. All right, go!"

And with sudden horror, Sloane realized the obvious.

Nick was going inside.

She wanted to scream, she wanted to beg, do anything to keep him from stepping over that threshold into peril. But all she could do was stand frozen while he slipped on his breathing apparatus and hefted his ceiling hook and Halligan tool.

Engine 58 was already stretching a line into the front door of the building. She heard the whine of the aerial ladder as O'Hanlan sent truckies from other companies up to the roof to ventilate the blaze. It didn't matter. None of it mattered except that Nick was walking toward the building with his team.

And she couldn't do anything to stop it.

Chapter Fifteen

Nick stopped in front of the service doors on the front of the building. Smoke thickened the air around them and he could feel the hot breath of the blaze. He turned to his crew.

"The stairwell is just to the left, straight across the corridor," he told them, raising his voice over the growl of the fire and the roar of the power saws on the roof. "Okay, the place is supposed to be abandoned and empty but we've got one or more civilians inside. Floor one was a club, three main rooms plus bathrooms, production rooms and a line of offices to the left." He squinted through thickening smoke. "Floor two is honeycombed with a bunch of private rooms, orgy rooms, dance studios, who knows. Floor three is the worst. It was a recording studio for a few years. It's a maze of sound studios and the baffling's still up in a lot of places. Knapp, Beaulieu, we've been here before, so we'll take the upper floors. Sixty-one, you take the bottom floor. Sorensen, you stay with them."

"Cap, you said I could go with you."

Nick looked at him and hesitated. *Stop being the older brother, let him loose.*

"You take Beaulieu and I'll watch over the kid," Knapp offered.

Nick slid on his face mask. "If he's going in, he's coming with me. Come on, Sorensen. You want fire, you got it. And switch on your Orienteer. We're going to need it." He set his own unit, watching the blue display spring up on the right side of his face mask. One by one, blue spots labeled with each crew member's initials popped up in a tight tangle. "Okay, watch yourselves. Keep track of your direction, make sure you know where you came from. And keep track of the time."

Nick looked across to where Sloane stood, eyes enormous, face pale even in the growing light of the flames. He ached to go to her but there way no way to fix this, no way but to do the job that was his life. The job that could save a life. Instead, he raised a hand in salute.

Then he turned toward the inferno.

Smoke hazed the air as they climbed the stairs, stepping around the hoses that snaked their way to the upper levels. The rasp of Nick's breathing mask echoed in his ears as if he were Darth Vader. They could hear the fire growling and popping through the walls. Feet pounded on the metal stairs above them. Nick didn't waste his voice on shouting, just motioned Sorensen to follow him out the fire door to the third floor.

Hose stretched ahead of them down to the end of the wide hall where the team from Engine 58 knelt, knocking down the blaze that burned a dull orange through the smoke. Pinpoints of light showed on the wall to his left where the wash of arc light from the fire equipment outside had searched its way through holes and gaps in the thick plywood sheets covering the windows. To his right rose the wall that hid the warren of sound studios.

They crossed to the vestibule halfway down the hall. He motioned to Sorensen and pressed their masks together. "Okay, we've got the doors to the rooms here. Three on each side. I'll take the doors on the left, you go to the right." To the right, away from the fire. "Be careful going through the doors. Make sure you keep track of your moves and don't get turned around. If you find something, shout on the radio." His voice sounded flat and muffled through the plastic of his mask. Sorensen nodded and they plunged off into the smoke.

Nick started with the door closest to him, fumbling for the handle with his thick gloves. The heat clenched him like a fist. He ignored it, intent on his task. Keep to a search pattern, he thought. Getting lost in the maze of doors and halls and smoke would be deadly.

Setting his shoulder to the wall, he moved around the perimeter of the room, swinging his ceiling hook across the floor in a broad arc to search for objects. To search for bodies. Amid the freight-train rumble of the flames, the creak and groan of burning wood, softening beams, he strained to hear a hint of a voice.

And on his display, the other blue dots moved in their own restless circles.

Sloane stared at the fire, reduced to watching and waiting. The LCD display on her master Orienteer gave her only the illusion of control. She concentrated on the blue dots, knowing that the image before her showed just a fragment of the picture. It might reveal the locations of the men in the bewildering tangle of rooms. It didn't show the heat and smoke and power of the flames creeping closer and closer.

The blaze reflected out of the service doors on the ground floor. Two engine companies were inside, working it with two-and-a-half-inch lines, but the temperatures were too high to keep it knocked down.

Glass shattered as flames broke through a window on the third floor.

Where Nick was. She saw the dot with his initials pause and her heart hammered against her ribs. An agony of tension gripped her as she watched and waited. Had he found something? Had he been hurt? It was excruciating, not knowing what was happening to any of the men she'd come to know and care for.

Not knowing what was happening to Nick.

"Chief!" She heard O'Hanlan holler behind her from the controls of the ladder. "Where are the other companies?"

"A drunk driver missed the siren and T-boned Rescue 1. Engine 29 was right behind them, couldn't stop in time." He had to shout to be heard over the throbbing engines of the pumpers and the ladder truck.

"Anybody hurt?"

"A couple got banged up. The apparatus is out of commission. We got more help on the way. I called in another alarm."

More pumpers, more trucks. There would be more hands but would they get the water into the maze that was the inside of the building?

And would they help the men inside get out?

The building groaned. It might have been brick outside, but the skeleton was wood, massive timbers, long stringers. And as the fire progressed, the building suffered.

Nick hardly noticed the bulk of his protective clothing, the weight of his helmet and breathing apparatus. The smoke thickened, banked down toward the floor. Life, normally so complicated, was reduced to utter simplicity—enter right, exit right, shoulder to the wall. Sweep the ceiling hook, strain to hear, strain to see, strain to keep a sense of direction.

The door had led to a hallway with two more doors, each with studios and offices behind. *Through the door, straight, right, door to the left, search, door to the right, search, through the door, search, then door, right, door, left, straight, right, left, straight, through the door.* And pray he'd find the vestibule.

The inferno grew hotter still.

The smoke was down within a few inches of the floor now, He couldn't see, searched by contact. Enter right, shoulder to the wall, sweep with the hook, move forward, sweep with the hook, move forward, sweep—

The hook jolted in his hand. He'd touched something. Or someone. Adrenaline vaulted through him.

And then he was scrambling across the floor. It was a man, passed out facedown. Facedown was probably the only reason the guy was still alive, Nick thought as he tore off his helmet and mask to give the man a breath of oxygen. Now he just needed to get the guy out. He dragged him to the hall outside, slipping into the rhythm of buddy breathing. He turned and passed through another doorway, turned again.

And found himself in a dead end.

The building shook with the sound of something—a beam, maybe—crashing down. Nick focused on keeping his breathing calm. A man hyperventilating could go through a sixty-minute tank in ten, and he was already sharing it. He retraced his path in his mind. It was important to get back to the original room, figure out an escape before the man in his arms died.

His stomach tightened. He stared through the swirling smoke.

And blinked at the blue lines in front of his face. The Orienteer. The schematic. The way out. He'd gone through the wrong door, he realized, a door he hadn't seen when he'd entered the room. He was in a hall now that led directly back to the vestibule. It would be quicker than retracing his steps.

If it were right.

Did he believe it? Did he trust it? Did he trust Sloane?

And it was that thought that had him tossing the man over his shoulder and following the blue lines.

Sloane stared at her monitor where Nick's marker had stopped. The building gave a rending sound and a wall of flame roared up from the roof. Her hands clenched convulsively. She could hear the deputy chief on the radio.

"Ladder 68, roof team, are you hurt?"

The radio crackled. "Negative. We nee—off quick."

McMillan cursed as the transmission was interrupted by a call for the motor squad to the back exposure of the building. It was the chaos of a fire scene with dozens of radios, any one of which could be keyed on at any time. "Say again, 68?"

"We need off. This whole damned thing is going to go."

"Comin' to get ya, guys," O'Hanlan boomed as he guided the aerial ladder to pluck the roof team off.

The deputy chief keyed the radio mike again. "All hands inside, the roof is unstable. Get out now." The air horns from the pumpers blared out the high-low tones of a mayday signal.

The radio crackled. "Ladder 67."

Adrenaline spurted through Sloane as she heard Nick's voice.

"I found our guy. He's hurt—"

His fragmentary words were stepped on by another transmission and Sloane bit off a curse. "He needs air. I'm getting him out."

Knapp's voice broke in. "Ladder 67, we'll meet you on the stairwell."

The building was unstable, Sloane thought in anxiety. They had to hurry.

The radio crackled again and another voice came on, this time coughing and choking. "Ladder 67, need assis—" Another transmission broke in for a moment. "—lost. Did you copy, Command?"

"Say again."

"—run out of air. I'm lost—"

And Sloane stared at her monitor, where Sorensen's marker sat unmoving, deep in the building.

"Ladder 67, inside, did you get that? Ladder 67?" The chief shook his radio in frustration, but there was no answer. "Trask, get your man out of there."

The universe was fire and black smoke, raging heat and rumbling fury. The engine company had pulled out. Nick stepped into the stairwell. "Knapp?" he bellowed and began pounding his ceiling hook against the metal railing.

He watched the blue dots of Knapp and Beaulieu coming closer and suddenly they appeared through the smoke like apparitions.

"This the guy?"

"Get him out." Nick handed him over. "I've got to go get Sorensen." Suddenly, Nick caught a breath. "What the hell? What is he doing?" he demanded, watching the blue dot that represented Sorensen burrowing deeper into the building.

And closer to the fire.

He didn't bother to say goodbye, just turned around and plunged back into the hall.

The smoke had thickened, furling around him like black velvet, so heavy that he moved blindly along, staying low. He wore the standard high-wattage shoulder lamp. It didn't matter. He might as well have turned it off for all the good it did.

"Come on, come on," he muttered to himself. The building shuddered as Nick drew near the vestibule. Suddenly there was a ripping sound and the ceiling at the end of the hall collapsed.

Nick dove into the vestibule, feeling the wave of heat shoot over him as the fire roared in triumph. He stayed by the floor, scrambling toward the door that his display told him led to Sorensen. Somehow the kid had gotten disoriented, crossing the vestibule and going behind the far door on Nick's side rather than toward the exit. The blue dot was motionless. Sorensen's personal alert siren would be sounding but it was silenced by the walls of acoustic shielding.

The door opened into swirling blackness. Nick moved down a short hallway, tracking his location on the Orienteer. Right at the end, then through another door. More smoke inside this one, and heat eddying around him, but no flames. It was here somewhere, though, stalking him with the relentless cunning of a predator.

Heading blindly across the room, Nick stumbled over something, cursing. It wasn't Sorensen, but a heavy light fixture that had fallen from the ceiling. Ignoring the ache in his shin, Nick plowed forward. Then his boot hit something else. Not a piece of the ceiling, this time, he thought, shining his light on it. Through the oily black smoke, he saw Sorensen's black leather helmet.

And his stomach tightened. He fought the urge to sweep his ceiling hook, looking for Sorensen. He couldn't afford to waste the time. The display said he was further in. Nick had to trust it.

There was a rumble ahead of him. His radio crackled. "Ladder 67, the roof is going. Get out, repeat, get out."

"Negative, Command. I'm getting my man."

"Ladder 67—"

Nick turned it off.

He went through the next door more cautiously, watching for fallen debris. Another hallway, another turn. His mask began a thudding vibration against his face, warning him he had only a handful of minutes left on his tank. The mayday signal sounding faintly from the pumper told him to get out and get out now. Not a chance. Sorensen's marker said he was behind this door and that was where Nick was going.

He put his hand on the final door, feeling the heat as he touched it. Taking a breath, he turned the knob to open it.

And walked into hell.

Her eyes stung and watered from the smoke. Her head pounded from the fumes. The heat had grown so that even she could feel it now as it turned the November night balmy. And Sloane didn't care, all she cared about was the monitor in her hand. On the display, she watched Nick fight his way through the labyrinth, closer to Sorensen.

Further from safety.

Negative, Command. I'm getting my man. He would never consider doing anything else. No firefighter would. She knew that, she knew it.

And still she wanted to scream as she stared at the display, watching the little blue dot with Nick's initials creep away from the salvation of the stairwell, inch by torturous inch deeper into the maze.

The building rumbled and she looked up to see flame shooting out of the windows on the upper floors. The plywood had been consumed now, leaving openings for the hungry flames, showing the line of fire that would cut off Nick's retreat. The tower truck poured hundreds of gallons a minute of water through the openings, fighting back the flames, fighting to leave him with an escape, a chance.

There was a crunch and a whoosh of flame as another part of the roof fell in and she had to fight not to cry out. Nick, she thought in agony.

I never told you...

Fire and brimstone. Heat and fury. The far end of the room was bathed in flame that spat and popped and snarled. Black smoke wreathed the blaze, making it seem as though he were looking into the fires of hell themselves. Melting paint dripped down the walls. Even down low the temperature slammed into him, making it nearly impossible to think, to move.

And Sorensen lay on the floor, edging toward a door that would take him away from the exit. His mask dangled from his neck, straps broken, faceplate cracked. A trail of torn and blistered skin ran up into his hair where blood poured from a gash on his scalp. He'd been trying to breathe the cooler air down low, coughing and retching from the smoke.

Suddenly, the flames up by the ceiling brightened. The orange shaded to sunburst yellow, a yellow bright enough to burn through the shrouds of black, a yellow that shimmered and spread fluidly across the ceiling.

And Nick's stomach clenched in fear. He knew the signs, every firefighter knew the signs.

The room was about to explode.

"Come on," he roared, vaulting into the room to grab Sorensen, throwing him toward the door and not caring because they had to get out of that room and get out now.

Or die.

He slammed the door and dragged the probie down the hallway, watching the blue lines for the route to escape. There was a whoof of explosion behind them and a rush of heat that sent the smoke before him roiling.

Sorensen was half-conscious, weak and heavy. Maybe head injury, maybe smoke inhalation, it didn't matter. They needed to get out. Nick dragged off his mask and put it over Sorensen's face, giving him several seconds of the rapidly dwindling supply of air before taking it back. Only a handful of minutes left. Only a handful of minutes to escape.

Passing the mask back and forth, Nick hauled Sorensen through the maze in grim determination, knowing it was only a matter of time before the roof went, the floor went and it all came tumbling down. If they didn't run out of air first.

He keyed his radio mike. "Ladder 67 to Command, we're coming out into the third-floor hallway. Low on air, repeat, low on air." He handed the mask to Sorensen and reached for what should have been the door.

And his hands hit a blank wall.

The building groaned. Cold fear swept through Nick as he spread his arms blindly, searching to either side for the way out. He knew it was there, he'd seen it on the display seconds before. They were not going to die in this building. It was not going to happen. His fingers touched a doorjamb and he moved to it in relief.

Until Sorensen caught at his sleeve. "Wrong door!" he yelled, handing Nick the mask.

For an instant, Nick froze, shaken at how very nearly he'd taken them back deeper into the maze. The mask chattered against his face, galvanizing him into action. There was no time to waste. The blue lines. The blue lines would take them to safety.

One more set of doors and they'd be in the vestibule. He sipped a little air and passed the mask to Sorensen, feeling the warmth of the door up top. It was a risk they'd have to take. They edged to one side of the doorjamb and Nick reached for the handle. The building rumbled around them.

Swiftly, he opened the door.

The freight-train roar of the fire outside staggered him. They were walking into an inferno. It rolled along the ceiling and licked down the walls, fed by air from the now-open windows. The mask jittered in Nick's hand as he handed it to Sorensen. Maybe they were walking into an inferno but they had no choice. They were out of time.

They scrambled out into the vestibule. Ahead, water pounded in through the windows. The torrent gave way before the growling advance of the flames, though, neutralized as a hissing steam that boiled back toward them as they lurched around the corner to the main hallway.

Everything to their right was a seething mass of fire. To their left, Nick caught glimpses of the fire door to the stairwell behind a flickering wall of flames. There was no good escape. An ominous creaking sounded overhead. And throwing Sorensen's arm over his neck, Nick plunged through fire, hauling ass for the stairwell door.

Then they were through and in the stairwell. Stumbling down the steps, Nick shared the very last gasps of air with Sorensen. Almost there. They were almost there. They were going to get out. Adrenaline spiked in his veins as together they hit the crashbar of the fire door at the bottom of the stairs.

And the world came tumbling down.

* * *

Don't let anything happen to him, don't let anything happen to him, please don't let anything happen to him. The words ran together in Sloane's head like a witch's chant.

Except that she had no power to control or protect. All she could do was watch the display in her hand. Every fiber of her being was bent on it as she watched the markers creeping closer, ever closer to the door. She was desperate to help him, desperate to see him, desperate to get him out.

And in that moment, she knew that she loved him. She couldn't say when it had happened, couldn't say how, only that her life was bound to his in some irretrievable way. And his life was hanging by a thread.

With a snarling roar, the rest of the roof collapsed and flames shot toward the sky, smoke boiling upward.

Sloane turned to stare at the inferno, a horror deeper than torment coming over her. She stared at her display, at the motionless blue dot. Nick was still inside. "No," she whispered, trembling. *"No!"*

She sprinted over to the door. Knapp caught her around the waist, turning her half-around, stopping her. His face was tight and drawn.

"He's right there, at the bottom of the stairs," she shouted hysterically, fighting to get loose.

"We know he is. They're going after him." He pointed to where the engine companies had doused the flames by the entrance.

The smoke blew back in her face, making her dizzy. Knapp shook his head. "You can't help," he shouted. "You're going to wind up in the hospital if you don't watch it. Now go back to the ladder truck and sit down."

Numbly, she watched the rescue team step inside with

their tools and hooks. How could it have happened? How could he be gone, and now, when she'd only just realized she loved him? She wanted to rage to the heavens, rage at the fates for giving her this bitter pill to swallow yet again. How could she have lost another person she loved?

Suddenly a shout went up. "Over there." Knapp pointed to where the rescue company was stepping out of the wreckage of the warehouse. With them, still on his feet, was Nick.

Adrenaline surged through her system, making her shake. She blinked back the tears that slipped crazily from her burning eyes. He was safe, he was whole, he was coming back to her.

For now.

Sloane sat abruptly down on legs that would no longer hold her. Suddenly she saw it, the pattern of the future. Day after day, night after night of having Nick make it through one more shift, never knowing which fire would be the one he didn't escape, never knowing which night she'd open her door to see the deputy chief standing on her doorstep, white hat in his hands as he searched for the impossible words.

The knot of men around Nick slapped him on the back, laughing and whooping. Her stomach rolled with nausea.

She couldn't not love him, it was woven into the fabric of her self. She didn't have to wait around to watch him die, though. The decision was swift, the need to escape immediate.

She turned to O'Hanlan, at the ladder behind her. "I have to go. Can you tell Nick that I won't be going back to the firehouse?"

"Hold on, are you sick?" he demanded. "Did you get too much smoke? Go to the medics."

"I'm fine."

"But—"

"Tell Nick," she said briefly, then ran.

* * *

It wasn't until he'd seen Sorensen to the ambulance to be taken care of by the paramedics that Nick gave himself the luxury of thinking about Sloane. Flanked by Beaulieu and Knapp, he headed toward the ladder truck. His shoulder ached a bit where it had been pinned against a wall, but that same wall had supported a layer of fiery debris, keeping them from being crushed and burned. The brush with death had left him giddy and supercharged.

"You were lucky, Nick old boy," Knapp said, slapping him again on the back. "Someone up there likes you."

"I'd like to think a lot of people like me, Knapp," Nick returned, looking around for Sloane. "Where's Sloane?"

"I told her to go sit on the ladder truck," Knapp said. "She was pretty upset when we thought you were trapped. She's probably in the cab."

Behind them, O'Hanlan shook his head. "She took off. Said she wasn't going to go back to the firehouse."

Nick frowned. "Was she sick? How much smoke did you get out here?"

"Not too much. She said she was fine."

"Then why did she leave, dammit? She didn't have any way to get out of here." Cursing, he unsnapped his turnout coat swiftly. "You didn't let her walk, did you?"

"I was stuck on the ladder. I couldn't very well run after her. She headed out that way." O'Hanlan jabbed a thumb down the street.

And Nick looked away up the empty sidewalk.

Chapter Sixteen

She walked up Columbus to Mass Ave. without seeing a cab. By the time she made it to the Back Bay, she'd hit a rhythm. As long as she walked, she didn't have to think. And if she didn't think, she didn't have to miss Nick and if she didn't miss Nick, she didn't have to face what she was walking away from.

So she just kept moving, down Mass Ave., over the Charles, through Cambridge and home.

It took her two hours of walking but finally she let herself into her flat with her hidden key, her head pounding—with the effects of smoke inhalation, not with the efforts of fighting back the tears. There was nothing to weep about. Nick had survived and she'd learned her lesson.

That walking away was the best thing for her.

The hour might have been late, but sleep eluded her. When she drifted off momentarily, it was to restless nightmares of fire and loss, running in terror down endless hallways only to look down and find her hands empty of the treasure she'd been trying to preserve. When the sky began to lighten, she rose, exhausted, to start her day.

The hot, sluicing water of the shower let her find a certain oblivion. The trick was to avoid letting her mind wander, to avoid thinking about Nick.

To avoid thinking about what she was giving up.

From her closet, she took whatever was closest at hand. She didn't spend much time on her makeup—there was a haunted look to her eyes that she didn't want to face.

Sometime that day, sooner or later, she was going to have to talk to Nick. She was going to have to find the words to tell him that their relationship—and it was, she could now admit, a relationship—was over. Tell him she loved him? Not possible. Not now, not ever.

A breath of pain whisked through her. Ignore it, she told herself. She'd kept her feelings locked down for all these years. She needed to keep them locked down now.

Because if she let them loose for one moment, she might fly all to pieces.

She slipped on her coat and picked up her purse. Going into work early was good. Putting in a few extra hours would allow her to catch up the time she'd missed. It was a way to keep focused. She'd catch a cab to the firehouse to pick up her car then hit the office. Check in with Bill Grant at the fire office, let him know that she'd seen enough so that testing could proceed without her on site. Move on with her life.

It was a beautiful day outside, a day to be savored by lovers. Something twisted inside her and she pressed it fiercely down. She was locking her door when she heard a sound behind her. She turned to see Nick striding up the stairs, his boots thudding hollowly on the gray boards of the porch.

And the numbness dissipated like early-morning mist.

"Where the hell have you been?" He stopped before her, anger sparking in his eyes.

Hold it down. Don't feel it. Sloane stared at him. "What are you doing here?"

"Trying to keep from going nuts. One minute the roof is falling in and I'm getting my guy out, the next I look around and you're gone. No clue where and your car's still at the station when we get back. We were there overhauling until one in the morning and I spent the entire freaking time wondering if something had happened to you."

"I told O'Hanlan I was leaving."

"And walked off into Dorchester in the middle of the night. You know the statistics on violent crime in that neighborhood? I called when I got back to the station, over and over, and you never picked up." His voice rose.

"I had my phone unplugged."

"Like it was unplugged this weekend? What's going on, Sloane? Last night you said it wasn't the time or the place. Well, it's sure as hell the time now."

A look at his face, at the lines carved by worry and fear took the punch out of her sharp retort. She let out a breath. It had to happen, she knew that. It might as well be now. "All right," she said. "Let's go upstairs."

By the time they'd gotten into her flat, some of the tension had gone out of his shoulders.

"Coffee?"

"Sure." Nick followed her into the kitchen. He took a deep breath. "Look, I'm sorry I jumped all over you. I was just really worried. You shouldn't have left that way."

"I know. I'm sorry." Honesty. She owed him that much.

The coffee she'd made that morning was still hot and she

poured each of them a cup before sitting down at the kitchen table. "How's Sorensen?"

"He's fine." Nick pulled up a chair to sit next to her. "He needed a few stitches and they wanted to keep an eye on him overnight because of the head injury. A light fixture dropped on him. It knocked off his helmet and his mask, which put his Orienteer out of commission." Nick tapped his fingers restlessly on the table. "He made it through, though. Couple of weeks, he'll be back raring to go."

Back to dance on the edge of death. Sloane's stomach tightened. "You were lucky."

"If we were lucky, it was because of you." He looked at her soberly. "If it weren't for your units, we would have died in that building."

"I know."

"If nothing else, you should have stayed around so we could thank you."

She gave a halfhearted smile. "I didn't need to hear it to know you were grateful."

"No? Then how about you should have stayed around because you were the only one I wanted to see when I finally made it out? I was so damned worried when I didn't know where you were." He kissed the palm of her hand, then laid it against the side of his face. "I don't think I could handle it if anything happened to you," he said softly. "I love you." His gaze was gentle, unwavering. And sudden tears swamped her.

"What is it?" he asked, as they rolled down her cheeks.

"Nothing." At first she battled them, dashing them angrily away and then it all just broke over her like a wave, the fear, the tension, the fight with Candy, the déjà vu of the fire.

And the anguish of watching the roof fall in, certain that she'd just seen Nick die.

The sobs racked her body. He said nothing, seeming to understand words were not what she needed. He simply pulled her to him, cradling her head to his neck, letting the salt damp of tears soak into his shirt.

When at last Sloane raised her head, long moments had passed. Nick kissed her hair. "Talk to me."

Sloane rose and moved away from him. If she continued to touch him she'd never be able to say what had to be said. She walked to the bathroom to wash her face with icy water. When she came back, She didn't sit but leaned against the counter. "I'm sorry about getting upset."

"Don't be. I get the impression it was long overdue."

"Maybe." She wrapped her arms around herself. "Nick, I..." The words lodged in her throat. It took an effort to force them out. "I can't be involved with you anymore."

His expression didn't change, he just looked at her steadily. "I can't say I'm surprised to hear you say that. You've been working yourself up to this for a while now."

"I haven't been working myself up to anything. It's just what I need to do. I'm sorry if it hurts you." She cleared her throat. "We talked about it at the beginning, remember? No promises."

Nick stared into space for a moment, nodding his head as though to music only he could hear. When his eyes cut to hers, it was with the impact of a punch. "That's right, no promises. No one's allowed to care for you, nothing's allowed to matter. It must get lonely in that little box where you live."

Her eyes narrowed slightly. "I live the way I have to."

"You're going to have to do better than that. Something happened the other night when we were together. You can't look at me and tell me that it meant nothing to you."

She gave him a level stare. "I wouldn't even if I could."

"Then why are you walking away? Why won't you try to

make this work? I know the fire was bad and it probably spooked you, but it's like anything else. You get used to it, you get past it."

"No you don't," she burst out. "I don't. I can't sit back and watch what you do. I lived with Mitch and his wife. I saw what she went through every single time he went off to work, every shift, never knowing what would happen. The night he was killed I was over at their house. I was there when the battalion chief knocked on the door." Her voice died away and she bit her lip, staring fixedly at her hands. He wanted to go to her then, but something held him back. "You have no idea what it's like to sit there, knowing that they're coming. Hearing the knock, and you don't want to answer it because you think if you don't hear the words it won't be true, that you can just sit in the dark and close your eyes and make it all go away except you know that it won't, and you know that it's real and there's nothing you can do to change it."

And she looked fixedly ahead but he knew she didn't see him. In that moment and that time, all she could see was the nightmare inside her head.

"My God, Sloane," Nick said helplessly. "Why haven't you talked to anyone about this? You can't just let it sit there and eat you alive. You've got to deal with it. You either get a hold on it or it gets a hold on you."

"Been tuning into radio psychology shows lately?"

He ignored her, knowing she was striking out at him because of her vulnerability. "You lost your brother in the worst way, the worst way, but it's part of life. And I know it hurts like hell but we all go through it. I've lost friends. I lost my father."

"Funny, so did I," she said in a brittle voice. "Only it happened to me when I was eight and I lost my mother at the same time."

"*What?*" His eyes widened in shock. "How?"

"Car accident. Mitch and I went to live with my grandparents, then, only my grandmother got breast cancer three years later. My grandfather lasted a little longer. With him, I think it was just a broken heart." Tears began slipping down her cheeks again. "Mitch took me in, gave me a place to live while I finished high school. And then I lost him, too." She looked up at him. "Oh God, don't stare at me like I'm some kind of freak. There's all kinds of bad luck in the world. It happens, isn't that what you said?" She swiped furiously at her cheeks. "I'll get over it."

"But you haven't really, have you?" He was just barely beginning to understand the magnitude of the disaster and how deep it all went. "This isn't just about firefighting, is it? It's about getting close to anyone." It twisted viciously at something inside him, knowing what she'd been though, knowing there was no way for him to fix it but to love her.

And that was the thing she feared above all.

Her eyes burned at him. "Every time, every time I've cared for someone, really loved them, I've lost them. I can't do that again."

"So you stay detached from people for the rest of your life?"

"I don't know. Right now, I survive." She raised her chin. "You risk your life and maybe you have to, but I can't watch while you do it. I can't jump every time the phone rings while you're at work. I love you too much to wonder every shift, Will this be the day someone knocks on my door? Will this be the night I get the call from the hospital? Will this be the night…will this be the night your luck runs out on you?" She shook her head blindly. "I can't, Nick, I just can't."

"What if you don't have to?" Nick crossed to her. "I took the promotional exam last month to get moved up to district chief." *Believe me. Trust me.* "I'll find out the results next week. If I pass, I'll be on the street supervising more than I'll be actually in the fires."

"And you'll hate it. You'll want to be right up next to the burn in every fire you oversee. I know it, it's like an addiction with you guys." Unable to hold still, she paced across the room.

"I've been fighting fires for thirteen years. It's time to do something else." And if it took giving up firefighting to be with her, he'd do it. Even if it meant giving up part of himself.

She turned back to him. "How can you be sure this is what you want?"

"I can't, until I try it," he said simply. "But the chances are good that I *will* get to try it. We're going to be losing half our district chiefs to retirement and promotion in the next five years. I can't promise that I'll hit the top five percent in the exam, I can't promise how soon I'll be promoted, but I will do my damnedest to get out of the day-to-day fires."

"And what if you change your mind once you're there and want to go back?"

"Then we talk about it. Yeah, you're right, I can't guarantee how I'll feel in the future. Then again, I can't guarantee I won't drive down the street and get broadsided. I could walk past a building and have a wall collapse on me."

Her eyes sparked at him. "Don't give me that. There may not be any guarantees but there are statistics, Nick. The more often you risk yourself, the higher the likelihood that something will happen."

"You know how many career firefighters in the U.S. died on duty in 2004? Twenty-nine—out of almost three hundred thousand, and half of those were natural causes. Less than a hundredth of a percent. It sounds scary but the reality isn't so bad."

"Tell that to my brother's widow," she snapped.

"Sloane." His voice was quiet. "I took the test. I think I can make a difference further up the command chain and I want to try it. I'd be lying if I tried to guarantee anything more, except that I love you and I think we've got a chance to be happy." He held his breath, willing it to be enough.

Sloane stared at him, eyes haunted.

"Please tell me you'll try." And in the space of a heartbeat his world reduced to the two of them, outside of space, outside of time, suspended only in the moment of her decision.

The seconds passed.

Finally, Sloane moistened her lips. "I can't, Nick," she whispered. "I just can't do it."

He wanted to wipe the shadows away. He wanted to take away the power of the past to hurt. He wanted to help her accept what had happened, put it aside and move forward into the future.

Sometimes wanting wasn't enough.

Slowly, reluctantly, he released her hands and rose. "I guess that's it, then." He pulled his jacket off the chair and walked back over to her. For a second, his fingertips touched her cheek. "You might not want to hear it but I do love you," he said softly. "If you ever change your mind, I'll be here." He paused. "Be happy, Sloane. You of all people deserve it."

And he walked down the hall and out of her life.

Chapter Seventeen

A second. A minute. An hour. Sloane had no illusions things would get better quickly. She had too much experience with loss for such naiveté, so she sat at her desk and forced herself to work, grasping at it like a lifeline. Concentration wasn't possible; she focused on rote tasks that didn't require any and ignored the occasional concerned looks that Dave, her intern, flicked her way.

The phone rang. "Sloane Hillyard."

"Ms. Hillyard, this is Gil Snowden over at the *Chronicle*. I'm doing a follow-up story on the Dorchester fire. I hear that there were a couple of guys who almost died last night, who would have died without some new equipment that you built."

Sloane closed her eyes. "I'm not the right person for you to talk to. You should check with the fire department."

"I did. They pointed me to you."

Because her job description didn't include falling apart, she took a deep breath. "What do you want to know?"

"The basics, for starters. What does it do, how does it work, how common is it. You know, the whole spiel."

So she gave it to him, the essential rundown that she could give in her sleep, drowning him in details she'd memorized long before while his computer keys clacked madly in the background.

...there were a couple of guys who almost died last night....

"Okay, I think I got it," Snowden said after a final burst of typing. "So this is the gear that Councilman Ayre was talking about before his reelection, right? Do you think he's going to continue to push it now that the election's over?"

"I wouldn't know. Again, I'd check with the department."

"You must be aware of his record of voting for departmental budget cuts," he said, ignoring her. "Any comments?"

"You'll have to take that up with someone else." A typical reporter, Sloane thought. If he didn't get an answer to his question, he asked it another way, poking and prodding until he got something he could use.

"Of course, funding cuts would affect the chances of the city buying your equipment."

"I'm a resident of Cambridge," she said with an edge to her voice. "I don't really follow Boston politics."

"Well you should. The firefighters really want this equipment. I just interviewed one of them, a Nick Trask."

And an iron band tightened viciously around her chest. Dropping her head down in her hands, she waited it out. It would stop, eventually, she knew.

Just not any time soon.

She raised her head to see Dave staring at her. On the

phone, Snowden was still talking. "…a big outlay." He paused expectantly. "Ms. Hillyard?"

She gathered her wits. "Yes, well, I hope that the department will get the funding for the units. They ought to be standard equipment for every fire department in the country." A nice, positive, meaningless quote.

"Of course, you've got a vested interest in that."

"Pardon me?"

"Well, it's nice business for your company. Exler's a start-up in need of a cash cow. No wonder you're pushing it to fire departments. Makes you look good if you succeed. More stock options for when the company goes public."

"Stock options aren't my concern. The gear is."

"And the gear is good for business."

Sloane's eyes narrowed. "It's got nothing to do with my company or with business."

"But it would be great for your revenue numbers. I mean, you're not doing this for your health, right?"

In a flash, her patience evaporated. "You want to know why I'm pushing this equipment?" she demanded. "My brother was a firefighter, and he died in the Hartford meat-packing-plant fire trying to save the guys in his company." Dave snapped his head around to stare at her. "I'm pushing this equipment so that that doesn't happen again to anyone, anywhere. This is not about business, Mr. Snowden. It's personal."

Nick walked down the aisle of the home builders' warehouse, the beeps of the forklifts echoing through the air, orange metal shelves towering on either side. By this time, he could probably navigate the aisles with his eyes closed. He'd been there a lot lately.

His house was the better for it. First the cabinets, then

paint, then new tile in the bathroom. He'd spackled and plastered and grouted and sanded, wired in light fixtures and refinished doors. When he wasn't at the firehouse or his side job, he was working on his living room, his kitchen, his study.

Not the bedroom, though. Too many memories lurked there.

And now he had a problem. After almost two weeks of knocking himself out, he was running out of things to do. Just the thought made his palms sweat. If he ran out of things to do he'd have time to think and if he had time to think, he'd think about Sloane and if he thought about Sloane…

He refused to go there. He refused to wonder how she was doing. Okay, he couldn't help wondering how she was doing, but he refused to miss her. Except he couldn't help doing that, either, which was why he found himself running to the home builders' warehouse to pick out handles for his kitchen cabinets, of all ridiculous things, just so he'd have a way to keep his hands busy.

Glass or ceramic? Copper or bronze? Knobs or handles, hooks or rings? He scowled at the fixtures and tried to forget that he'd planned to bring Sloane to help him pick out hardware because they were the kinds of things that women cared about, and he'd wanted her to walk into his house and see something she'd chosen.

He'd wanted her to walk into his house and feel at home.

The omnipresent ache for her sharpened. And he grabbed a handful of plain white knobs because it just didn't matter.

An hour. A day. A week. Sloane drove herself relentlessly, working into the night until her neck ached and her vision blurred, driving herself pitilessly at the health club until her muscles refused to continue. Each morning, she set herself an impossible schedule in the hope that by night she'd be exhausted enough to fall into the oblivion of a dreamless sleep.

And each night she was disappointed.

Now, nearly two weeks after the fire, she stood in the hallway outside the city council chambers, waiting for Bill Grant.

"Sloane." Bill Grant strode up to her, beaming. "Glad you made it. You sounded kind of iffy when I called you last week."

"I'm still not sure what I'm doing here. What does the Ways and Means Committee need from me? They've got all my reports and all the specs. They've got the data from the rest of the fires. What happened in Dorchester should speak for itself."

"They don't just want to hear facts and figures, they want to hear about you. They want to hear about your brother."

She stiffened in outrage. "I'm not going to talk about that to a room full of strangers. It's personal."

"Sloane," Bill said in a low, urgent voice, "it's what it takes to get the message through. I know it must be hard and I'm sorry, but if you really want to be sure it doesn't happen again, then tell these guys what it's like. Make them understand the reality. Your buddy from the *Chronicle*'s out there. He'll make sure people hear about it."

She moved her head. "You don't understand."

"No, Sloane, *they* don't understand. And you're the only one who can make them. You of all people should know how much rides on this." The door to the chambers opened. Grant looked at her. "It's your chance to make a difference. Will you do it?"

A chance to make a difference. An appeal to let them paw over her soul. Could she live with herself if she did it?

Could she live with herself if she didn't?

Sloane took a deep breath and walked into the chambers.

* * *

Nick sat on his couch turning the envelope over and over in his hands, staring at the seal of the Boston Fire Department. A few weeks earlier, he'd have torn it open in anticipation and curiosity, waiting to see how he'd fared and what his future might look like. Now, he knew what his future looked like.

Without Sloane, pretty damned lousy.

It would get easier with time, of course. Everything did. Eventually, he wouldn't think of her every waking minute. He wouldn't seize up when he walked down a sidewalk past someone wearing her scent. Eventually, he knew, he'd get past her.

Sure. In a decade or two.

Ripping open the envelope impatiently, Nick pulled out the papers inside. The cover letter didn't matter; all he cared about was the list of results. And in a spurt of jubilation, he saw his name among those at the top. Not a perfect score but a ninety-nine percentile with a rank of second. Second out of more than two hundred. Not bad. The promotion would be coming as soon as a position became available.

And the one person he wanted most to call with the news was the one person who didn't want to hear from him.

The problem was, Sloane thought, there were too damned many ways for a person to be reached. Even when she slipped out for an hour-long meeting, she had to slog through a dozen messages when she returned. She clicked on her e-mail, reading text and deleting spam as she punched her way through voice-mail menus.

And sat bolt upright when she heard the first message.

"Sloane, George O'Hanlan of Ladder 67." The voice boomed out of the receiver into her ear. "Nicky got some good news about his exam so we're taking him out to celebrate Friday night. Thought you might want to come along. We'll be at Big John's in Southie about eight. Come on by if you get a chance."

Come on by if you get a chance.

And suddenly she found herself missing the men at the firehouse with a fierceness that surprised her. She missed their noisy good humor, the laughter, the ribbing, the warm crowded evenings in the firehouse kitchen. The unquestioned support. She'd only spent a few weeks around them. How had they gotten to matter to her?

Connections. They were suddenly all around, tripping her up everywhere she turned.

Sloane closed her eyes briefly and punched Delete.

The next voice mail was an interview request from the editor of *Fire Engineering.* He'd want to talk about the Orienteer. They all did. The *Chronicle* coverage of the Dorchester fire and the budgetary meetings had made Sloane the crusader of the month. There were the requests for demos, for test systems, for testimonials.

And the questions, always the questions. Her grief had gone from a very private thing to front-page news. In the first few days, walking into the Exler offices had made her want to cringe, colleagues gazing at her with eyes bright with sympathy, or worse, curiosity. She'd been through it back in Connecticut, in the aftermath of the fire, and had loathed it. The move to Cambridge had been a chance to get back her privacy—and her anonymity. And suddenly here it was, public all over again.

It was less difficult this time, though. Perhaps it was that time had passed. Perhaps it was because there was a purpose behind letting people know. Bill Grant had been right. If it was a way to bring attention to the Orienteer, a way to get people to look twice and to listen, it was worth it. And as the days went by, she found it hurt a little less.

If only losing Nick were that way.

She talked with the *Fire Engineering* editor briefly to schedule the interview. As she hung up, out of the corner of her eye she saw Dave watching her. "You need something?"

"No. I just, I uh…" He cleared his throat. "I just wanted to tell you that I'm sorry about your brother."

Since that day he'd heard her on the phone with Snowden, Dave had studiously avoided saying a word about her revelation. In the days after the news had been made public, days of questions and well-meant condolences from the other staffers, he'd respected her privacy, allowing Sloane to slip gratefully into the peace of the lab each day.

Until now. Oddly, it didn't make her uncomfortable. He was able to say it as if he meant it. Like Molly Trask.

Like Nick.

Her throat was suddenly tight. "Thank you. It was a long time ago," she said. And a longing for closeness hit her like a physical ache. She needed to be close to someone, she needed to be held, loved. To avoid thinking about it, she punched the next message up. Only to be buffeted again.

"Sloane, Candy. Sorry to bother you but I saw an article in the paper about you and your gear and Mitch. I just wanted to be sure you were okay."

Connections…

And abruptly she ached for them, for Candy, for Pete, for the people who'd been her family.

For Nick.

She was in her car and on the highway before she even knew what she was about.

* * *

The house looked different. Once slate blue, it had been repainted a cheerful yellow with white shutters. Flower boxes hung below the windows, empty now, but full of promise for spring. Seasons passed—chill autumn, barren winter—but sooner or later the ground quickened.

Sooner or later, everything was renewed.

Sloane rang the bell. She turned to look at the dogwood in the front yard, the one they'd planted together when she'd graduated high school. It had grown so much. They all had.

Behind her, the door opened and a rawboned teenager stood looking back at her, his eyes almost level with hers. Her jaw dropped. "Pete?" she breathed.

He studied her a moment, frowning. "Aunt Sloane?" he asked. His voice gave an adolescent squeak.

She nodded.

"What are you doing here?"

The suspicious note in his voice broke her heart. "I was in the neighborhood and…" She stopped. In the face of suspicion, honesty. "Actually, I wasn't in the neighborhood at all. I drove down because I missed you guys. I wanted to stop in and say hi."

He stared at her awhile and nodded finally. "That's cool," he said and stepped back from the door.

She wanted to hug him, but she wasn't sure how to handle this new, grown-up person. When she put out her hand to shake, he took it awkwardly, unused to the ritual. The hell with it, she thought and used his hand to pull him close. He was stiff against her for a moment, then yielded and hugged her back. "I've missed you, Pete," she murmured.

"Yeah," he agreed and gave her another squeeze before letting her go.

"So I hear you liked the guitar."

"Yeah. I was just upstairs practicing. You want to hear me play?" His tone was offhand but he watched her closely. His hair hung down into his eyes. The hems of his new-looking jeans ended around his ankle bones, as if he'd already grown out of them. He was no longer a little boy, he was a teenager on his way to being a man and she'd almost missed it.

"I want to hear everything," she said.

Pete had gone through his blink-182 and Green Day books and had moved on to U2 when they heard footsteps downstairs.

"Pete?" Candy called from the kitchen. "Whose car is that?" Sloane headed for the stairs just as Candy came up, only to watch her jaw drop open in shock. "Sloane?" She frowned. "What are you doing here?"

She'd made a mistake, Sloane thought with a sinking heart. *Home is the place where, when you have to go there, They have to take you in.* But too much time had passed and maybe this wasn't her home any longer. "I thought I'd drop by and say hi. It's Friday night, though. You probably have plans."

"Hey, Mom." Pete stuck his head out of his room. "Sloane's going to take me to see blink-182 next time they come to town."

"She's going to..." Candy held up her hand. "Hold on, let me catch up a little. Pete, you need to get the leaves up outside."

"Ah, Mom."

"You've got an hour before dusk. Get to it. Sloane, can you come downstairs a minute?"

Sloane bit her lip at Candy's tone and followed her down to the kitchen. "I'm sorry I stopped by without calling. I'll get out of your hair."

"Don't be crazy," Candy told her fiercely and pulled her in for a long hug. When they stepped apart, she was blinking a little. "I'm just surprised to see you. I didn't think I was going to for a long time, maybe never." She sat down at the kitchen table, rubbing her temples.

Sloane took a deep breath and sat across from her. "About the other day when we talked…"

"I was out of line," Candy said quickly. "I said a lot of stuff I shouldn't have. I'm sorry."

"No. I've been thinking a lot about it and you were right. It was a wake-up call. I was asking for it."

"No one asks for anything, Sloane. We're all just trying to get along."

"I haven't been, though." The words came out slowly. "I've been hiding out for way too long."

"It was a lesson you learned pretty young."

"I outgrew the clothes I wore as a kid," Sloane said. "I should also have outgrown that. I thought it would make things better. It didn't. I know that now."

"Good. I'm glad." Candy rose and opened a cabinet to remove a pot. "Are you staying for dinner?"

Sloane hesitated. "Sure, if I'm invited."

"Only if you chop the onions," Candy said, blinking again. "I always cry."

"So what's going on with you?" Candy stirred the marinara sauce she'd thrown together from diced tomatoes, garlic and spices.

"What do you mean?"

"There's something wrong. I could hear it when we talked the other week but it's worse now."

Sloane filled a pot with water to boil the pasta. "It's a man I was seeing. We broke up."

"That would have been my guess. Who is he?"

She should have known Candy would get right to the point. "A firefighter."

Candy snapped her head around to stare at Sloane. She shook her head. "You don't pick the easy ones, do you?"

"I didn't pick him at all." She set the pot on a burner and turned it up high.

"No. Sometimes the picking's done for you. So what happened? It just didn't work out?"

"Nothing had to happen." Sloane leaned against the counter. "You of all people should understand that. Look what you went through with Mitch."

"Yeah, let's look," Candy said slowly, covering the simmering pot of sauce. "Eleven years of thanking my lucky stars every morning when I woke up next to him. A wonderful son. The sister I never had by blood." She reached out to squeeze Sloane's hand.

"But God, Candy, what you went through every night when he was on the job. And now."

"Sloane, that was you." Candy's voice was gentle. "*I* decided not to think about it. I learned really early on to leave it to fate. One of the accountants at work died of a heart attack a couple of years back. Safest job you can imagine. He was sitting on the couch watching a football game when it happened." She gave a brief smile. "The clock's running on all of us. That doesn't mean you tuck yourself away and hide from life, that means you reach out for it while you can. Like I did with Mitch. After a while I wasn't scared every night when I watched him leave. I was proud. He was my own personal hero."

"I can't lose him, Candy," Sloane whispered. "I love him too much."

"But you've lost him as it is, haven't you?"

The words shivered through her. She missed Nick so much it ached. Automatically, she tried to push it down but it bubbled back up again, worse than before. Desperation choked her. After years of denying her emotions, of bottling up grief, loss, anxiety, she'd abruptly lost the ability.

She sank down at the table, face in her hands. "I can't do it, Candy, I can't do it."

"You can't do what?" Candy sat by her, rubbing her shoulders gently. "Love him or live without him? You're hurting right now and you have been for weeks. Gone is gone."

Sloane shook her head blindly. "No. I know he's out there."

"So you're choosing to hurt instead of having it forced on you. God, you talk about what it would be like to watch him go off to work every day, but how are you going to feel if you hear a report that something's happened to a firefighter? Do you think for one minute that you're not going to tear yourself apart imagining it's him? Imagining the worst?" Candy's gaze delved into her. "And what if the worst does happen? Are you going to feel any better reading about it in a newspaper than hearing the news face-to-face? Is it going to hurt any less?"

She'd thought she could avoid hurt by walking away. She'd never guessed how deep the loss would go. And for what? Sloane thought suddenly. She didn't have to be feeling this emptiness. She didn't have to be without him. All it would take was reaching out. "My God," she whispered, her eyes meeting Candy's. "I've been such an idiot. I've got to go find him. I've got—"

The lid began ticking on the boiling pot of water and she paused. Dinner. More than anything else she wanted to go to Nick, but how could she run off when she'd only just begun to repair the damage with Candy and Pete?

Candy rose to stir the marinara sauce. "You know, I don't think there's enough here for three of us," she said, peering into the pot.

"What are you talking about? You've got a ton of it."

"Pete's a big eater. You know how they are at his age. We'd better play it safe. How about if you go back to Boston tonight and we plan on a real dinner next weekend?"

Trust Candy to understand. She always had. The grin spread across Sloane's face until her jaws hurt. "Oh, I missed you so much." Sloane threw her arms around her. "I'll see you soon, I promise."

"We'll hold you to it." Candy kissed her on the cheek. "Good luck with your man. Call and tell me how it goes."

Sloane stopped at the door and gave her a brilliant smile. "Count on it."

Nick leaned out over the pool table and eyed his shot. He made one, two practice strokes and tapped the cue ball, which rolled across the table to nudge the eight ball into the corner pocket.

He straightened. "Looks like I win, O'Hanlan."

"Aye, that you do. That earns you the right to buy a couple more pitchers, Nicky, me boyo."

"O'Hanlan, how is it that the more beers you have, the more Irish you get?"

"The ale loosens me tongue, brings back the mother country."

A corner of Nick's mouth twitched. "Nice trick, considering your mother country is Southie."

"And if a man can't pick up a good Irish accent there, then where can he?"

"I don't know, but for the guest of honor, I seem to be running up to the bar an awful lot."

"Well, once you're promoted you won't be able to go drinking with us, so we'd better do it now."

Nick snorted. "Yeah, right. Hey Beaulieu, why don't you come along and help me carry?"

Set in the working-class neighborhood of South Boston, Big John's sat by the side of the railroad tracks in a beat-up wood frame building. Inside, a man could get good food, cheap beer and play pool at a few dozen of the sweetest carved oak tables Nick had ever seen.

And every time he'd been there, John Feeney had been behind the bar pulling beers, his wizened face never seeming to age from year to year.

Nick tossed down some money. "Three pitchers of Sam's."

"Coming up."

It was good to be out for a change. And if his heart wasn't entirely in it, it was still better than recaulking his shower, which was about the last thing left to do at his house.

"Hey." Beaulieu nudged him. "You've got a fan club."

A few feet away, a curvy blonde whispered into the ear of her girlfriend and gave Nick a playful look.

Nick frowned and rubbed the back of his neck. As far as he was concerned, the beer could come any time.

The blonde leaned his way. "Having fun tonight?"

"Good enough."

His terse reply set her back only for a minute. She stared at the gray T-shirt he wore, with its Ladder 67 shield. "So are you really a firefighter?"

"He really is," Beaulieu supplied.

"Thanks, Todd," Nick said under his breath.

"This is where you start offering to show her your hose," Beaulieu murmured.

"Funny."

She tossed her hair and moved toward him, managing to inject maximum hip sway in just a few steps. "Our table just got called. Want to play with us?"

Nick looked at her. Blond hair, clear eyes—and about as much character as a glass of water. "Not right now. Thanks for the offer, though." He shoved his change in his pocket and grabbed two of the pitchers John slid across to him. "Hey Beaulieu, you want to get the other one?"

"I can't believe you just did that," Beaulieu said aggrievedly when they were back at the pool tables.

"What?"

"They were complete babes, man, and her girlfriend was giving me the look."

"Maybe she had dust in her eyes." Nick refilled his glass.

"You don't just turn around and walk away on women like that. What's gotten into you?"

Nick took a brooding sip of his beer. It wasn't a question of what had gotten into him but who.

And her name was Sloane Hillyard.

Sloane stood at the doors of Big John's trying to calm her jitters. It had been nearly three weeks since she'd seen Nick. Perhaps he hadn't been out of her mind for more than a minute at a time, but he might have gotten past her a lot more quickly. Or he might still be furious with her.

If you ever change your mind, I'll be here. He'd said it, she reminded herself. Surely his feelings wouldn't have changed that quickly. He was a steadier man that that.

At least she hoped so. The only way to find out was to go through the door and do what she'd come there to do.

Inside, the room was noisy and clouded with smoke, the buzz of conversation punctuated by the clack of pool balls smacking together. Old George Thorogood played on the jukebox. A voice over the PA announced tables.

And Sloane stood inside the door, scanning the room for faces she knew.

Looking for the man she loved.

Glass in hand, Nick watched O'Hanlan set up a shot. The burly Irishman sighted the angles and stroked his cue decisively.

And the ball went well wide.

"Great partner you've got there, Nick." Sorensen hooted. "Way to go."

Nick winced. "For Chrissakes, O'Hanlan, we've got five bucks a piece riding on this game." He looked away in disgust, reaching out for his beer. And froze.

At the table, Beaulieu sank the five ball and scratched. Groans and cheers erupted around the table.

"Now who's the one to talk about partners, Sorensen?" O'Hanlan needled. "Your shot, Nicky." He turned. "Nicky?"

But he was talking to thin air because Nick was already moving purposefully toward the door.

Their eyes met with a snap of electricity. When she saw him, it was as though the rest of the room receded in some way, leaving only Nick. The longing for him was a physical thing crouched in her throat. It paralyzed her, so she could only stand, staring, as he walked up. Her pulse hammered.

"Hey," he said.

She couldn't stop the grin from spreading over her face. "Hi. Having a good time?"

"It's just improved immeasurably." He wore just jeans and a T-shirt, nothing special. And he looked perfect, absolutely perfect. "So what brings you here? Did you just happen to be in the neighborhood?"

"Maybe I was just out for a walk." She tried for a joke.

"All the way from Cambridge?"

Her heartbeat thudded in her ears. "If that's how far I have to go to find you."

"Well, you've found me."

Suddenly she couldn't find air. The whole drive from Hartford she'd thought about what to say to him. Now that the moment had come, she was tongue-tied. *Just do it.*

"Let's get some privacy." He reached out for her hand and tugged her to the door.

Outside, the air was frigid. "Nick, you can't be out here without a jacket," she protested. "You're going to freeze."

"I'm not worried about it. Talk to me."He reached out for her hand. "What's on your mind?"

Somehow, the dim light and the quiet released her. "I was an idiot the other day," she told him, the words tumbling out in a rush. "I've been an idiot the whole time and I'm sorry, sorry for everything."

The overhead streetlight set his eyes in shadow, carved deep hollows below his cheekbones. "Sorry for what?"

"For trying to walk away. I was so afraid of what might happen. I can't live my life that way, though. I know that now. You helped me understand." Her voice shook a little and she tried to steady it. "You told me if I changed my mind I could look you up. Well, I'm looking you up now. I want to try this out. I want to be with you."

For long, excruciating seconds he was quiet. "Are you sure about this?" he asked finally. "It isn't just because of all the stuff you went through with the papers, is it?"

She shook her head. "I'm sure, as sure as I can possibly be. I don't guarantee that I might not get scared sometimes but it doesn't matter. It's life. I don't want to be without you." She locked her eyes on his. Everything rested on this, everything. "I love you and I want to take a chance." She swallowed. "If you haven't changed your mind."

For answer, he swept her against him and held her close. Long minutes went by while they just absorbed the feeling of one another's bodies again, the closeness. "Being without you the past month has been hell," Nick murmured against Sloane's hair. "I love you so damn much."

Being in his arms again was everything she'd ever needed, Sloane thought dizzily, and she laughed that everything that had been so wrong could suddenly be so right. "I'm sorry it took so long. I just had to figure things out."

"Don't be. You're here now. That's what matters." He leaned back and frowned a little. "Just exactly how did you wind up coming here, anyway?"

"O'Hanlan told me you were going to be here."

Nick raised an eyebrow. "Oh, did he?"

"He said you had something to celebrate." She kissed him lightly on the lips. "He didn't say what."

"Ranking second on the exam. I'm in line now for promotion."

"Nick, that's wonderful. You must be thrilled about it."

"Not nearly as much as I am about this. Don't get too excited," he cautioned, "I still have to wait for an opening. It could be soon, it could be awhile, there's just no telling."

"It doesn't matter." She brushed the backs of her fingers

against his cheek. "It's not about whether you're promoted or not. This is about us. You, me, together."

And the kiss was like coming home.

"Ah, young love," said a voice nearby.

"Don't it just get you all choked up?"

They looked up to see O'Hanlan and Knapp leaning out the door, grinning at them.

"Now, didn't I tell you there was a reason Nick was so grumpy?" O'Hanlan said to Knapp.

"Now that we've fixed things up for him, he'll start being human again," Knapp agreed.

"Seems like that ought to be worth another pitcher of beer," O'Hanlan commented.

"You're an operator, O'Hanlan," Sloane told him, grinning.

Nick laughed and swung her around. "And I'm so glad of it."

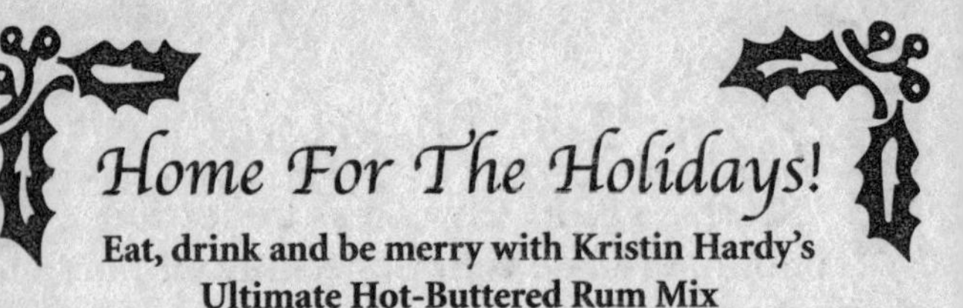

Home For The Holidays!

Eat, drink and be merry with Kristin Hardy's Ultimate Hot-Buttered Rum Mix

Treats make the holiday bright

One of my favorite holiday treats is hot-buttered rum. Not just any old hot-buttered rum, though. This is the ultimate, as revered by J. J. Cooper in *Under the Mistletoe* (Special Edition, December 2005). You'll be seeing J.J. again, so keep an eye out for him.

Hot Buttered Rum Mix

1 lb butter
1 lb white sugar
1 lb brown sugar
dash salt
1 qt light cream
1 tsp vanilla

add:

Hot Buttered Rum

1 tbsp Hot-Buttered Rum Mix
1 shot dark rum (Myers is good)
Hot water

Cream butter, sugar and salt until emulsified. You want it light and fluffy, as if making a cake, so don't rush. Combine cream and vanilla. Add about a half cup at a time and let blend in thoroughly before adding more. It should have the consistency of buttercream at the end. Makes about four cups.

To make hot-buttered rum, add the hot-buttered rum mix and a shot of dark rum (I like Myers) to a mug. Fill the rest of the way with hot water. Delicious.

Note:

This recipe makes enough to share. I put it in glass jars with a pretty label on the front with directions and a ribbon around the lid. It's an instant holiday gift, and one that almost everyone will love. For more recipes, go to www.kristinhardy.com.

Home For The Holidays!

While there are many variations of this recipe, here is Tina Leonard's favorite!

GOURMET REINDEER POOP

Mix 1/2 cup butter, 2 cups granulated sugar, 1/2 cup milk and 2 tsp cocoa together in a large saucepan.
Bring to a boil, stirring constantly; boil for 1 minute.
Remove from heat and stir in 1/2 cup peanut butter, 3 cups oatmeal (not instant) and 1/2 cup chopped nuts (optional).
Drop by teaspoon full (larger or smaller as desired) onto wax paper and let harden.
They will set in about 30-60 minutes.
These will keep for several days without refrigerating, up to 2 weeks refrigerated and 2-3 months frozen.
Pack into resealable sandwich bags and attach the following note to each bag.

I woke up with such a scare when I heard Santa call…
"Now dash away, dash away, dash away all!"
I ran to the lawn and in the snowy white drifts,
those nasty reindeer had left "little gifts."
I got an old shovel and started to scoop,
neat little piles of "Reindeer Poop!"
But to throw them away seemed such a waste,
so I saved them, thinking you might like a taste!
As I finished my task, which took quite a while,
Old Santa passed by and he sheepishly smiled.
And I heard him exclaim as he was in the sky…
"Well, they're not potty trained, but at least they can fly!"

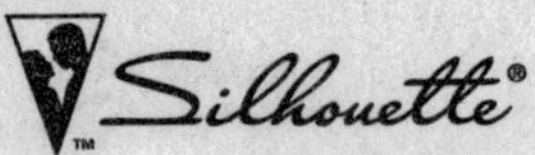

SPECIAL EDITION®

COMING NEXT MONTH

#1723 THE SHEIK AND THE VIRGIN SECRETARY—Susan Mallery
Desert Rogues
Learning of her fiancé's infidelities the day before her wedding, Kiley Hendrick wanted revenge—and becoming mistress to her rich, powerful boss seemed like the perfect plan. At first, Prince Rafiq was amused by his secretary's overtures. But when he uncovered Kiley's secret innocence, the game was *over*—the sheik had to have this virgin beauty for his very own!

#1724 PAST IMPERFECT—Crystal Green
Most Likely To...
To Saunders U. dropout Rachel James, Professor Gilbert had always been a beacon of hope. So when he called asking for help, she was there. Rachel enlisted reporter Ian Beck to dispel the strange allegations about the professor's past. But falling for Ian—well, Rachel should have known better. Would he betray her for an easy headline?

#1725 UNDER THE MISTLETOE—Kristin Hardy
Holiday Hearts
No-nonsense businesswoman Hadley Stone had a job to do—modernize the Hotel Mount Eisenhower and increase profits. But hotel manager Gabe Trask stood in her way, jealously guarding the Victorian landmark's legacy. Would the beautiful Vermont Christmas—and meetings under the mistletoe—soften the adversaries' hearts a little?

#1726 HER SPECIAL CHARM—Marie Ferrarella
The Cameo
New York detective James Munro knew the cameo he'd found on the street was no ordinary dime-store trinket. Little did he know his find would unleash a legend—for when the cameo's rightful owner, Constance Beaulieu, responded to his newspaper ad and claimed this special charm, it was a meeting that would change their lives forever....

#1727 DIARY OF A DOMESTIC GODDESS—Elizabeth Harbison
With new editor-in-chief Cal Paganos shaking things up at 125-year-old *Home Life* magazine, managing editor Kit Macy worried her sewing and etiquette columns were too quaint to make the cut. So the soccer mom tried a more sophisticated style to save her job...and soon she and Cal were making more than a magazine together!

#1728 ACCIDENTAL HERO—Loralee Lillibridge
After cowboy Bo Ramsey left her to join the rodeo, words like *commitment* and *happily-ever-after* were just a lot of hot air to Abby Houston. To overcome her heartbreak, Abby turned to running the therapeutic riding program on her father's ranch. "Forgive and forget" became her new motto—until the day Bo rode back into town....

SSECNM1105